FINAL CUT

STORIES

KORY M. SHRUM

Cover Design by Christian Bentulan
www.coversbychristian.com

Editing by Toby Selwyn

ISBN: 978-1-949577-75-4

FINAL CUT

FINAL CUT

1

———

Dried leaves blow across the concrete, scratching the pavement as they tumble. Bare branches crack and groan overhead in the breeze. As I turn my face up to the three-quarters moon, a creature howls in the distance.

Not a werewolf.

But Mrs. Bates's wolfhound two blocks over, with its soulful cry, certainly makes me think of werewolves. Frankly, I want to think about anything except the ghost squatting in my house.

Her house.

I turn my attention back to the Halloween display in my front yard.

The three ghouls, contorted, bare their jutting and bloody teeth at me.

I rip off the closest hand and reattach it, trying to fix its crooked angle. I redo the purple strands of twinkle lights entwining the bush, knowing full well that they're fine.

All of it is fine. The graveyard. The rising ghouls, the flaming pumpkin head with her blade held high. The werewolf. I'm by far the best-decorated house on this sleepy street.

It's two weeks until Halloween and the most my neighbors have conjured up are some sheet ghosts hanging from the trees and a few pumpkins waiting on their porch steps.

A total lack of ambition.

At least they aren't hiding outside of their own houses, I chide myself, adjusting the fake tombstone so that it sits at a slightly different angle.

Despite the growing chill of the October night, I'm reluctant to go inside for one simple reason.

My house is haunted.

She's in there.

No sooner do I acknowledge this than the windows of my little Cape Cod fill with blood-red light and Michael Jackson's "Thriller" begins blaring from the living room stereo. She must've turned the radio up to full blast because I can hear the opening sequence clearly all the way out here.

I watch as the light glows brighter in the windows. Eerie. I'm still frowning at the house, considering my next move, when a boy sidles up the sidewalk with his ancient and arthritic golden retriever. He stops beside me.

Great, I think. *Now there are witnesses.*

And she always did love an audience.

Sure enough, the light begins to pulse in the rhythm of the music.

"Whoa." The boy's jaw unhinges as only a ten-year-old boy's jaw can unhinge. "So cool! How'd you make it do that?"

"A timer," I mumble.

"My dad won't even let me watch scary movies. He says the devil can reach you through the television screen."

I snort. That sounds exactly like the kind of thing Victor Johnson would say. Last semester I had the misfortune of being on the same English Department committee with him

—most of the faculty at the community college where I teach live in this neighborhood—and more than once he rolled up to meetings with a Jesus-themed coffee mug in hand.

Coffee gets me started. Jesus keeps me going.

What would Jesus brew?

But he favored his *Y'all need Jesus* mug above all.

"Did your mom let you watch scary movies?" the boy asks.

My heart clenches. "Yeah, my mom loves—loved them."

"You're lucky then," the boy bemoans. "Being a grownup is so much better than being a kid."

"Sure," I say, not wanting to disillusion him. "If you say so."

"Are you sad that she's dead?" he asks.

Ah, gotta love kids and their unflinching honesty.

"Sometimes." I pick my satchel stuffed with ungraded papers and half-eaten Halloween candy up off the lawn.

"You'll see her again." The boy winds the leash around his wrist. "That's what Dad says."

"I'm sure I will," I say, now beginning to move toward the house.

In about thirty seconds.

I ease open the front door with an abundance of caution.

The song changes from "Thriller" to the *Ghostbusters* theme song. I close the front door behind me.

I put my satchel on the armchair at the edge of the living room, practically tiptoeing into the room as if this will save me from the oncoming jump scare.

A clown with a knife.

Carrie covered in blood.

The *Exorcist* kid.

A vampire—and not the sexy kind.

Sometimes she'll break with the movie monsters and appear as something generic like German shepherd–sized spiders.

But by the time I reach the stereo and turn it down for the sake of my eardrums, nothing has happened.

That's suspicious all on its own.

Only, I don't have to wait much longer.

Thump.

Drag.

Thump.

Drag.

Thump.

Drag.

Thump.

It sounds an *awful* lot like a body is being dragged down the staircase.

I know whatever I see coming around the corner from the foyer into the living room will be an illusion, but the noise is unsettling all the same.

I'm still trying to decide on my next move when a zombie shambles into the living room.

Damn it. She knows I hate zombies.

One of its eyeballs is swinging from its socket. A stream of bloody drool trails over its chin and chest, suggesting it's recently had a good meal. One arm is gone. The broken and twisted leg must have been responsible for the thump and drag noises. Or maybe she made those separately, just for the effect.

The zombie closes in.

It chatters its teeth in excitement, sniffing the air as if it can taste me already.

The groans turn more desperate as it approaches.

When it reaches out for me, I press a finger into each of my temples.

"Mom, we *talked* about this."

The zombie stops just short of me, its outstretched hand hanging in the air.

I try to make my voice as firm as possible despite the fact that she has crafted a disturbingly lifelike creature this time. "You're *not* allowed to terrorize me for the first hour that I'm home from work. Please. My sanity demands it."

The zombie's lower jaw falls to the carpet. The voice still works fine. "But this is pretty good, right? I've been working on it all day. Look at the skin."

Reluctantly, I lean forward, peering at the details of the decaying flesh. She's managed to make the gray tissue pull back in places, like an actual corpse's.

"Actually—" I begin.

The zombie lunges and I scream before I can stop myself. But there's no contact. Just a puff of cold air washing over me. That's because the zombie no more exists than does my love life.

I throw up my hands. "*Mom!*"

"I knew you were scared!" The disintegrating corpse laughs at me. "You put on a brave face, but I *knew*. A mother always knows."

"You promised," I say, taking a seat on the sofa. I hope I look annoyed. I mean, I *am* annoyed. But she's also right. She got me. My heart is pounding in my temples. I truly do hate zombies above all other movie monsters. If I watch a zombie movie I have nightmares for a week.

"And we agreed," I add, as if this is a prayer I can use to inoculate myself against my mother's antics.

"The hour before bed, the hour upon waking, and the hours before and after work are blocked off from all scaring," my mother dutifully recites. She's little more than wispy blue light now. An ethereal orb. "But when you're gone *all* day, that doesn't leave much room for scaring, pumpkin. I need to squeeze it in *somewhere*."

My mother was a prankster in life. Death hasn't changed that.

When I was a child, she used to kiss me goodnight and tuck me in, only to sneak outside and stand at my bedroom window with one of those creepy silicone masks on. As soon as I started screaming bloody murder, she'd come in and pretend not to know what was going on.

Out here, my darling? Why there's nothing at all! That's why we keep the windows locked tight.

She got away with this for years until one December, when I was searching the house for my hidden Christmas presents, I found her stash of masks in the back of her closet. That's when I knew it had been her tormenting me all along.

But by then I was already indoctrinated. She'd successfully cultivated my fascination of all things horror with late nights spent watching *Tales from the Crypt* and *Twilight Zone*. Wes Craven, Alfred Hitchcock, John Carpenter, George Romero—we'd watched it all, curled up under my grandmother's handmade quilt with a giant bowl of popcorn between us.

It was because of my mother that I became obsessed not just with the horror genre but with horror films.

When I told her I was going to college for screenwriting, she never told me to grow up. Never told me to get a real job or pull my head out of the clouds.

She was excited for me. She always showed interest in what I was working on, let me talk through my ideas and brainstorm with her. She loved what I was doing.

After I graduated and moved to LA, she was the one who helped keep my dreams alive. During the day I was doing everything I could to meet the right people, get my work in front of the right eyeballs, but I probably don't need to tell you that Hollywood isn't a game for the faint of heart.

Often I called her upset and discouraged, and when I did, she would fill my head with dreams about the day one of my scripts would be turned into a movie. How we would go to the premier together, walk the red carpet together. Maybe even visit the movie set together.

She believed in me even when I couldn't.

But then one unsold script became two. Became three. Became *eight*—and I ran out of money. I was spending more time working to pay for my LA apartment than I was writing. It wasn't sustainable anymore.

I turned thirty and felt like I had nothing to show for it but some credit card debt and a miserable dumpster fire of a love life. Let me just say dating LA girls was not easy.

When the last one dumped me, I had no reason left to stay.

I called Mom and told her it was all over.

It's not over, she'd said. *You just need a break. Come home.*

So I did. I moved back to Michigan and I reclaimed my old bedroom. She even set up a desk for me and everything.

I wrote two more scripts that also didn't sell.

Keep writing, she said. *You'll make it, I just know it. I've got a feeling that when you break out, it'll be big. You just gotta keep going.*

By then I was starting to think about novels. If I could get a novel to make it big, maybe I'd be asked to write the script for it.

"Sweetie, what's wrong? Why do you have that face?" Mom asks. Or what's left of her.

I can't tell her the truth. I can't say, *It's hard to keep my dreams alive now that you're gone.*

So for a moment I don't know what to say. I stare at the pulsing ball of light in front of me. Finally I manage, "It's nothing. I'm just tired. It's been a long day."

"Should we order a pizza and watch a movie?"

My heart clenches. She asked me the same thing the night she died.

Should we order a pizza and watch a movie? A classic? It might give you inspiration.

I'd said yes, and she'd left for her evening walk.

Only she didn't come home. Not that night anyway.

I look toward the dark kitchen. The stove looks back at me accusingly. It's been doing that ever since I made the resolution to clean up my diet and stop eating out so much.

But I'm in no mood to cook.

"I pick the pizza, you pick the movie?" I ask.

She lets out a little squeal of delight and the TV turns on. As the channels flick, I dig my cell phone out of my work bag.

Mom turns on *The Lost Boys*, one of her favorites.

"Men with long hair are just so *sexy*," she says.

"If you say so." I call the pizza place and order the meat lover's deluxe with extra peppers.

The energy of the room crackles with her excitement.

"This is going to turn your whole night around," Mom promises. "Just you wait and see."

Despite Mom's efforts to cheer me, by eleven I'm crying in the shower when really, I should be tackling that stack of ungraded papers on my desk. It's a good thing my Introduction to Creative Writing course doesn't meet again until Tuesday.

I prefer crying in the shower because it hides the evidence and spares me from her probing questions. But I may have gotten too carried away because by the time I climb into bed with my fresh bat-covered jammies and jack-o'-lantern socks, a sharp headache is forming behind my eyes.

I'm searching the nightstand for aspirin when I catch movement in the corner of my vision. I turn to find that my bedsheets are rising.

Something is slowly creeping toward me under the covers. Something the size of a basketball. The hair on my arms rises.

"*Mom.*"

The shape under the covers continues to advance.

The primal urge to escape overtakes me and I leap up, throwing the blanket away, only to stub my toe on the nightstand.

A string of curse words pours from my mouth.

"Oops," Mom says, giggling. The shifting sheets deflate.

"We talked about bedtime, Mom. You've got to respect my boundaries."

"But you're in bed an hour early," her disembodied voice whispers.

"It doesn't matter. A rule is a rule." The pain in my toe is finally dissipating, leaving behind an unpleasant warmth. I climb back into bed and adjust the covers around me once more.

"I'm just trying to help, honey."

"How is scaring me helping *exactly?*" It's more of a demand than a question.

Mom's wispy light pulses, fading just a bit. I don't know why, but I feel like that's what sadness looks like. At least when you're dead.

"Because you can't be scared and sad at the same time," she says, voice fading out again.

Then she is gone.

I know because silence hangs in the air. My ears ring with it.

For a long time, I lie in the dark, her words replaying in my head.

You can't be sad and scared at the same time.

I don't know if that's true. I'm pretty sad *and* scared most of the time. Scared about the future. Sad about losing her.

Just like when she was still alive, she thinks a good scare is the best way to cheer someone up.

But I can't be cheered up. And I don't have the heart to tell her that.

There's also the other thing I haven't been telling her.

That I've been looking for her killer. I'm determined to find out the name of the piece of shit who hit her and fled the scene, leaving her to die on the side of the road like fucking roadkill.

"Mom?" I whisper to the dark.

Her orb of light burns back into existence, just like I knew it would.

"Yes, pumpkin?"

"You don't have to hide," I tell her.

"I thought you might want to be alone, darling."

"No, it's okay. You can stay if you want to."

Nothing is okay. I'll never be okay again.

And just like that, the tears are in the corners of my eyes again.

"Of course I want to," she says, a draft of cold air moving across my cheeks. She probably wants to wipe away my tears, but she can't do that anymore. There's a lot she can't do anymore.

"I always want to stay with you, pumpkin," she whispers.

Then the waterworks begin in earnest.

2

———

When I wake, sunshine is accosting me. It pours through the bedroom window, cutting a line across my face. I groan, trying to block it with my elbow. I check the clock on my phone. It's almost ten in the morning. I overslept again. I've been doing that a lot since the accident. There's just a part of me that has no desire to move. If I could grow a cocoon-like sac like in *Species*, I'd totally do it. Because convincing that part of me to do anything has been a hell of a challenge.

But today is a writing day.

If I don't get my ass up and to the computer, if I let another zero-word-count day creep up on me, then the self-loathing will set in.

Maybe self-loathing would be a nice change of pace from depression?

Don't be silly, my mind says. *You can always have both.*

That gets me up and moving.

"Mom?"

I wait. I stand in the middle of my bedroom, hair undoubtedly shooting in all directions, one eye cracked open.

"Mom?"

Nothing.

At least I can get ready in peace, I guess. Once, I asked her where she goes, and she said that she hasn't gone anywhere. This raises many questions. Is she lying? Possibly. Or is time moving differently for her? Or maybe she goes unconscious sometimes and just doesn't know it?

She hasn't come back even after I shower, brush my teeth, get dressed.

God, I do miss Mom making breakfast.

It's almost noon by the time I sit down at my desk with a couple of pieces of toast and a mug of hot coffee.

I open my email, check my socials, all of this a mere warm-up to the big event. Don't ask me why writers are so averse to just sitting down and doing the damn writing. But everyone I've ever asked has said the same thing. We each have our own process, an internal begging and pleading that has to run its course before any words actually get typed onto the page.

I'm no different.

Just open the document.

I do.

Just type a word, any word.

"Word," I say, my fingertips striking the keys. Then I delete it.

I try reading the last scene I wrote to get me back into the rhythm of the story. That does the trick. Once I finish the reread, I'm ready.

Up next: my final girl—though she doesn't know she's the final girl yet—is about to make the mistake of stepping into the woods with the mysteriously hot chick who joined their little party at a cabin. Her friends are dancing around the bonfire in the background, music blasting, most of them drunk or high out of their minds.

She's too smart to be doing this—following some beautiful stranger into the woods in the middle of the night. My heroines aren't stupid. Usually.

But she's depressed because her twin sister just died.

Even smart people do stupid things when they're drunk and heartbroken.

The scene is moving at a pretty good pace until I hit a decision point—I've got to decide if the killer is a yet-to-be-introduced psychopath or if it's her jealous best friend. Or maybe this stranger leading her into the woods.

The second option fits the arc of the narrative a little better. As well as the big reveal I want to add later on.

But it's a big decision.

While thinking, my eyes slide lazily to the trinkets clotting the windowsill behind my computer.

There are rocks, feathers, dried flowers. A snail's shell.

I lift up a shiny black rock. When I turn it in the light, it shimmers, iridescent.

Each one is a treasure that Mom brought back from one of her walks. She didn't always come back with something, but most of the time she did, and when she handed it over, I always inspected the gift and declared that it was *a fine specimen for my collection.*

My stomach is in knots again, my heart sinking down into it.

I put the shiny rock back on the windowsill.

Beyond the window, a little patch of woods rests behind our house. It was Mom who'd put my desk in front of the window, claiming she read an article that said views of nature activate creativity.

"Mom?"

I listen to the silence ringing in my ears.

I wish she was here to talk out this scene with me. When

she was alive, she always gave me thoughtful critiques, always pushed me to try new things.

"Mom? You around?"

I rub my eyes, leaning back in my writing chair, and try to relax the knot in my chest.

The hair on the back of my neck pricks to attention. The temperature has dropped at least ten degrees. I see a shadow in the corner of my eye and turn.

The mirror beside my desk reveals a gruesome sight. Behind my chair, just *inches* behind me, is a grotesque mummy. I recognize it as a replica from one of our favorite movies.

"*Mom.* What *are* you doing?"

"You're sad again, pumpkin," the mummy's reflection says. "How can you be sad when your mummy is a mummy?"

I snort despite myself. I'm about to ask for her feedback on my scene but stop.

It doesn't feel the same for some reason, and it hurts a little to realize that.

"It's time to quit for lunch anyway." I stretch my hands overhead. "Or maybe I should just quit forever."

I mean this remark to be nothing more than dramatic cynicism. But Mom has never let me get away with comments like that.

"Don't give up," she says, a cold breeze pushing through my hair. "The greats never do."

I'VE GOT TACO SHELLS WARMING IN THE OVEN AND GROUND beef sizzling in a pan when I get a text.

I've got something. Want to meet?

My mind goes ten directions at once.

Yes! I write back. *When?*

You free now?

My heart takes off like a shot in my chest.

"Your face is getting red," the oversized spider on the wall above the stove tells me. "Are you talking to a *girl?*"

I don't answer, which only encourages her more. The spider bursts into a hundred smaller spiders.

"Tell us, please. Tell us! Tell us!" a chorus of little voices beg as they scramble over the cabinets. "Is it a girl?"

I wave them away. I don't want to tell Mom who I'm talking to for many reasons. Kaitlyn being a hot girl is the least of them.

Thirty minutes? I'm making lunch.

I can come to you, she replies. *You at home?*

"We want to meet her," the spiders say. "Bring her here."

"Mom, be serious. I can't bring her over here for obvious reasons."

The spiders gasp in a high-pitched voice. "Are you *ashamed* of us?"

I try to keep focused on the message I'm typing despite the spiders crawling *all* over me now.

Sorry, no. I'd rather you not—because my house is currently being haunted by my dead mother—*neither me nor the house are in presentable condition. If you can wait, I'll meet you at the Fleet Street Diner at 4:30.*

Thought you were eating, smile emoji.

"Oh, a *smile* emoji," a cluster of spiders coo from my shoulders. I realize that they climbed up here to better see the phone. "You *do* like her."

"No," I say, perhaps too quickly. "It's a professional smile emoji. Now get all your legs off of me."

I manage to finish making my tacos, but I have to take them to go.

Mom won't shut up with the questions, and it's worse when she's excited about something. She basically just cycles through every movie monster she knows while interrogating me for details about *the girl*.

It's like she can't manage a single form when her emotions are running high.

Have you ever been interrogated by Nosferatu before?

Or Ellen Ripley's alien queen?

The creature from the black lagoon?

"It's just someone I'm working with, Mom." I pull on my shoes and a coat, moving my tacos from one free hand to the other. "It's just work, I swear."

The pale man from *Pan's Labyrinth* says, "Why would you lie to your mother, pumpkin? Don't you trust me?"

I grab my keys off the hook and turn to find Frank-N-Furter standing there in his black garters and thigh-highs.

I take a breath. "I'll be back later. Please stay away from the windows."

Before I pull the front door closed behind me, it's Pinhead who says, "Fine. We'll talk when you get home."

KAITLYN IS ALREADY SITTING IN A BOOTH BY THE WINDOW when I whip Mom's Mini Cooper into a parking spot. I watch her for a moment, admiring her sleek back hair, the way it's pulled back behind her ears in a loose ponytail. A few strands have fallen forward into her super-cute face, and she brushes them away with an absent-minded wave of her hand. Her eyes are trained downward, but I can't tell from this angle what she's looking at. Her phone, maybe? Or a menu?

I notice, not for the first time, a sudden urge to wipe my clammy hands on my jeans and to check my breath. Then I grab a tin of mints from the center console.

It's not like that, I tell myself. *You hired her to do a job. She's doing it. That's it. Don't make it weird.*

My ex-girlfriend's assessment lives rent-free in my head until today.

You were weird at first. You can't flirt for shit.

Thanks for that, Valerie.

I give my face and teeth one more inspection in the rearview mirror before I climb out of the car with my satchel.

Kaitlyn spots me the second I enter the diner. Her face lights up and she waves me over.

My heart lifts a little, hopefully.

Stop it. Keep it professional. You don't even know if she's into you, and if she's not, then you're being a creep.

"Hey," Kaitlyn says. "Thanks for coming. It's good to see you."

Her voice is very warm. I've *got* to pull myself together.

"Of course." I push my satchel into the corner of the booth.

Kaitlyn lets out a little nervous laugh.

"Do you want a coffee or something? I already ordered."

"Oh, okay." It takes me a minute to catch up. I order a coffee while Kaitlyn digs around in her bag, pulling out her computer and a sleeve of papers from a manila envelope. She turns her side of the booth into a desk, placing a folder marked *Laurie* to the left of the computer.

"I like the way you write my name," I say.

I like the way you write my name? What the hell is wrong with me?

"Thanks," she says, a little smile quirking her lips. "It's a pretty name."

"My mom named me after Jamie Lee Curtis's character in *Halloween*."

For a moment Kaitlyn only blinks at me.

Maybe that's why I feel compelled to add, "She loved horror movies."

"Explains why you write them," she says. "It's like my dad and true crime."

I try to remember what Kaitlyn has said about her dad.

He was a cop at the local precinct for many years, but when he almost died after getting shot, he left the force and opened a private investigation agency. He ran the agency for fifteen years before dying of a heart attack two years ago, at which point Kaitlyn took over full time running Park's PI Services.

He'd liked sports—something that I have *zero* understanding of—and he liked taking Kaitlyn back to South Korea once every other year to see family and remind her where she came from, even though she's lived in America all her life.

I'd initially contacted Park's PI Services because it's the best-reviewed private investigation agency in town. I'd decided to stay on because Kaitlyn was nothing short of gorgeous.

A superficial reason, I know. Shoot me.

"Dog walkers are predictable," Kaitlyn says. And the words feel so abrupt that I'm very sure I've missed something.

I blink several times. "What?"

"They usually have routines. They walk the same routes at the same time of day. In addition to Ms. Grier, I got three of those walkers to confirm that they'd seen a dark blue sedan speed off around the time of your mother's death."

Her smile is still sly when she slides a photograph across the table. "Up the road from where your mom was hit is a roundabout with cameras. I've got someone checking the history to see if we can match a car of that description to the time of your mom's death. If I can get a plate number, then we can work to identify the driver."

"Are you saying we might actually catch the asshole?" It isn't until this moment that I realize I'd given up.

Kaitlyn struggles to keep her face neutral. "It's too soon to say. Maybe the cameras didn't capture anything, or we can't pull a plate number. Or the driver has an alibi. Or it might not have been the owner who was driving. Or the car was stolen."

"It only matters that we keep trying," I tell her. But I have to admit that I'm not sure if it matters anymore. Especially not when my dead mother spends her days shapeshifting into her favorite movie monsters, pranking me. She doesn't seem the least bit bothered by the fact that she's dead. I don't think she cares.

"I think this is just for me," I say.

I hadn't meant to say that part. But I've noticed that around Kaitlyn my inside thoughts keep becoming my outside thoughts. Professional relationship my ass.

"I know." When I look up, I find that Kaitlyn's face is soft. She adds, "And if it matters to you, that's enough for me."

My face burns.

Her expression is gentle. "How are you holding up?"

"I don't know how to answer that," I admit.

I haven't told her—or anyone—about my mother haunting me. What would I even say? I haven't decided how I feel about it myself.

Am I glad she came back?

Yes. I think…?

I don't know. It would've been harder if she'd just left, right? If she'd been killed in a hit and run and then I never heard from her again, never knew if she was okay, you know, emotionally.

I'm sure my very overactive imagination would have served me up all sorts of horrible scenarios.

My mother lying in the street, bleeding out, brains half

out of her head, feeling alone and unlucky as the last of her life left her.

Kids know their parents are going to die. But I guess I always imagined it would be later, when she was old, and I would be with her, at her bedside, reminding her of all the wonderful times we had together. And it would definitely have been after I'd had a long and illustrious career as an undisputed master of horror.

That's never going to happen now.

Kaitlyn is still looking at me, expectantly. Still waiting for an answer.

"It's just hard to concentrate," I say lamely.

"On your writing?" she asks.

I think of the mummy standing behind my chair bleeding sand onto the floor while it reached toward me with crusty bandages.

"All of it. I got a past due notice a couple of days ago about the water bill because I didn't even *know* that Mom had paperless statements. It's fine. I paid it. But it makes me wonder what else I'm missing."

She twirls her straw in her water glass. "You're going through a period of adjustment."

That is an understatement. And it isn't just getting the paperwork and the financials and everything else in place, it isn't even the hauntings, which are distracting all on their own.

It's also the missing her.

I miss my mom.

It's probably hard to understand since I still see her—or some version of her—every day.

But it's not the same. What's left of my mom can't hug me. What's left of my mom can't kiss the top of my head and tell me everything's going to be all right.

Tears stand out in the corners of my eyes before I can will them away. How embarrassing.

At least Kaitlyn doesn't look grossed out. Her features are only pinched in concern.

She takes a breath and says, "I wasn't okay for a long time after my dad died, and I *knew* he was headed for the boneyard given how that man ate. He could put away some chili cheese fries with extra bacon like the world was ending tomorrow. I didn't even know it was possible for a human to put that much cheese in their mouth at one time."

I laugh despite myself.

She seems pleased to hear it, her lips tugging into a beautiful smile.

She reaches across the table and takes my hand. She squeezes it.

"It'll get easier," she promises. "Give it time."

3

———

Aᶠᵗᵉʳ saying goodbye to Kaitlyn at the diner, I head to work. I don't teach today, so I don't need to be there. But let's be honest, I'm avoiding my mother's questions. The whole reason I took this job was to give myself an excuse to get out of the house twice a week.

That's probably the *real* reason why I haven't left Michigan.

The job and the house.

This is where I grew up. This is where we lived together, made a home together. I don't like the idea of someone else moving in here and making it *their* house. I don't want to get rid of any of her things. And what if she isn't tied to her urn? What if it's the house, and I sell it and pack her ashes thinking she'll come with me to LA only to find out it doesn't work that way.

Then again, I'm sure one week with my dead mother will make them sell it back to me at a discount, but that's not the point. It does me no good fantasizing about things that will never happen anyway.

I linger on campus, staring out the copy room window at

the courtyard below, hoping Mom's short attention span—death hasn't changed this in the *slightest*—will make her forget all about my meetup with Kaitlyn. I don't need another round of interrogations from the *IT* clown or whatever she conjures up.

I sort of want to tell Mom that I hired Kaitlyn to investigate her death. She would've thought that kind of thing is cool. But there's a part of me that worries it might upset her, to know I'm looking into what happened.

My mother, the ever-forgiving type, would tell me to let it go. She'd say that the driver probably hit her on accident and feels horrible about it.

There's no point in making it worse. Forgive and forget.

That is—was—her motto.

I've never been forgiving or forgetful. I'm still pissed at Britney Jenkins for setting my favorite Barbie on fire in the first grade. Later she got arrested for arson, so that tracks. But I wish my doll hadn't been one of her earliest victims.

I've tried to find out what Mom remembers about the night she died, but she won't give me any details. I don't know if that's because thinking about it upsets her or if she's afraid she'll upset me.

Or maybe she's just having too much fun terrorizing me to be upset. She no longer has to rely on rubber masks or hiding in the closet to make me jump out of my skin.

Without a body, she can pull off tricks never before possible. More than once she's declared it the absolute best thing about being dead.

I'm still hiding in the copy room, making copies for my next class, when the sun finally dips behind the horizon. It's time to quit stalling and head home. I grab my satchel, the mail from my faculty mailbox, and the handouts. The traffic is light on my way home.

When I pull up in my driveway fifteen minutes later, there

are at least ten kids standing on the sidewalk outside my house, and they're squealing in delight.

"What the—" I put the Mini Cooper in park and turn off the ignition.

The stuffed werewolf that I staked to the front lawn is throwing his head back and howling. The three ghouls are floating—*floating*—several feet off the ground. The pumpkin head's jaw bobs up and down as she releases a menacing laugh.

The house itself is the most surprising of all. The two front windows of the Cape Cod are full of monsters. The one that *should* be showcasing my living room furniture is covered in zombies pressing themselves against the glass. The other has the mummy that visited me while I was writing this afternoon. Behind them an eerie purple light pulses. She's got "Monster Mash" blaring this time.

Jesus, Mom.

When I get out of the car, one of the boys asks, "How are you doing that?"

"A timer!" the Johnson boy answers.

"Your house is hella cool!" another confesses.

"Thanks." I throw a self-conscious wave.

"We've only got a stupid witch on the porch," another laments.

I escape inside as quickly as I can, hissing, "*Mom!*"

I don't know which of the monsters to direct my attention at, since she seems to be projecting several at once. I throw my satchel on the armchair closest to the front door.

"Mom, what if someone files a complaint?"

"But they're *so* appreciative," Mom says. Her voice comes from thin air, the definition of disembodied. "It reminds me of when you were little. It was so easy to impress you then. Every time I showed you a new movie or told you a new story, you thought it was the most incredible thing in the world."

I look out at the delighted faces. She has a point. There's a lot of joy out there.

"Okay, but you're setting a very high bar right now," I tell her. "The neighbors are going to hate me."

"Pfft. Who cares. Everyone needs to lighten up."

I stand in the foyer, looking from the zombies to the mummy. "Mom, how are you doing all this?"

"I don't know," she says, sounding both breathless and excited. "I feel like I'm getting stronger. I might figure out that banshee scream after all."

"I won't be sad if you don't." The last thing I need is my mother screaming like an actual banshee and splitting my eardrums in half. I consider it a small blessing from the universe that she hasn't been able to manage it yet.

"But you like this, don't you? It's cool?"

"Of course. It's very cool. I just don't want to answer any questions from the neighbors. Or the police," I say.

I don't know how I'd answer them.

A pulse of concern shivers through me, tugging at my guts.

I feel like I'm getting stronger.

Should a ghost be getting stronger?

I think about asking her to try for a hug then. Maybe we can manage it if she really is getting stronger. Then I change my mind. If we try and fail it'll ruin the mood.

I leave Mom to her scaring and go about the task of making dinner. Too bad my ghost roommate can't cook or clean. Despite all her theatrics, Mom doesn't seem capable of *actually* moving objects or touching things.

It's all show and bluster. Like, literal wind. That's it.

There's the breeze I feel when she moves through me or past me, when she tries to touch me. The television and radio seem to be the exception. She can turn them on and off but not with the remote. She can also flicker the lights. So there's something electrical going on too.

Fifteen minutes later, I've got a bowl of mac and cheese thrown together and I'm in front of the TV. Mom has *Halloween* playing. I feel her moving close, cooling the air around me.

"Why do you love this movie so much?" I ask her, spooning cheesy noodles into my mouth.

"They did so much with such a small budget," she says. "Don't you love it?"

Love is a stretch. "Sure, but there are other movies I like more."

I think she's going to let it go, but I'm mistaken. Twenty minutes later she's still in full critique mode.

"See, look what they did here with the angles," Mom says. "Nowadays they would've had to—"

My eyes are fluttering closed. It's dark outside and my stomach is full of noodles. The weight of the day is pulling me toward slumber. It always does this as we move toward winter.

With my eyes closed like this, a movie playing in the background and Mom prattling on about it—it's almost like she's alive again. Apart from the cold spot turning my legs to frost, it's quite cozy, and it makes me miss her all the more.

I wish I could ask for that hug.

She's not gone, I tell myself. *She's right here.*

I almost believe it.

I open my eyes when the music rises suddenly. Jamie Lee Curtis has just discovered the bodies. She backs out of the room screaming, falling against the wall, unaware that Michael is coming up behind her. She's trembling and carrying on—until Michael stabs her, that is.

Mom's orb sighs. I can't tell if it's a pleased or disappointed sigh.

"Why stumble around in the dark like that? Especially if you're just going to be crying and making all that noise? You know the killer can hear you." I sit up, putting my empty bowl on the end table. "Why *did* you name me after a victim, anyway?"

"Pumpkin. I didn't name you after a *victim*," Mom says. "I named you after a *survivor*. There's a big difference."

4

———

I'm pushing in chairs when my bag begins to vibrate, playing the "This is Halloween" tune. I walk back to the desk and dig it out to find Kaitlyn's name scrolling across the top of the screen. My heart skips a beat.

"Hey?"

"Hey!" She sounds a little breathless. And like maybe she's outside. Pretty sure that's the sound of traffic and wind. "Is your class over? I hope I'm not interrupting."

I'm only surprised for a second. Then I remember that she's a private investigator. Obviously she knows where I am and what I'm doing.

"The class ended a few minutes ago. I was just trying to tidy up a bit. I always feel so bad for the janitors."

"Do you have plans afterwards?" she asks.

My mind flatlines. It does that when I talk to girls I like. A very annoying habit.

For a moment there's only silence on the line.

She fills it by saying, "Because I was wondering if you wanted to come with me. I'm paying a visit to a witness."

Okay, so she's not asking me out on a date. Of course not.

She's too professional to be mixing business and pleasure. I don't know why I got my hopes up. There also remains the fact that she has expressed *zero* interest in me.

"Should I really be going with you?" I ask before switching the phone to the other ear. "Won't I just be mucking up a crime scene or something?"

Kaitlyn snorts. She has a *very* cute snort. "There's no scene to muck up. *If* by some stroke of luck we do come across physical evidence, I won't let you touch it."

"*Let* me," I repeat. "Well, as long as we know who's in charge."

There's another beat of silence. God. Why did I have to go and make it weird?

"Will you come?" Kaitlyn asks. "I'd like it if you did."

That settles that. "Sure. Just give me an address and I'll meet you there."

"Actually, I'm outside," she says.

I peek into the hallway, but she's not there.

"Outside your building," she clarifies, as if she can see me. "In the east lot."

"That's where I'm parked," I say dumbly.

She humors me. "I know. Come on down and we'll ride together."

It isn't until I'm out of the building and I see her in the parking lot, leaning against my car, that I realize she'd said *come down*.

Not *out*, but *down*.

Did I tell her my classroom is on the upper floor at some point? I don't think so.

We lock eyes and she throws me a wave. God, she's cute.

WE'RE CRUISING DOWN THE HIGHWAY TOWARD THE WEST

side of town when I crane around, looking into the backseat of her SUV.

"I already checked for a killer," Kaitlyn says with a big smile. "There's not a body either. I got rid of it before I picked you up."

I laugh, hoping to hide my nervousness. She's probably joking, but her delivery is perfect. She even widens her eyes to suggest a hint of playful crazy.

You read too much horror, I tell myself.

It's true that the novel I *just* finished was about how the killer had been the cop who'd rescued the final girl. After stabbing her and murdering all her friends, he pretended to worry about her, care for her, protect her, for *years*.

God, stop it, I chastise myself. *I picked Kaitlyn. I called her. She did not kill Mom with the intent of finishing me off next. Why would she do that?*

"You're quiet today," Kaitlyn says.

Quick, say something.

"I was just thinking you couldn't fit a body back there with all that paperwork." This is true because her backseat is full of cardboard file boxes. "Unless you chopped it up. But then your boxes would be soggy."

Kaitlyn's brows go up and don't come down, like she's considering this thoughtfully.

Is that what you call flirtatious banter, you freak?

"Sorry. That was probably too graphic," I say.

Kaitlyn shrugs before turning on her blinker and switching lanes. "You realize I read a lot of true crime, right? Those writers can get very graphic when describing the crime and what was done to the body. I don't like it when they're dehumanizing though. That was someone's loved one, you know?"

"Totally. Makes sense."

"As for the boxes, they're old files. I'm trying to clean out the agency. Dad was a total packrat. But I need to go through everything, maybe digitize it, before I throw anything out. It's going to take forever."

"Sounds like it."

"What about you?" she asks.

"No, Mom wasn't a packrat. I'm probably the hoarder in our relationship."

Kaitlyn snorts again. "No, why do you love horror so much?"

"Oh. I don't know. My mom loved it, so I had a lot of exposure to it growing up."

Kaitlyn looks unconvinced. "In addition to true crime, my dad was really into birding and golf. I can play a mean round of it, but that doesn't mean I love it. You *love* it. I can tell. Why?"

The question forces me to think.

"Honestly, I don't like the same kind of horror she does—did."

She looks over her shoulder to switch lanes. "There are different kinds?"

"Oh my god, *yes*."

Her lips twitch, amused by my outburst. "Go on then. School me."

I sit up straighter in the passenger seat. "Horror is a *very* broad church. There's traditional horror or slasher films, but there's also horror thrillers like *Silence of the Lambs*."

"Oh, I like that one. Very cat and mouse."

I'm starting to see a pattern. She likes scary when there's a psychological or crime element. I file that away for—what?

What are you going to do exactly, Laurie? Ask her out to dinner and a movie? Netflix and chill? You haven't the guts.

I push on. "There are horror comedies like *Scream* that make fun of horror while being horror. My mom loved the gory stuff, which isn't my favorite. Slasher films. Psychos with knives. Killer clowns. We both loved monsters. Creature features. That's probably one of my favorites, the supernatural stuff."

"Like ghosts? Demonic possession?"

"Not demonic possession so much. Witches, vampires, werewolves. Or body snatcher things are fun. *The Puppet Masters. The Invasion. Aliens.* Pretty much anything that makes you wonder what else could be out there in the world."

Now she's smiling at least. "You like mysteries too then."

"And comedy. My favorite horror movies are funny."

"*Funny?*" She glances away from the road long enough to give me a skeptical look. "Horror movies are never funny."

This unleashes a torrent of words.

"Oh my god, *yes* they are. Ryan Reynolds was hilarious in *Life.*" I start ticking movies off my fingers. "*The Cabin in the Woods. American Psycho. Jennifer's Body. The Blackening. Shaun of the Dead. Zombieland. Trick r' Treat. The Menu. The Lost Boys. What We Do in the Shadows.*"

Kaitlyn's brows are up again. "I stand corrected. And I liked *The Menu.* That's another one I've seen."

"Ralph Fiennes and Anya Taylor-Joy—" I make a dramatic chef's kiss with my fingers, pun intended. She laughs like she gets it. This only encourages me to press on. "Nicholas Hoult gets an honorable mention. He's also hella funny in *Renfield.* Have you seen it?"

The car slides to a stop at a red light.

"No. But hearing you go on like this makes me want to. Sounds like I've got quite a few new recs to check out. That's good, because I'm almost done with the series I'm watching."

My cheeks warm. I'm very aware of how excited I get when I talk about horror and my excitement isn't usually well met. I either run into bros who think horror is a dudes-only club, no girls allowed, or girls who think it's super weird for a girl to be into such things.

Girls like my ex, Val.

I sink in the passenger seat. "Sorry. I talk a lot when I'm into something."

"I love listening to you talk about it," Kaitlyn says. "Don't get shy on me."

Now my face is on fire for a different reason. My arch-nemesis: compliments.

"You probably don't like horror since you always see the worst in people."

"The best in people, you mean," she counters.

I frown. She catches it before I can fix my face.

"It's true that I see people's dark side sometimes. Like in the case of your mom's death. Hitting someone and taking off is unforgiveable. But the ambulance came because someone saw it happen and called for help. So there's also that—someone doing good. What you focus on matters. I try to focus on the helpers."

I don't know why, but she's trying to make me feel better. Maybe because my face is the color of a tomato in late August.

"Don't hide your love of horror," she says, smile still bright. "I really do like to hear you talk about it. I want you to finish what you were saying. Tell me why you prefer comedy horror above all the horror out there."

Her profile in the last light of the day is almost too beautiful. The curve of that jaw, her slender throat. Her bright eyes meeting mine. A few minutes ago, I was wondering if she could be a killer herself. Now look at me. Pathetic.

I fight for concentration, tearing my eyes away from the woman driving me god knows where. Actually, we're not far from the house. I could leap from the car and run through those woods if I had to.

"Horror isn't always about *horror*," I say. "It makes us think about our fears differently. Take zombies, for example."

Kaitlyn wrinkles her nose. "Not my fav, but go on."

"Mine either. Zombies are more about the unstoppable march of death, how no matter what we do, we can't escape it. Or they can represent our fear of contagions, of getting sick, or of losing our free will. Fears about survival. It's not really about zombies. It's about the things we're so scared of. Then add comedy to it. In *Shaun of the Dead*—that's a zombie movie—they make fun of those fears, play with them, while also looking at Shaun's relationship with his girlfriend, Liz. They're supposed to be trying to survive a zombie apocalypse but really it's about a guy trying to get his girlfriend back and breathe new life into their relationship."

Kaitlyn snorts. "You really love puns."

I'm pleased she noticed. "I'm just saying it's a story about love. Friendship. Forgiveness. That's what the movie's *really* about. The zombies are just there to help the viewer see things differently."

Kaitlyn thinks about this and says, "The book you're writing. What's it really about then?"

My chest compresses. It feels incredibly intimate all of sudden, sitting together in her car. This feeling is intensified as she turns into a parking lot and pulls up outside a set of baby-blue apartment buildings. Two mourning doves take flight from the roof at the sight of us.

She's looking at me, waiting for me to answer. "If you don't want to tell me, it's okay. Maybe it'll ruin your creative process."

"No. It's just—First of all, I don't know if it's a book or a screenplay. I keep going back and forth. Secondly—" Why not? What have I got to lose? "It's about grief."

When she doesn't ask for more, I feel compelled to explain myself.

"Beth—that's my main character—she's grieving the death of her twin sister, who died in an accident. Only Beth doesn't really believe it was an accident. She was there that night and saw something, even though she isn't sure what she saw. Really she just wants to be with her sister again. She's—she's suicidal and heartbroken, and the killer comes back to finish her off. He knows she wants to die and taunts her about it, but she decides to fight back at the last moment, and she pulls through. Surviving that encounter is what proves to Beth that she really wants to live, even though her heart is broken and probably always will be. Oddly enough, fighting for her life is what gives her the strength to go on."

For a long time Kaitlyn says nothing. She's looking at me with those deep blue eyes again. I can admit it hurts a little to look directly into them, so my gaze slides away.

I'm staring at a row of mailboxes when she says, "That sounds like an amazing story, Laurie. I hope you'll let me read it when it's done."

My face catches fire for a third time. I swear I'm going to combust if she keeps this up.

She leans across the center console toward me, and my heart climbs so far up my chest that I think it's going to explode out of my mouth.

I'm about to lick my lips just in case this turns into a kiss, but before I can, she whispers, "I have to admit it doesn't sound very funny though."

A surprise laugh bursts from me as she withdraws.

I clasp the back of my neck and rub it. "Yeah, I'm struggling with that part. Comedy is harder than you think. Maybe I'll throw a PI in there to spice things up."

"Just make her cute," Kaitlyn says. "That's all I ask."

With a wink, she throws open her door and climbs out, leaving me in the passenger seat to compose myself.

I do not manage it.

My face is still burning as we mount the stairs to the

second floor of the apartment complex. We stop outside a door. Number seven.

Kaitlyn knocks.

I just stand beside her looking like a total creep. Because there's a big picture window beside the door, I've got no choice but to stare through it, watching a woman walk the *entire* length of her apartment toward us.

She's somewhere between my age and my mom's. Forties, maybe? She's got coppery-blond hair with dark roots. Her brown eyes look comically large behind her thick glasses and her lips are little more than a thin line just above her chin.

I note all of this wondering just how weird I must look staring in her window like this, but she opens the door. I can't be looking too crazy.

That or she's a *very* trusting person.

Kaitlyn says, "You know, there are a lot of Korean horror movies I should introduce you to. They scare the shit out of me."

Before I can answer, the woman opens the door and says, "Can I help you?"

"Hi, Ms. Grier, I'm Kaitlyn Park. We talked on the phone." Kaitlyn turns to me with a bright, very professional smile. "This is Laurie."

The woman's face softens. "Oh, you poor thing. Come in, come in."

I won't lie. The moment she says *you poor thing*, I almost burst into tears. Not a proud moment, I know. But grief is weird. Ever since Mom died, every time someone is really nice to me about her passing—maybe they say something kind, or give me a few gentle words, whatever—it makes me want to cry.

This sudden urge comes to a head when the woman puts a plate of freshly baked chocolate chips cookies down in front of me and says, "When Kaitlyn said you were coming,

I decided to make you these. I'm so sorry about your mom."

"Thank you."

That does it. Now I'm eating a cookie with tears on my cheeks. I use my free hand to pet a very old, very fat pug who blinks up at me with uncomprehending eyes. I think it is more interested in the cookie I'm holding than in me, but I'll eat my shirt if there's more than two brain cells floating around behind that seal-pup face.

"Ms. Grier, if it's not too much trouble, I'm hoping you can take us through that night one more time. I know you've already told the police everything and—"

Ms. Grier waves Kaitlyn's concerns away. "I'm happy to tell it all again. You probably want to know what it was like, don't you, dear? Your mom's last moments?"

I feel like I've been horse-kicked.

"You were with her when she died?" It's really a question, but the words come out as more of a shocked wheeze.

"Yes," she says tenderly. "I saw the whole thing happen. I'm just so glad I was able to get across the street to her before she passed."

She wasn't alone when she died.

I barely feel tethered to my body as Ms. Grier tells her story. Some very distant part of me is registering that I'm eating cookies in a stranger's house while she tells me about my mother's murder.

I'm not sure if this qualifies as an out-of-body experience, but it's certainly surreal as hell.

"I was walking up Birch with Fettucine in the lead and I saw this dark car speed past, tires pealing. I thought, *what an asshole*, driving like that. It's a busy road, lots of people walking. And it's close to the school. It was too late for the kids to be out, but still. Someone could get hurt—Lord. What am I saying? Someone *got* hurt."

I'm holding half of a crumbled cookie. The geriatric pug, Fettuccine, sees his opportunity and takes it from my hand. I put up no fight.

"After the car passes me, that's when I see her about half a block up. I thought, *Oh my, someone's fallen in the road.* I thought it was a little old lady. That's what made me take off at a run. Those curbs are so steep! I was afraid somebody else was gonna come by and—well, Fettuccine isn't much of a runner, so I had to pick him up."

"Sure." I don't know what I'm saying *sure* to exactly. It feels more like a punctuation mark than anything. A word that tells Ms. Grier that I want her to go on with her story though I have zero idea how I'm supposed to respond to it.

"I could tell she was a sweet woman," Ms. Grier says.

By the way her brains were thrown across the pavement? I think darkly.

"Do you want to know the first thing she said to me, when I got to her?"

No, I think. "Yes."

"She said, 'Can I pet your dog?'"

I gotta say, if this is made up, Ms. Grier really pegged my mom.

She is—*was*—one hundred percent the kind of person who could be dying and still want to pet the dog.

"I called 911 and stayed with her until the ambulance came. I held her hand the whole time and Fettucine sat right beside her too. It was so peaceful that I didn't even know she was gone until the ambulance pronounced her dead on the scene."

This feels like a stretch.

I did the very morbid thing of watching videos on YouTube demonstrating what it was like for a person to get hit by a car. I saw *countless* mannequins get tumbled under and over vehicles traveling at various speeds. You wouldn't believe all the ways a body can make contact with pavement.

The medical examiner went over the most likely scenario with me after she'd finished the autopsy report. I know from the autopsy that the car clipped Mom's left leg from behind. She hadn't seen it coming. It's possible the driver saw her at the last minute and tried to swerve to miss her but wasn't quick enough.

Mom's leg was shattered by the impact, and she was thrown. It's not clear if she went up over the top of the car or to the side across the hood, but either way, when she came back down, she hit her head on the pavement at the left temple. There had also been a lot of scratches and road burn on her skin from the tumbling, but those two injuries—the shattered leg and head injury at the temple—were the worst of it. The medical examiner thought it was probably shock that killed her rather than the injuries.

When I feel especially sorry for myself, I try to remember that even if Mom had survived, it's unlikely that she would have ever walked again with a leg like that, and she would've hated it. Apart from scary movies, her walks were her favorite thing in the world.

The geriatric pug has dropped into sleep, snoring.

"I'm sure she was thinking about you when she passed," Ms. Grier says.

When I'd asked, Mom told me she'd been thinking about pizza. She hadn't even mentioned a dog. But I appreciate the effort that the woman is making to help me feel better.

I force a smile. "Thanks."

TEN MINUTES LATER I'M SITTING IN KAITLYN'S CAR AGAIN with the remaining cookies wrapped in a napkin on my lap.

I ask, "Is it normal to bring your clients with you for ride-alongs?"

She hesitates for a fraction of a second, but I still catch it.

"Oh yeah. Totally," she says.

Her expression leaves me with a strong feeling she's lying. In fact, I have the distinct impression that the entire conversation with Ms. Grier was for my benefit alone and held no value when it comes to solving the case.

I resist the urge to call her out on it.

"Was it helpful?" Kaitlyn asks, searching my face. "Hearing her talk about your mom?"

I nod. I don't trust myself to speak yet, not without crying again.

Maybe I would have if there wasn't a ghost in my house rattling my bed at night, giving me all kinds of new definitions for *restless spirit*.

What if Mom came back because petting a dog as she died wasn't enough to help her pass from the world peacefully?

"Were there other witnesses?" I ask. Mostly because I want to know if I'm going to be met with another round of sympathetic faces and stories. And possibly cheesecake. I wouldn't be sad if the next person had cheesecake. Just saying.

"No, the other two dog walkers on the road can't meet. One's a travel nurse. The other is playing hard to get. Witnesses can be like that. Flaky."

Suspicious, my mind thinks reflexively. *Being out of town.*

"The nurse emailed me the written statement of her testimony. She also mentions a car speeding down this road at the time your mom was hit. She got a better look at the driver. Male. Looked tall and thin with dark hair. It's the same dark sedan description as what Ms. Grier reports."

"That doesn't narrow it down much." I rub my cold hands

together. "How many tall, thin, dark-haired guys do we have in the city?"

"It still helps. Written statements hold up well in court," Kaitlyn replies, turning on the car and blasting the heat. She reaches across me to the vents, angling them toward me. "Better?"

"Thanks." I hold my hands over the vents, letting the warm air heat my icy fingers. It's really feeling like October tonight. "I appreciate what you're doing, but it doesn't sound like you have enough to move a case forward."

Kaitlyn smiles. "Ye of little faith. I have something else to show you."

She leans between the seats to rummage in one of the file boxes in the back.

I'm *very* aware of her ass in my face.

I look away, trying to find something else to fixate on.

Finally, she settles back into the driver's seat with a set of photographs in hand.

"My contact came through. The traffic cam at the intersection *did* get shots." She points east toward the roundabout up the road. She hands me the photographs.

I look through them. In each one is a dark car, slightly blurry to suggest speed, I guess. I've never been much of a car person, but I can't help but think Mom might've been a little offended to be run over by such a plain car.

It's hard to tell much about the driver from the photos, though. There's no clear picture of their face.

"Can you do anything with these?" I ask, unable to hide my skepticism.

"They're working to clear up the license plate. They need to outsource it since they don't have an in-house program strong enough to do it. They'll get back to me in a few days. Once I have a plate number, we can look into identifying the owner of the car."

"Are the cops aware you have this?"

Her gaze slides down and away.

"*Do* they know you have this?"

"They don't. They're also not actively investigating your mom's death. They *should* be, but they're not. It's going to take something solid—like what I'm putting together—before we can light a fire under the DA's ass."

All of this sounds legit, but I have no idea if it really is. I'm no PI.

Yet Kaitlyn is searching my face for something. I'm not entirely sure what she's hoping for, so I just say the only thing that's in my head.

Just one more inside thought becoming an outside thought.

I hand back the photos. "I trust you."

5

———

By the time I get home it's almost nine. I'm dead on my feet. My body is weary, but my mind is alert for whatever welcome-home trick my mom planned during my absence.

The house is menacingly quiet. The Halloween decorations on the lawn are being too normal. No synchronized song and dance. No flashing lights. The radio and TV are off.

I put my bag on the armchair by the door and stand in the living room for several moments waiting for—I don't know. *Something.*

"Mom?" I call out. I'm tense. I'm *ready*.

Nothing happens.

The air rings with silence.

There's no cooling or warming, or even the sense of air passing over my skin, which sometimes happens when she's getting ready to pounce.

I'm met with only silence.

Just silence.

For some reason, that's worse.

I'm still looking around, suspicious, as I call in Chinese

food and pay the exorbitant delivery fee to get them to bring it to my house rather than get back into the car to go pick it up.

I know I swore I'd eat better now that I'm in my thirties, but it's hard to be tired, hungry, *and* disciplined at the same time.

Once dinner is taken care of, I fall back on the couch and cover my eyes with my arm.

That's when I feel it.

A presence.

"I knew it," I mutter under my breath. I don't even open my eyes. "Did you *have* to wait for the moment I sat down?"

Nothing.

"Mom. *Come* on. I'm so tired. Let's just turn on a movie."

I roll open my eyes. I don't know what I'm going to see. A monster, a ghost. Whatever it is, I'm prepared to show her the full level of my annoyance.

Except what I see is *not* my mother.

There's some sort of shadowy figure hovering beside the couch. The hair on the back of my neck stands on end.

"Mom," I say, knowing damn good and well that is *not* my mother. No matter what shape my mother takes, or how silly, monstrous, or gross she becomes, she always—*always*—feels like my mom.

Still, I find myself saying, "Very funny. You can stop now."

Of course, nothing happens because it's not my mom. It's not going to listen to me. Hell, maybe it can't even hear me. I don't know. I've never encountered an ominous shadow before.

Worse, I'm scared to get up.

I have no choice but to remain pinned, paralyzed where I lie on the couch.

What will it do if I get up? Will it bum rush me? Suck me into its darkness?

Because *that's* a terrifying thought. Very *Scary Stories to Tell in the Dark*.

Maybe Mom has a friend? Maybe she's just got a ghost friend who can't take other shapes? Or speak? The shadow doesn't feel evil per se. But it does feel like it wants something.

I'm still trying to figure out my next move when my doorbell rings and I scream. I can't help myself.

"Ma'am?" A concerned voice calls through the door.

"Yes!" I don't know why I scream this, but I do. "Can I help you?"

I know damn well it's my dinner. Why am I yelling at the door?

Fortunately, the shadow remains fixed where it is, tracing the same path back and forth in front of me.

"Yes, uh, I've got your order," a voice replies, the poor, confused delivery driver sucked into—whatever the heck this is.

"I'm fine," I call out. Why did I say that? Maybe because I can't say, *Actually, I think I'm being held hostage by a spirit. Please assist.*

"Uh, that's nice, ma'am. Can you please come get your order?"

Not exactly.

"I'm not feeling well, so could you possibly leave the food on the porch and I'll get it after you leave? I don't want to expose you—" To *what*? Whatever the hell is happening in here?

There's a pause. He's probably checking to make sure that I paid already.

I'm very glad that I did.

"Okay," he decides at last. "I'll put it between the doors so it won't get wet."

I wonder if my generous tip is what earned me this VIP treatment.

"Thank you," I call out. My voice is *way* too high and shrill.

The storm door opens and something rustles and scratches at the inner door—presumably the sack of food.

My eyes remain fixed on the floating shadow.

"Have a good night," the guy calls, and the outer door creaks closed.

That still leaves me trapped in the living room with a freaky phantom and my dinner cooling on the porch.

I pull my knees up to my chest.

Mom, I'm scared.

No sooner do I think this than the temperature shifts. I feel Mom before I see her.

"Don't be afraid, pumpkin."

I've barely registered the soft blue orb of my mother's presence when the shadow leaps forward. I move away, too afraid to actually make a sound. When I whirl, ready—what the hell I'm going to do against a shadow I have no idea—I find that the shadow hasn't chased me.

It's squaring off with my mother.

She's dodging it.

There's something playful about my mom's movements, almost a *you can't catch me* vibe to it. That is until my mom lets out a banshee scream. It's so loud, so complete, that I feel it vibrate my bones.

The bulbs in the two living room lamps blow. Her light blue orb form tears from the room out of sight. The black shadow rockets after her.

I'm left standing in the dark living room, with the hair on my arms and neck standing straight up. The static in the air is thick enough to touch. My hands are clasped over my heart as if that will keep it in my chest.

"Mom?" I whisper.

Why the hell am I whispering? I don't even know except that now I have the terrible idea that she might be running from the shadow.

I mean, if there really is a spirit world—confirmed—then it stands to reason that there is more than one kind of spirit, right? My mom is a benevolent trickster, but that doesn't mean they all are. What if there are bad ones? Or hungry ones? Oh my *god*, what if there are ghost *eaters*?

"Mom!"

I search the house high and low for her.

I look in all the closets—a favorite hiding place of hers. I look under the bed, behind the shower curtain, in the basement—my least favorite place in the house by far because it's creepy as hell.

I even go out to the garage and look in the attic space above it.

Nothing. I can't find her.

I don't even feel her.

By the time I give up and get my food off the porch, it's cold.

At the dining room table, I eat mushu pork, lo mein, and enough crab rangoon to kill an elephant.

The exhaustion that I came home with is completely gone.

When I finally go to bed, I'm only able to lie there as a tense bundle of nerves. I'm convinced I'll never sleep again. I scroll on my phone for hours until I doze off.

Suddenly my eyes fly open, and sure enough, there she is.

"Mom! Are you okay? Where did you go?"

"What do you mean, pumpkin?"

"What do I mean? What was up with that creepy shadow? Why did it chase you? Why the hell was it even here?"

"I don't know what you're talking about."

She absolutely knows what I'm talking about. How could she forget an encounter like that so quickly?

"Whatever it was, I'm fine now, pumpkin."

"You were not okay when that thing chased you," I say calmly.

"I'm fine, see? Don't worry."

Dead is not fine. Before I can say this, the closet door creaks open slowly—that's what I get for not closing it all the way. Just like that, Mom is back to her old tricks again.

But even as the curtains begin to fan menacingly and girlish, creepy-as-hell laughter circles the room, I know she's trying to cover her lie with distractions.

The question is, *why*?

6

———

I finally find enough conviction to drive to the grocery and buy honest to goodness food. Like plants. I turn out of our neighborhood onto the main road and imme-diately spot a car pulled over at the curb. Almost in the exact spot where Mom died.

"Who the hell—" Then I recognize the car.

After a pickup rolls past, I pull a U-turn in the street and park behind the burgundy SUV with the decal *Park's PI Services* stenciled on the side.

I get out and walk along the curb toward the dark-haired figure kneeling down, inspecting—what? The concrete?

"Hey. I saw you when I was driving by." *Obviously.* If I hadn't seen her I wouldn't have stopped.

Kaitlyn stands, smiling. "Hey."

I gesture at the concrete. "What are you doing?"

"I think I have a match for the car that hit your mom," she says, frowning at the curb.

"Oh, wow."

"I have to prove it's the right car. Burden of proof, you know."

I don't follow, and she must realize that by the look on my face.

"The plates don't match the car. But there's an owner who reported his car stolen the day before your mom was killed and I think *that's* the one that hit her, except *that* car was *red*, not dark like what we've got on the camera. The plates were stolen too, but I think I've tracked them to a garage in the next town over. I'm waiting for the paper trail on that to come through."

I nod like I understand any of this. "This might sound dumb, but I still don't know what you're doing staring at the curb."

"Not dumb." Kaitlyn smiles. "I was looking to see if there was anything here to prove that the dark car is really red. A nice chunk of bumper with a red interior or an edging of red paint would be nice. No chance your mom had a titanium leg, did she?"

This surprises a laugh out of me. "No. Not that I'm aware of. I think the medical examiner would've mentioned it."

Looking at this stretch of road brings back sore memories, clear and bright.

My mother, the way she looked in the foyer, pulling on her walking shoes. The way she turned to me, smile bright, and said, *Should we order a pizza and watch a movie?*

When I'd agreed, she'd added, *Call it in and I'll race it home.*

Then she went out the door.

And out of my life.

Later I would be certain that the click of the door behind her that night had had a heavier sound to it. More likely it's something I added retroactively, knowing what I know now.

But I can't get that image of her out of my mind.

The last moment I saw her alive. In the flesh.

How beautiful she was. How bright and infectious her smile. How mischievous her eyes. Even when she wasn't up to anything, she could make you think she was with a smile like that.

I remember listening to an ambulance siren growing closer. Hearing it pass by the house. I'd said the same silent prayer I always say when I hear an ambulance, a simple, *Good luck. God speed.*

Only later I realized it must've been the ambulance on its way to her. They wouldn't have used the siren after picking her up if she was dead already.

I hadn't known any of that while I was waiting for her to come home.

The night stretched on.

The pizza came.

Then the police.

When the officer had rung the doorbell and I found him on the porch holding his hat, I knew. I knew even before he said, *Are you Laurie Bell?*

What followed was the haze of going to the morgue, identifying her body. By that point a fugue had settled over my life. I'd stopped eating. Sleeping.

I think I'd all but given up. In spirit, certainly. It was just my body that wouldn't let go.

I stopped leaving the house. I stopped getting out of bed.

Then my mom came back.

She came back as if she'd never left.

Get up Laurie, she said. *Get up and throw me a party.*

I hadn't given her a memorial when I'd got her ashes back. I hadn't had it in me to do it even though my mom's friends had called and asked, promising to do all the work—she'd had *so* many friends.

They'd brought casseroles. They'd even tried to clean the house a few times.

I thought they'd be pissed that the memorial was happening months after her actual passing. But they were thrilled. Amy, my mom's closest friend, said it was a good sign.

I knew you'd pull through. You're strong like her.

I didn't tell a single one of them I was only throwing this party because my mother was back from the dead and demanding it.

I hadn't the heart to tell any of them she's still here.

So I threw a party and they came. Mom hadn't learned to do any tricks yet, or maybe she was too shy with her old friends. In either case, I felt her there that night, but never saw her until after they left and I was cleaning up the plates and glasses and cake.

For some reason, thinking about all of this, I've begun to cry.

"Oh, Laurie. God, I'm so stupid." Kaitlyn's face crumples. All the humor is gone. "I'm so sorry. I shouldn't have made jokes. That was—"

"It wasn't the jokes," I say. "I like your jokes."

This earns me a wan smile. Her hands hang awkwardly in front of her. She's pulled her sleeves over her wrists. Clearly her intention was to wipe my tears away but she's stopped herself.

Slowly she returns her hands to her side. And I'm left wishing that she would have done it.

"I was just remembering the last time that I saw her," I say. "When she left for her walk. She took them every night. I never thought she'd not come back from one, you know?"

She nods. "I do. Yeah. I remember the last time I kissed my dad bye and told him to have a great day. We never know."

"Is that why you invited me to meet with Ms. Grier? Because it didn't seem like you really needed to interview her. Or at least, she didn't give you anything new."

Kaitlyn gives me another shy smile. "Not so smooth, am I? I thought talking to the last person who saw your mom would help give you closure. That maybe it would be better to know she didn't die alone. That had been the hardest part for me, knowing Dad was alone, and probably really scared."

"I'm sorry," I say. Because what else can you say when confronted with someone else's grief? And I feel like I owe it to her. She's been so gentle with mine.

She shrugs as if to say, *It is what it is.*

"It did help," I tell her, and I resist the urge to reach out and take her in my arms. To let her rest her head on my shoulder while I squeeze her tight. The urge is strong, but I have no idea if that would be welcome. And there's still this damn question of professionalism.

But if that were true, then why is Kaitlyn tracing the outline of my lips with her eyes before looking away with quite a bit of color in her cheeks.

It's the cold, I tell myself. *Her cheeks are only red from the cold.*

"I'm glad it helped," she says, her attention on the curb once more.

WHEN I GET HOME FROM THE GROCERY, I ORDER TAKEOUT. I know, *I know*. I'm doing my best, okay? I'm too tired to cook. Besides, I have a hit of inspiration and I want to work on my screenplay. So I brew a pot of coffee and sit down at my computer.

I've decided to add a hot detective as my final girl's love interest after all. I want to do a switching back and forth between the detective and final girl POVs, where the detective thinks about the person she killed and we won't know until the end if she's the actual killer or just rolling in guilt over a bad guy she killed in the recent past. I think it'll add a nice layer of tension and misdirection to the story.

I'm sketching the details of this outline into my notes—trying to make sure it doesn't clash with my earlier idea of it being unclear which of the twins actually died—when the doorbell rings and I get my lunch.

Indian today. Chana saag and buttered chicken and an order of garlic naan.

I fall deep into the writing—but it's still a mess—half of it is screenplay format, half reads like a novel. Still I'm feeling that lovely flush of warm energy that always comes with good, smooth writing. I punctuate sentences with bites of saag, but otherwise, it's quiet.

Just me and the typing.

Autumn sunlight dances on the window and I lose myself in the process. Maybe that's why I don't notice the shift. The blooming stillness.

When the energy leaves me and I feel the writing session coming to a close, I sit quietly for a moment, enjoying the exhaustion that comes at the end of a good session.

Next door, my neighbors' three little kids are throwing themselves into a leaf pile over and over again while their golden retriever jumps in after them, digging out one kid after another as if it's a search and rescue game.

I look up and see Mom is there. Not as any kind of crazy monster or gory crone, just as her own blue-white semi-transparent orby self.

"Hey," I say. "When did you come in?"

"I like it when you're happy." There's a dreamy quality to her voice. "I feel at peace when you're at peace."

Then I remember the shadowy figure. "Are you gonna tell me what that thing was?"

She pretends not to know.

"Come on. I know you know something. What is it?"

"I don't know," she says. "Just like I don't know exactly what I am right now."

A terrible thought strikes me, and I see the soft light of my mother's being shimmer as if struck.

"Don't get upset," she says.

Too late for that. "Does it hurt you to be here, Mom? Is it hard for you to be—the way you are?"

"It hurts more to see your heart breaking, pumpkin. No mother wants to see that."

She is uncharacteristically thoughtful today. I've got to admit that scares me more than any zombie.

I ask, "Mom, why did you come back? Why didn't you go where—wherever it is all the other de—others go."

I almost said *all the other dead people*, but that seems harsh.

"I heard you crying."

The hair on the back of my neck rises again. I think I see something move in the hallway. Something beyond my mother's formlessness. Was it a shadow? Am I imagining it?

My mom goes on as if she hasn't noticed. "I heard you crying, and I couldn't leave you, pumpkin. I just couldn't. Not like that."

That's the real reason she came back? It hurts to hear her say it, but I'm not surprised. I am—was—blessed with a loving, affectionate mother. Why wouldn't she come back and try to cheer me up with her silly pranks?

I pick up a feather from my desktop. I look at all the trinkets, all the gifts she's given me over the years. My mother's endless efforts to put a smile on my face.

I look into the hallway again, certain I saw a shadow this time, but there's nothing.

"If it hurts you to be here, Mom, you should go. I'll miss you, but I don't want you to be in pain."

She comes closer, her light a little brighter now that the sun is dipping below the horizon.

"Oh, I could never be in pain if I'm with you, pumpkin."

Static crackles along my skin.

I know that *thing*, whatever it is, is back even before it glides into the room.

"Mom," I whisper, afraid to make any sudden movement.

"It says I can't be here," she whispers, as if she's also trying to go undetected. "It says this isn't where I belong."

The shadow moves closer.

"Is it evil? Does it want to hurt you?"

Before I get my answer, the temperature of the room shifts, a flash of heat followed by an icy, arctic blast. Then my mother tears from the room, through the closet door and out of sight, another banshee scream rattling the windows and my nervous system as she goes.

The shadow follows her.

So shadow has no interest in me. It only lingers near me because it knows my mother is close—that she'll remain close until—when?

When I stop mourning her? Stop crying myself to sleep?

Stop crying out to her like a scared child in the night?

And what happens if it catches her? Will it hurt her? She didn't answer me as to whether or not it could cause her pain.

There's also the matter of her staying at all.

What happens if she doesn't *cross over*, as they say? Is it bad for her? I can't help but feel like there must be negative repercussions of some kind.

It's not just her improved scaring skills that are changing.

I've also noticed the forgetfulness. When alive my mother was an encyclopedia of information. She could give you dates, times, and extensive details for every aspect of our lives.

Now she remembers less and less about her old life, as it's becoming little more than a distant dream to her. Two weeks ago I asked her what Amy's birthday was so I could send her a card. Not only did she not remember the birthday, but she couldn't remember Amy.

Amy! Her best friend of twenty-three years!

Will there become a point when she doesn't remember me, too? What then?

Will she be trapped here, wandering the earth, unable to remember why she was ever here?

I'm still thinking about this as the last of the day gives itself over to night. As I watch part of the Halloween Scream-Fest marathon on TV, killing the hours between dinner and bedtime. As I go up to shower, change, brush my teeth. As I carry on with this business of living—Mom stubbornly absent.

She's still not back after I climb into bed and pull the covers up to my chin.

I lie in bed remembering the little trick she did with the curtains the night before. I should add that to the screenplay. It was a great visual, very atmospheric.

I imagine—as I sometimes do—someone interviewing me about my latest work.

Where did you get the inspiration for that incredible scene, Laurie?

For the first time I imagine saying, *My mom. She came back and haunted me because I was depressed that she'd died.*

I can't imagine what the interviewer would possibly say to that, so the fantasy dissolves and I turn over onto my side, pulling my knees up to my chest.

As I doze off to sleep, the house is still quiet.

Mom doesn't come back.

7

———

My class doesn't meet on Halloween night, so the day before, I throw them a bit of a Halloween party. I know this is silly since they're all adults, but I'm pleased to find they're as into it as I am.

They wear costumes. I pass out candy. We tell each other scary stories in a round-the-campfire fashion, with the desks arranged in a circle. For a minute I forget that I'm a teacher and this is my job. I'm having so much fun that I'm reluctant to let them go at the end of the two-hour session.

This is where their loyalties end. No matter how much fun they were having fifteen minutes before, they're absolutely ready to ditch me.

After they file out of the room, I stay behind to put the desks back in order and pick up a few stray candy wrappers from the floor.

Not so adult after all, I think as I toss the trash in the can under the teacher's desk.

I'm packing up my bag when my cell phone starts to ring.

For a second, I half expect it to be my mother. Impossible.

She hasn't been able to call me since she died. But it's weird how slow the brain is to accept that someone is dead. My brain continues to expect her to call me like she used to at this time of day, to ask me when I'm heading home or to run dinner plans by me, or let me know that she'll be out late with her friends.

I *think* it's her because there's some part of my brain that refuses to accept that she's gone.

Maybe because she hasn't really passed on, has she? a little voice says. *And whose fault is that?*

My guilt has been rampant since Mom confessed that the reason she came back was because she heard me crying.

My throat is tight when I answer the call.

"It's me." Kaitlyn. I'm surprised to hear from her. It's been over a week since I had my strange emotional breakdown on the side of the road. There was definitely a part of me that thought she'd been avoiding me thanks to *that* waterworks display. That either the tears had turned her off or maybe she was just trying to erect a stronger barrier of professionalism between us.

Smart move considering I'm a crazy hot mess.

I was flirty and then I was crying. *No one* is going to find that attractive.

"Hey," I say. *Be cool.* "What's up?"

"Are you done for the day?" she asks.

"You know I am," I say. "Are you outside again? Got someone else you want me to meet?" Because that's the only reason she would call me, right? She must have some sort of update about my mother's case.

"No one to meet, but we do need to talk."

"And here I was hoping my ex would be the last woman to ever say that to me," I joke.

Kaitlyn doesn't return my laugher, and that makes it *so* much worse. I don't even get one of her cute snorts.

"That serious, huh?" I say.

"I'm afraid so," she says.

Well, damn. "I'll be out in a second."

"I'll wait for you here. No rush." She ends the call.

By the time I get to the parking lot my heart is pounding so hard I feel sick and a little lightheaded. My mind is making up all kinds of wild scenarios of what she might want to tell me. Fortunately, she can't tell me someone I love is dead. Too late for that.

Apart from some distant cousins in Florida that are little more than strangers to me anyway, I don't have any family left. Our dog, Cujo, died two years before Mom did, and she never had the heart to replace him. I think the only bad news that might *actually* land is if Kaitlyn says she is dropping my case and never wants to see me again.

Or maybe Kaitlyn has cancer.

Or she has a secret lover who wants her to drop the case because she can tell that the two of us are on the brink of falling in love—which is delusional, I know, but the mind—especially *my* mind—can come up with all kinds of stuff, especially in a panic.

These theories evaporate when I see her.

She's got a fat lip and a bruise across her cheek.

My fear has folded completely into anger. "What the hell happened to your face?"

"It's nothing," she says, and forces a smile. "You should see the other guy."

"Yes, *actually*, I would like to see the other guy," I say, feeling very hot in the head suddenly. "I think I've got quite a bit to say to that asshole."

Her eyes slide away. "Laurie, please. I need to tell you something."

It's the use of my name that gets me. Exhaustion hangs from her like a heavy winter coat. Her shoulders sag, her face is sallow. I realize that my anger isn't welcome here. At least, not right now.

"I'm sorry," I say, adjusting my satchel strap across my chest. "I'm listening."

"The guy I've been following—the suspect—he came to my agency," she says.

"Did he do that?" I nod toward her busted lip and darkened cheek. "Did he threaten you?"

Not only did he run over my mom, but now he's hitting the girl I like too?

God, as if I need another reason to bury this guy in my backyard.

It doesn't help that grief amplifies my self-destructive tendency. I don't even care who wins the fight. I just want the chance to hurt him as much as he hurt me.

Kaitlyn takes a steadying breath. "Please let me finish."

"Sorry. Go on."

"I found where he was staying, and I found the car. I staked out his motel room and got some shots of him there, and lots of photos of the car. I was able to follow him for a solid three or four days before he spotted me. That's how this happened."

She points at her bruised cheek.

"He didn't hit me," she clarifies. "He was trying to take the camera, but I wouldn't let go. When *he* let go, it came back and popped me in the face, fell on the pavement, and broke. I lost my last batch of photos, but it's fine. I have enough from the first few days saved on my computer and backed up."

I don't know if she's lying to calm me down. I feel like she's totally the kind of person who would downplay an injury so others don't worry about her.

"Doesn't sound stupid to me," I say. "Sounds like you put yourself in danger for me. I don't want you to do that."

Her cheeks are turning red. She presses on. "That's not what I'm worried about."

I hold up a hand. "Excuse me? Getting into a confrontation with a possible killer *isn't* what you're worried about?"

Now she looks truly apologetic. Like someone who screwed up big time.

My pulse is rocketing at the base of my throat again. "What else happened?"

"When he came to the agency, I thought he just wanted to confirm that I'm the one working your mom's case. Why else would I be taking pictures of his car, right?"

"I don't know how he would connect you to my mom just because you took pictures of his car."

"*He* knows he hit someone, and your mom was the only hit-and-run case in the city in the last year. There's been a notice in the press for months, asking for anyone with information about her death to come forward. He could've gotten her name from that. With her name, it wouldn't have been hard to get *your* name. In her obituary, you're listed as the only surviving relative. You don't have to have any investigation skills to put your name into a search engine and find out all about you. Your position at the college is the first result that comes up. And your home address is in the faculty directory."

I'm trying to put all this together, while also wrapping my head around the idea that Kaitlyn probably knows *a lot* more about me than I realized. If she could do all that, then she probably also found all the photos of my ex in my social media albums.

"Laurie, do you understand what I'm saying?" She's searching my face.

"You're saying the killer might have my name and home address."

"He absolutely has your name and home address. He told my receptionist as much."

I can only blink at her.

"He approached Brandi, clearly fishing for information."

I don't interrupt, though the urge to do so is *monumental*.

"He said, 'Is Ms. Park the one working the hit-and-run case for Laurie?'"

"Shit."

Kaitlyn held up a hand. "Brandi's not an idiot. She knows not to give info to strangers off the streets. But when she was reluctant to respond, he added, 'Laurie Bell. From Pine Street. We're friends. She recommended a PI for my lost wallet, but I wasn't sure this was the right place.'"

"I would never recommend a private investigator for a lost wallet. It's too expensive," I say. "It's cheaper just to replace everything."

What a dumb thing to say. It's right up there with I like the way you write my name.

But it's honestly the first thing I think of.

"I'm not saying you're too expensive. I think you're worth every penny."

She interrupts my mounting panic.

"I know." Kaitlyn snorts, either thinking what an idiot I am or to humor me. "It wasn't a great cover story, but you can see the problem, right? He knows your name, he knows you live on Pine. And he came to the office less than twenty minutes after our altercation. That's not enough time for a thorough search. That tells me he was already keeping tabs on you."

"Why?" I ask.

"I don't know." Her gaze slides away again. I can't tell if she's lying or just protecting me from something. Maybe both? "I reached out to the police department this afternoon. I pressed charges even though the injury is *technically* my own fault. But they don't need to know it wasn't his fist that did this."

"Shit." I don't know what else to say.

"I'm not above lying if it gets a killer in handcuffs. They issued a warrant for his arrest. It's a good start."

"I'm sensing a fluid moral code," I say approvingly.

"I wanted to give the police a reason to pick him up. I also turned over all my evidence and case files to the DA this afternoon. That's what I was doing when he came by the agency. I'm hoping the assault charge will be enough to hold him until the hit-and-run charges are up and running."

"I have so many questions." And this is true. My head is swimming with them. "What's his name? What's he look like? Where the hell is this motel?"

"Marcus Steiner is the name he gave the receptionist at the motel. He's white. Six feet tall. Lean. Dark eyes and hair. He wears it in a little ponytail at the back of his neck. Pock-marked cheeks and tattoos on his hands. There's no local record of him anywhere. No job, no papers. He's paying for that room in cash. I got the station to pull a print from my camera, where he grabbed it. They're running it now."

"If he's staying in a motel that makes it sound like he's not from here." I'm still trying to sound calm, chill. Like I'm totally fine with what's going on here, but in truth, hearing her describe the guy makes me nervous. I feel like I've seen someone like that lurking around, but I can't quite place where I saw him.

The grocery? The post office? Outside of Ms. Grier's apartment?

Or am I just being paranoid? Possibly, given the rapidly rising anxiety overtaking my body.

"He's got an East Coast accent, not as strong as Boston but somewhere in the vicinity," Kaitlyn goes on, clearly unaware that I'm fighting off a would-be panic attack.

I'm all but clutching the base of my throat. "If he's not from here then why didn't he leave town after hitting my mom? Why stick around?"

Kaitlyn blows air through her lips. "I've been asking myself the same question. What's keeping him here? He's already proven that he's a runner. So why stay? It's strange."

For a moment, ominous silence hangs between us.

She ends it by saying, "As soon as I realized he had your name and address, I had to see you. I wanted to know if you're okay."

God, she's looking up at me through her lashes with those gorgeous big blue eyes again. My panic actually gets worse, not better. But it feels a little *lustier* now.

She's searching my face. "I've asked the police to keep a watch on your house in case he comes around. I didn't want you to freak out if you saw a cruiser circling."

"I can take a punch, too, you know. Maybe my bruise won't be as cute as yours but—"

Bruise as cute as yours...? I cringe. Seriously, what is wrong with me? Why do I even try to flirt? It's painful for everyone.

But she's giving me this strange little smile. I can't tell if she's annoyed or if she pities me.

"Okay, Muhammad Ali. Just promise me you won't open your door to strangers until they pick him up," she says.

I scoff. "Tomorrow is Halloween. I'll be opening my door to *all* the strangers."

"No chance you'll cancel?"

"Zero."

"Do you want company for the night?" She's watching me closely again.

Do I? There are few things I want more than Kaitlyn at my house, on my sofa with those pouty lips of hers, but there is no way in hell I can invite her over. Can you imagine what my mother would do?

"Sorry," Kaitlyn says. "I shouldn't have sprung that on you."

"No, it's okay." *Fix it, fix it, fix it.* "I do want you there. I do. But my house isn't—It's not guest appropriate at the moment."

"You don't strike me as a slob."

"I'm not," I say proudly. But then I don't have a good excuse to counter that with. I finish lamely by adding, "Now's just not a good time."

She seems disappointed, but whether it's for my safety or romantic reasons remains unclear. I can't deny the physical tension though. I'm usually *very* good at reading women.

"Then promise me you'll be careful." She gives my hand an affectionate squeeze.

I have a disturbingly clear image of opening the front door with my candy bucket to find Steiner—as Kaitlyn has described him—standing on my porch, knife in hand. He sinks it into my gut before I can close the door. It goes right through the eye of the plastic jack-o'-lantern candy bucket with a satisfying *thunk*.

That's how I'd write the scene anyway.

"Are you listening?" Kaitlyn says. Now she looks annoyed. "I like your face how it is. So don't go looking for trouble, even if it's tempting."

She likes my face.

My cheeks are on fire.

"I'm not convinced he'll come after me," I tell her. "The fact that he ran from the scene screams coward to me."

"Not necessarily." She leans a hip into the door of my car.

I feel my body lean toward hers for a fraction of a second before I come to my senses.

"If he's got a record, he might run to avoid getting caught for another crime. It could be the reason he left that other town," she says. "If that's the case, it's a crime with a stiffer penalty than a hit and run."

That gives me pause. What's worse than killing a person with your car?

Kaitlyn sees me puzzling it over and nods, clearly pleased that I'm taking it seriously.

Joke's on you, I think. My anxiety makes me take *everything* seriously.

"I'd hate it if anything happened to you," she says.

My god that's some heavy eye contact. And such pretty eyes.

Immediately I think of the ending scene from *Jeepers Creepers*.

Way to ruin it, brain.

I swallow. "Would you really?"

Are we back to flirting? *Is* this flirting? I'm not convinced it is flirting because Kaitlyn's smile is a little sad at the corners again. Can you look sad and flirt at the same time? I didn't think so, but the eye contact is at one hundred percent.

"Yes," she says. "I would."

8

———

om wakes me on Halloween morning in the form of that disturbing clown toy from *Poltergeist*.

"It's here," she says. "The best day of the year."

Then she cackles, and the toy's head spins on its neck and the doors to my armoire and closet begin to blow open and closed. She even makes the closet shine with a bright light like it did in the movie. I'm actually impressed.

I sit up on my elbow and squint at it. "How are you doing that?"

"Trade secret," the clown says. "Also, there's a man outside. He keeps looking at the house."

My heart rockets, causing my temples to pound and arms to feel weak. Of course, I immediately think of Kaitlyn's warning from yesterday. Is it Steiner? Has he come to finish me off for some bizarre reason I can't even begin to understand?

Maybe he's just a completionist—killed the mother, gotta finish off the daughter.

Like watching *all* the *Friday the 13th* movies. You don't

really want to. By the time Jason makes it to space, you're over it. But you gotta finish because at that point it's the principle of the thing.

You're *committed*.

I throw back the covers, rush past the clown, and head downstairs. Very slowly, I peek around the curtains and search the street.

I don't see anyone.

Mom's cold spot settles in beside me.

"There's no one out there," I say.

"Yes, there is. Look."

She's not pointing exactly, but I do see a man come around the side of my neighbor's house—the one cattycorner from mine. "That's just Mr. Johnson. You know him. You hate —hated—him, actually. Why call him 'a man'?"

"He's staring at the house," my mother says, as if this answers my question. "He has a menacing expression."

"Of course he does. He thinks Halloween is Satan's birthday and our yard is the work of devil worship."

I scan the street but see no one else. "Was he the guy you meant? No one else?"

I turn to find my mother has disappeared.

The radio in the living room kicks on and "Day-O" by Harry Belafonte blasts from the speakers.

A burst of cold air pushes at my back, making the curtains flap around me.

"You can't lift me, can you?" This is as much a prayer as a declaration.

"Why!" she laments.

"I'm heavier than curtains and bedsheets and doors, maybe?"

She groans, disappointed.

I know she'd be forcing me to dance if she could.

"Maybe you'll get better with practice," I reassure her.

I follow her orb to the living room, where the TV flickers on. The channels flip until they stop suddenly on *Coraline*.

"You know this movie is far scarier for adults than for children," Mom says.

She has said this before and recently. Again, I get the feeling that maybe her mind is unraveling more the longer she stays here, the longer she tries to stay with *me*.

"Mom, how do you feel?" I ask.

"I don't feel much," she says. "But more than you'd think. It turns out a lot of the feeling is created by the mind. But all that's on my mind these days, pumpkin, is you."

The channels start flipping again, pausing next on *The Rocky Horror Picture Show*.

She'll have a hard time picking a channel today. All the stations will be capitalizing on the Halloween theme. Her favorites will be competing with themselves.

"You should work on your story," she says. "You'll be too busy to do it tonight. You still need to carve a pumpkin. You know you've got to get it out before dark or the demons will come."

That makes me think of something. "Mom, can you see other ghosts?"

"Yes," she says.

"*Really?* So is the stuff about the veil being thin today true?"

The flicking channel stops on *The Simpsons*. It's a "Treehouse of Horrors" anthology episode.

"Yes, the veil is very thin," she says as Bart puts a flashlight under his chin, giving his face deep shadows. "That's a good thing. He's too busy to worry about me today."

That sends chills down my spine.

"Who's too busy? The shadowy thing?"

She doesn't answer.

"Go work on your story, pumpkin."

"But—"

"Go on," she says. "There's no time to waste."

I have a clear sense that I'll be getting nothing else out of her.

I sigh, turning away. "I'll make some coffee first. And maybe some eggs."

My mother groans. "*Oh*, what I wouldn't give for a cup of coffee."

I SPEND THE DAY AT THE COMPUTER. THE SUN RISES HIGH then begins its descent, throwing shadows across my desk and windowsill as the day passes me by. A few of the rocks that my mother had brought home from her walks spark when the light hits them. When the furnace kicks on in the bowels of the house, one of the feathers is blown forward by the heat coming from the vent—not by any ghostly means.

I put it back in its place and write on. I'm in another beautiful flow state. The words come easy, the scenes dancing fully formed behind my eyes. My heroine has just come up with a brilliant way to dispatch the killer even though I was afraid I'd written myself into a corner.

I love it when they do that.

It's the buzz of my phone that finally breaks my concentration. That's when I realize how low the sun is now. I've only got an hour until sunset. Tops.

"Shit." I answer the call while also frantically saving my progress. "Hello?"

"Hey, it's Kaitlyn."

"Hi." Why am I smiling like an idiot? What is wrong with me? I haven't had this big of a crush on a girl since Val broke up with me. Then again, she cheated on me with her tennis instructor, so I guess that left a pretty bitter taste in my mouth. Especially since she'd tried to make me seem like a paranoid jerk when I'd tried to tell her that I was one hundred percent sure she wanted to bang the guy.

She'd volleyed with a *you just don't like tennis*.

"We got a match on the print they pulled from my camera. It was only a partial, but it matches two unsolved murder cases in Pennsylvania. The suspect in those cases is Dennis Smart, and he matches the description of Marcus Steiner. Laurie, they think this guy is a serial killer."

I feel strangely separated from my body. "Is this your idea of a Halloween prank?"

"No prank. If they're right and he *is* a serial killer, then it explains why he hit and ran on your mom. He's avoiding life in prison or the electric chair. Those penalties are far more severe."

I feel the pathways in my brain dilating, giving everything a dreamy, abstract tinge.

"My mother was run over by a serial killer and this serial killer has my address and name. Are you *sure* this isn't a Halloween prank?"

"This isn't a prank." Now she sounds mad. "Please take this seriously."

"Okay, but what the hell is a killer from Pennsylvania doing in Michigan?"

"They're working on that," she says.

I don't even know what to say to that. "And what am I supposed to do?"

"They got a warrant for his arrest, they just need to find him. You have to be careful until they do."

"What are the names of the women he allegedly killed?"

There's a pause and a shuffle of papers. "Megan Barten and Cosette Tracey."

I can't resist. Before she even hangs up I've got the internet up and I'm searching for the girls. Kaitlyn is going on about the warrant, but I barely hear her. I'm reading everything I can about Megan Barten, twenty-eight, and Cosette Tracey, thirty-four. How they went out one night, just like my mom did, how they kissed their families goodbye and promised to be home soon, just like my mom did—but that promise wasn't kept by any of the women.

They're calling this guy the Late Night Nabber. He stabbed both women over ten times while raping them.

Just lovely.

At least my mom didn't go through that.

"Do you think this guy targeted my mom?"

"No," she says. "I think it was an accident. Most killers get caught because they make a mistake like that. Maybe he looked away from the road or maybe he was drunk. He has a couple of DUIs and drunk and disorderly charges on his record. That's why he's in the system."

"But why is he *here?*" I ask again. Of all the places this guy could flee too, why Michigan?

"I'll let you know when they figure that out," she says. "But you realize the danger?"

I realize the danger all right.

Because I'm looking back and forth between Megan's picture and Cosette's picture and there's something blaringly obvious.

They both look like *me.*

Like my mom.

That's why I'd really asked whether Kaitlyn thought she was targeted on purpose.

I've watched enough horror movies to know that serial killers have a type. This Late Night Nabber's got a thing for brunettes with small dark eyes and a smattering of freckles across their nose. Pointy chins and mousey ears.

And I got all of those features from my mom. I am much taller than those girls though. I'm 5'9, while Megan was 5'1 and Cosette was 5'3.

"Laurie?"

"I'm here," I say, and sensing that's not what she wanted to hear, I add, "I'll be careful."

"Good. I hope you will."

"If you really think I'm in danger," I say, "there's a spare key you could use to get into my house."

What are you doing! my brain screams.

A beat of silence.

"Is it too soon to give you a key to my house?" And just like that I've gone right back to being a creep. "I mean, don't use it if you don't have to. I'd rather you not but—"

But it'll be easier to explain my ghost mom to you than be stabbed to death if it comes down to that.

"Are you sure you want to tell me where it is?" Kaitlyn asks. "That's pretty personal. What if I'm the bad guy? Or an accomplice? I could've bruised my own face, you know. I guess I did. Technically."

"If this was a scary movie, I would be the bad guy," I say.

"Why?"

I like the amusement in her voice.

"Because I'm positioned as the victim. The one you don't expect. You'd come to save me and find ten bodies walled up in the basement or something. Turns out me and my mom were eating all the neighborhood children the whole time."

She laughs. "I'll be sure to check the basement before I leave then."

"Good. The guilt is killing me."

"If that's the case then you better tell me where the key is so I can take all those bodies off your hands." The humor fades from her voice a little. "I promise only to use it if it's an emergency."

I say it for the second time. "I trust you."

And I tell her where to find the spare key.

9

———

I carve a very hasty Jack Skellington into my pumpkin while *Trick r' Treat* plays in the background. Another Laurie—in the movie—is pretending to be a vulnerable Red Riding Hood while a killer stalks her through the woods.

"Why couldn't you have named me after her?" I ask Mom, pointing my carving knife at the TV. "She's cool."

"You were born before this movie came out, pumpkin," Mom says. Her orb flits past me toward the window again.

She's excited for the night to begin.

"Now that you're dead, do you know secrets to the universe? Like if werewolves were real, would you tell me?"

She ignores this, zipping from one window to another.

"Fill up the candy bucket!" Mom says. "They're coming!"

No sooner do I open a new bag of Halloween candy and fill the plastic jack-o'-lantern bucket than the doorbell starts going off.

With Kaitlyn's warnings in my ears, I peek through the peephole before opening the door.

No grown men. Just a cluster of little goblins.

I pull down my Freddy Krueger mask and open the door.

The kids squeal. "Trick or treat!"

All but one. That little smartass says, "Where's your knives hand? You're supposed to have knives for fingers."

Look here you little punk— "I took it off so I could give you this candy. Should I have kept it on and *tricked* you instead?"

"No!" The kids run off the porch, back to their parents, who wave from the sidewalk.

I return the wave.

For the next round it's a dad carrying his toddler on his hip with the tiniest of candy pumpkin buckets in her hand. I can only push two mini candy bars through the top.

"Got to start 'em young," I say.

"Your decorations are amazing," the dad says. "Must've taken you forever to get those up. How are you doing the window display?"

It takes me a minute to realize that it's my mom back at the window, putting on another performance.

"Oh, uh—holograms," I say, and shut the door before he can question my paper-thin alibi.

The candy is going fast. I don't know if it's the yard display that sends the message that I definitely have candy, but whatever it is, I feel like I get every kid in the neighborhood twice. I go through the first bag and into the second while managing the endless parade of little hobgoblins coming to my door.

Lots of costumes I recognize are from the superhero universes that are hot right now. We also get some classics— vampires, witches, skeletons, Disney princesses, Dorothy complete with red shoes. A mime. I'm hella impressed by the Transformer who can turn from boy to cardboard car—and he demonstrates this ability on my leaf-covered sidewalk, staying in his car shape until his mom collects him from the sidewalk with apologies.

I'm also pleased to see Lock, Shock, and Barrel from *The*

Nightmare Before Christmas, though they say nothing about my pumpkin.

Missed opportunity there, kids.

On the TV, *Trick r' Treat* ends and *Casper* begins. I'm about to change it—wondering if ghosts will upset Mom—but she is giggling.

"You used to love this movie so much," she says. "You could quote it from beginning to end."

"I still can." And I wouldn't mind asking Kaitlyn if I can keep her. Just sayin'.

My eyes are focused out the window. I can't stop myself from looking up and down the street, searching for a man who matches Steiner's description. But I don't see anyone.

Or at least, I don't see anyone *out of place*.

I see dads with their kids. I see big brothers carrying candy bags and adjusting costumes. But there's no one with a creepy mask staring at my house. No lurking shadows.

I do see the police cruiser slide by not once but twice, and I feel a little better for it.

A light rain begins to tap at the windows and the wind chases stray leaves across the street. Jack-o'-lanterns flicker, their illuminated insides bright in the encroaching darkness. The kids are thinning out, probably discouraged by the change in weather.

I check the clock. Only thirty minutes left for trick-or-treating anyway. This little group coming up the driveway will probably be my last.

I slide the mask down over my face again and push open the door.

An inflatable T-rex cries, "Trick or treat!"

It's accompanied by an angel and a devil. The quartet is rounded out by what I can only assume is—a caterpillar? Lots of green and a red nose.

I give each a heaping handful of candy.

I'm about to put the last fistful into the caterpillar's bucket when another one of Mom's ear-splitting banshee screams cuts through the air behind me.

I turn just in time to see her light blue orb disappear through the living room ceiling, the shadow in pursuit.

"Whoa," the angel says. "How'd you do that?"

My heart is hammering in my chest. It takes me several seconds to recover.

"It's the TV," I say. "It was the movie."

"Casper isn't scary!" the dinosaur says. "It's a dumb movie for girls."

"Excuse me," I say. "I'm a girl."

"Ew."

This little shit.

"Stop looking into my house. And how the hell can you see through that thing anyway?" I shove more candy in their bags. "Take this. Now go on. Keep a lookout for—"

I don't even know how to finish that. Killers? Shadowy ghost eaters?

"Weirdos," I finish lamely.

I usher them away from the porch, casting nervous looks over my shoulder.

Mom, please be okay.

From the driveaway the devil yells, "You're the weirdo, lady!"

He and his friends run off into the night laughing. As long as they don't come back and TP my house or smash my pumpkin, I don't care.

I shut the front door, cutting their laughter short.

"Mom?"

For a moment, I just stand there listening. My ears strain to hear even the faintest sound.

The banshee scream has dissipated, leaving only more of that ringing silence in its wake.

I don't know how to explain it, but it feels like the air is thick with electricity.

"Mom?" I whisper.

Why am I whispering? Couldn't tell you.

"Mom, are you okay?"

Nothing.

I search the house high and low for her again, but just like before, I don't find any sign of her. Not so much as a cold spot.

The doorbell rings once during my search but I ignore it. I still need to check the basement, and we're past trick-or-treating time anyway. They'll get the hint. And I guess they do because the doorbell doesn't ring for a second time. If there's a knock, I don't hear it.

When I come upstairs from the basement—the absolute last place I wanted to check—I find the front door is open ever so slightly.

This gives me pause.

I pushed the last batch of the kids out the door pretty quickly when Mom screamed. It's possible I didn't close it all the way.

Or, a little voice says, *someone opened it, snuck in, and didn't close it all the way behind them because they were afraid it would make a sound.*

There is a little mess of water and leaves on the mat, but that could've blown in with the last trick-or-treaters, or even through the open door.

"Hello?" I call out.

Nothing. Of course. What psycho is going to come out and say, *Oh why yes, you got me. How clever you are.*

I listen for a full minute more, but hear nothing.

No one is here.

I'm just freaking myself out. This house is like eighty years old. The wood floors are super creaky and I was downstairs. If someone had come in, surely I would have heard the footsteps overhead.

Unless they're a ballerina.

"There is no killer ballerina in my house," I say definitively, and shut the door. Then I spin the deadbolt for good measure.

There. Safe and sound.

I turn my attention to cleaning up the mess. Pumpkin guts, my Krueger glove, the pile of candy wrappers that accumulated on the little side table. I do the dishes in the sink, and when the house is back in order, I check all the doors—and a few suspicious windows, just to make sure all is locked tight.

"Mom?" I call out again. I wait, listening to the silence.

The floorboards creak upstairs, and I stop dead.

It's not a killer, I tell myself again. *You know this is an old house. And the storm is picking up.*

That is certainly true. The wind is tearing at the windows, howling at the panes.

Still, I wait for another long moment, but there's nothing.

No killer.

No Mom.

Even her shadowy pursuant remains MIA. No other ghosts, for that matter.

I sink onto the sofa to watch the end of *Casper*. Devon Sawa and Christina Ricci are about to dance. I finish off the popcorn bowl while they do, turning my head every ten or twenty seconds, hoping to catch a glimpse of Mom.

Halloween has always been our night. It doesn't feel right ending it without her.

This is the first Halloween I've been alone.

And what if it's also her last night on earth?

What if that shadow caught up to her after all? Or what if there's something to that whole thinning veil thing and

Halloween is like a reset button? What if it's not just a certain three Salem witches who disappear with the coming dawn? What if it's *all* lingering ghosts that do, like an eraser sliding across a chalkboard, clearing the slate?

This thought terrifies me.

I haven't prepared for this possibility that maybe she came back but wouldn't *stay*.

I haven't said goodbye.

"Mom!"

No one answers me.

"Mom, stop messing around! If you're here, come out now!"

She doesn't.

The movie ends, the popcorn is annihilated, and the first crack of serious thunder sounds overhead. The lights flicker but stay on.

I take that as my cue to turn in for the night.

That and the fact that I'm feeling like a good cry, which really is best done in bed or in the shower. Maybe both.

I pour myself a fresh glass of water, grab a couple of *Goosebumps* books off the shelf in my office, and carry them upstairs with me. Why yes, I still have my entire collection from when I was a kid. All my Christopher Pike books too.

I pass the dark guest bedroom, Mom's old office, and go into my bedroom.

There I put the water and books on the nightstand and grab my pajamas—Halloween themed, of course—and head for the shower. But not before I put my phone on the charger.

The tears feel *close* in the shower, but don't come.

That's fine. I'm more in the mood for an under-the-covers cry anyway.

I can even think of at least three videos I've got saved on my phone that will surely trigger the waterworks.

One is the video that Mom took of me in high school, directing my first play. A play *I* wrote. At the end she turns the camera on us in a selfie mode, gives me the biggest hug and kiss, and tells me how proud of me she is.

There's also the video from her last birthday. We went to Creole Corner, a local restaurant that focuses on, you guessed it, creole, and Cajun cuisine. Her favorite was their shrimp cakes and pimento mac and cheese. I've got a video of the waitress bringing a little beignet with a candle in it.

"Make a wish," I'd commanded.

"What could I possibly wish for?" she'd said, stretching her hand across the table to take my free one. "When I already have everything I've ever wanted right here."

Oh yeah. That'll do it. My sinus cavity is swelling as we speak.

A shadow passes by the opaque shower door.

I freeze. The tears I'd been summoning seconds before evaporate with the shower steam.

I saw that, right? Something moving from Mom's office to the bedroom.

"Mom?"

No answer.

Suddenly the shower isn't half as warm and inviting as it was. I'm covered in gooseflesh. I can't decide if it's better to step out of the shower or stay in it.

But I didn't hear any footsteps, so it's got to be Mom, right? Mom or her shadow stalker. It can't possibly be a big guy like Steiner.

"Mom, the bathroom is off limits. We agreed."

Mostly because I am still traumatized by the bathroom scene from *Thirteen Ghosts*. Of all the jump scares, *bathroom* jump scares are the worst.

It occurs to me how foolish I was to think my mom would miss a big scare on Halloween night.

"If I slip, fall, and break my neck, that's on you."

I step out of the shower, then shut and lock the bathroom door.

I don't think this will stop her or the creepy shadow that's been trailing her, but it makes me feel better. At least now I can finish washing my hair. Still, I do it with my back against the wall, both eyes open.

My phone rings in the other room.

Who the heck would call me after ten on a weeknight?

Kaitlyn is my first instinct. And my heart flutters at the possibility. Maybe she just wants to check on me.

And if I could answer, what would I tell her?

I can't figure out if the killer is in my house or if my dead mother is just trying to capitalize on the terrifying Halloween atmosphere in order to scare the shit out of me. There's also the possibility that it's the shadowy ghost who's trying to catch her and drag her screaming to the other side.

When one call ends, the phone starts ringing again right after.

That sounds important. Who double calls unless there's an emergency?

Yet I'm still too nervous to go out there. Principally because I'm *naked*.

Nothing good happens to naked women in scary movies.

I rush through my skincare routine, put on my pajamas, brush out my hair, and exchange my contacts for glasses. I go back and forth on this last step. If there *is* someone in my house—which I just can't believe since I've heard nothing—I'd rather have my contacts.

Glasses can get knocked off your face. They can break.

"Fuck it." I put on the glasses.

Then I open the bathroom door, a plastic hairbrush in one hand, aimed high like a hatchet.

I peek my head out into the hallway.

Nothing.

"Mom?"

I know I saw something. I *know* it. I'm not hysterical. I just don't know *what* I saw.

Still holding my hairbrush, I creep into the bedroom. My goal is to just get my phone. Get to my phone, see who called, find out what the emergency is.

But I only take one step into the bedroom when I see it.

On the floor, shining in the light thrown by my bedside lamp, is a boot print.

One, two, three, four—a whole line of them. They cut across the bedroom floor, disappearing at my closet door.

Is this the trick? A visual trick to increase my fear?

Mom loves closet scares. It's not off-brand for her. I kneel down and touch it.

It's wet.

Actually wet.

Mom can't do that.

If this was one of her tricks, it would be all visual.

The wetness is a human thing. Also, the size of the boot. I realize now that my hand is pressed flat beside it that it was made by a *big* boot.

Bigger than my hand. And a very wet boot for it to still be shedding this much water. The boot of someone who stood outside in the rain for quite a while before coming up here. Or maybe just a boot that walked through a couple of decent puddles.

My gaze slides to the closet door.

It's not closed.

It's open a crack, and that crack is widening.

A tall lanky guy with pockmarked cheeks steps out of my closet.

"Fucking ballerina," I whisper.

And he lunges, with a blade.

10

———

An actual *fucking* blade.

I stumble back, connecting with the wall. But as clumsy as this is, I do sidestep the strike. The sound of the blade dragging over the plaster sets my teeth on edge.

I'm up over the bed a second later. He positions himself on the other side. I try to remain focused on his face. I learned that much from tae kwon do as a kid. If you want to know what your opponent will do next, watch their face, their eyes, their torso. Never watch the hands, feet, or extremities. They'll only distract you.

But man, I gotta say. It looks like a *very* big knife even in my peripheral vision.

"Where you going to go, honey?" he asks.

His voice is disturbingly nice. Like a late-night radio DJ's.

"Up your ass."

I groan inwardly.

Up your ass? Really? That was the best I could do for a comeback?

One life-and-death situation and I'm using the same crappy dialogue I make fun of in B movies?

I'm so disappointed in myself.

"That might be kind of hard to do," he says. "I don't really think you're in the position to manage it."

He's not wrong.

Both sides of the bedroom have two windows, but to my back is the steep side with only a two-story drop behind me. Well, there's also a decorative wheelbarrow that holds—held —Mom's petunias in the summer.

I'm sure it would do a fine job of breaking my legs or neck if I jumped into it.

Meanwhile my would-be killer got the side with the roof above the sunroom. If I were on *that* side, I could throw open the window and crawl out and into the redbud tree before making my way down. Much shorter drop and no metal obstacles.

He's also on the side of the bed with my phone.

It occurs to me that the only thing between me and a murdering rapist is my bed.

Shit.

"Can you just, like, look at that and tell me who called?" I point at my cell phone slightly to his right.

I can't believe it, but he actually glances that way.

As soon as he does, I grab my end of the mattress and flip it upward.

Laurie's first rule of survival—keep them guessing.

Also, no bed now.

I shove hard with all my might and keep driving forward until I hit the wall, the killer pinned.

Never in my *life* have I been so grateful for my shitty mattress. I've been meaning to replace it for years, but never got around to it. And if I'd really gotten the memory foam mattress I've been wanting, then I would probably be dead right now.

No way in hell I could've lifted it.

"You stupid bitch!"

The curtain falls down and the rod hits me on the top of the head. Ouch. Forget about it.

The killer is getting his bearings and the mattress is now pushing back. There's also the matter of the knife. I can't see it.

I need a clear path to the bedroom door. I pivot the mattress ever so slightly, sliding it along the wall so that I can get to the door.

I manage it, and when I reach the door and try to open it, he shoves hard, using the mattress to force the door shut again. My elbow connects with the handle and sends a bolt of electricity up my arm.

I shove him back, get the door open, *lock* it, and slip through the crack, pulling it closed behind me.

I scrape the hell out of the back of my heel—the worst feeling, but I'm sure it's better than a knife to the guts.

Let him fight his way through a mattress *then* a locked door.

I run as fast as I can down the stairs to the front door. Halfway down I realize I didn't grab my phone. Damn it. My body starts turning back.

"No! What the hell am I doing?"

I've never experienced anything like this. I think part of my brain can't even believe that such things as psycho killers in my house is a possibility.

That's movie stuff. Silly, funny movie stuff.

Not anymore.

Tonight the shadow that slid past me while I was in the shower wasn't Mom getting into position for a good scare. It was her *murderer*.

Now that I'm standing on the first-floor landing, a new feeling overtakes me.

It's less about my safety and getting out of the house alive.

It's more about the fact that *that* asshole is the one who killed my mom.

That prick in *there* was the one who ruined *my* life. Not only that, but he has the *audacity* to come here and try to finish me off? *Me?*

I look up the stairs. I'm so angry my skin feels like it's on fire.

Don't do it, a little voice warns. *Your mom doesn't want revenge, she wants you safe.*

Is this my conscience? It sounds a little bit like Kaitlyn.

Fine. I'll live to get my revenge another day.

I reach up to grab my car keys off the hook.

My fingers swipe only air.

For a moment all I can do is stare at the empty hook.

"What the fuck?"

I'm a thousand percent sure that my keys were here when I went up to bed. They're always here. I'm militant about it.

"Did you steal my car keys, you fucker?" I shout up the stairs.

He was planning to steal my car—my *mom's* car—after he'd stabbed me to death?

Asshole.

He screams upstairs—a very pissed-off kind of battle cry —and a thunderous *crack* ricochets through the air. I think it's the sound of my door being ripped off its hinges.

Whoa.

Pounding footsteps overhead, and I have exactly *zero* seconds to decide my next move.

I wish I could say that my anger overtakes me and I become a souped-up powerhouse who eradicates her enemies.

In fact, my anger leaves me completely the instant I

realize two things. For one, I have no weapon and he does. Secondly, he has experience killing people—I do not.

It's the cameraman who never dies.

I'm just the writer and I don't even have a plan.

My plan was to get into my car and drive to the nearest police station and to stay there until Steiner was in custody. Or maybe at Kaitlyn's place. That wouldn't be such a bad alternative.

But now I don't have my keys or a phone.

That leaves me with only two remaining options. And they're the ones I always ridicule the most when I see the final girls do it on the big screen.

Run or hide.

Oh, how the mighty have fallen.

I bolt out the front door, letting it slap loudly against the frame after me.

"Help!" I scream. "There's a murderer in my house! Somebody help me!"

My god, the dialogue. It needs to be rewritten. All of it.

Still I scream at the top of my lungs. Not because I think anyone is going to help me.

Come on. It's Halloween. The chances of someone believing that my cries aren't some prank are slim to zero. I could *literally* be covered in my own blood and someone would think it's a costume.

If I did want someone to help me, I'd have to lie and say my house is on fire, maybe even that some idiot kids lit my house on fire.

That they would believe.

They'd let me in and call for help if for no other reason than to make sure the fire doesn't spread to their own houses.

I consider this option as I hide behind my neighbor's shed, with a view of my front door.

After a few calming breaths, I realize I can't go to the neighbors.

What's stopping the guy from following me in there and killing them as well? Absolutely nothing.

Getting them to unlock their doors for me might be the very last thing they ever do.

Horror movies love to kill the bystander who just wanted to help.

I have no choice, really.

I'll hide here in the dark until that fucker comes outside looking for me. Then—depending on what he does—I'll make my next move.

If he comes outside and gets far enough away from the house, I can sneak in behind him and lock him out. Then I can go upstairs, get my phone, and call the police.

If the police cruiser comes by again—*please, please, oh please*—I'll run out and try to stop it. Though I won't let them put me in the back where I can't get out.

If the cops don't come by and the killer *doesn't* get far enough away from the front door, then I'll stay here. I'll wait.

I take several breaths. I take several more.

Nothing.

That guy hasn't come out yet. The police cruiser hasn't slid by.

What the hell? Where is he?

And what am I going to do if he doesn't come out? I can't just go back inside and ask why he isn't chasing me. How anticlimactic.

Headlights sweep my lawn. My heart lifts. But it's not the police.

It's an SUV that slides to a stop beside Mom's, and the driver hops out.

I know her at once.

"Kaitlyn!"

She doesn't even look my way. She's ducking low as if she's trying not to be seen.

"Kaitlyn!"

Still no response. She's talking to someone. Who? Herself? That's when I see the earbuds.

"Yes, 2814 Pine Street. And send an ambulance in case she's hurt."

I'm guessing it's a dispatcher that she's giving my address to. Also, she has a gun.

Wow. I'm surprised. I hadn't pegged her as the type.

Giving this reaction, I'm guessing it *was* her that called when I was getting out of the shower, probably to make sure I was safe and sound at home. And when I didn't answer she came to check on me. Only now she's going into the house where my mother's killer is while I'm out here in the freezing rain like a dummy, squatting behind a tool shed.

She's going into the house.

Into the house.

With *him*.

"No, no, no, no!" I abandon my hiding place and run after her.

She's halfway across the living room when I push open the door and yell, "Kaitlyn. Get out of here. He's in the—"

She turns toward the sound of my voice, gun lifting.

She's going to shoot me. Oh my god, she's going to shoot *me*.

She pulls the trigger. The report is incredibly loud, head-splitting.

I have a terrible moment where I think, *This is it. I'm going to die now.*

But the pain of the bullet tearing through my skull never comes. Instead, a dark figure stumbles in my periphery. I turn in time to see Steiner slump to the floor.

Kaitlyn wasn't trying to blow my head off. She was trying

to shoot the killer creeping up on me. And he still has the knife in his hand.

Nothing like having a hot girl with a gun in the room to give me a boost of confidence.

My spine straightens.

"*Really?*" I frown at the guy with my best disappointed face. "That's the best you've got? You shouldn't bring a knife to a gun fight, compadre."

Jesus, Laurie. Just stop talking.

"Drop the knife, Dennis," Kaitlyn says. "The police are already on their way. They know you're here. They know who you are. Don't make this any harder on yourself than it has to be."

Okay, her dialogue isn't any better. But she looks very sexy saying it over the barrel of a gun.

Sweat has broken out on his face. There's too much color in his cheeks. He rolls those dark eyes up to mine, and there's nothing but hate in them.

"What the hell did I do?" I ask. "*You're* the one who ran over *my* mom."

"Dennis," Kaitlyn says again in warning.

He ignores her. He's still looking at me. "I won't go to jail if there are no witnesses."

"Laurie! No!"

Hearing her scream my name makes me turn toward Kaitlyn, a question half formed on my lips.

That's my mistake.

I should have never taken my eyes off the killer.

I'd already forgotten how light on his feet he was.

Fucking ballerina.

A white-hot fire tears through the side of my body. My mind dilates completely, obliterating all thought, and in its place is only a scream of flaming pain.

I stagger into the end table behind me and the lamp goes

down, shattering on the floor.

I suck in a breath, but I can't. My lungs refuse to expand.

He twists the knife.

I scream again, and that's when I feel her.

My mother.

An arctic blast of cold air the size of a tidal wave washes over me. The killer stumbles back. Now he's the one screaming. I think there are some curse words in there but mostly it's just inarticulate terror.

My mother has become the big skull head from *Poltergeist*. She's put herself between me and the killer, chasing him back while she snaps her furious mandibles at him. The wind blowing off her is the most intense it's ever been. Pictures are torn from the walls. Frames and figurines from the mantle crash to the floor.

My hair flies around my head as I collapse to my knees.

Blood is pouring from my side. It's hot and sticky and my vision is darkening at the edges.

I feel sick.

Holy shit. I think I'm actually dying. I mean, if we're being honest, I kind of wanted this ever since Mom died, but now—now I'm not so sure.

A shot fires and then the killer isn't screaming anymore.

Burning-hot hands cover mine. "Laurie, no. Stay with me. Laurie!"

"I—I don't think I can," I admit, looking up at her face. It's Kaitlyn. "God, you're so beautiful."

A little choked sound escapes her. I can't tell if it's a sob or a laugh. It hardly matters. The world is rapidly elongating, being pulled away from me, stretched like a funhouse mirror.

"Laurie, stay with me!" Kaitlyn screams, real fear in her voice. *"Please."*

A dark shadow approaches. For a moment, I think I see a

face in the darkness—a kind of terrifyingly beautiful face—as that darkness reaches toward me.

Instinctively, I reach out in return.

"No!" My mom's voice cuts through. "No, not yet!"

The shadow says something I don't understand. It floats like music at the edge of my comprehension. Like if I only tried a little harder, I'd get it.

"I don't believe that. She's got time. So much time."

More inarticulate music.

"No, you listen to *me*. You were right. It was my fault for being here. I'm the one that should go. I'll go with you now. No more tricks. Just please let her stay."

Kaitlyn's hand squeezes mine harder, but her voice sounds so far away. Like she's talking underwater.

"Laurie, listen to me." The stretching of the world stops. "It's Momma, pumpkin. *Look* at me."

The darkness is gone and in its place is my mother. Her face comes into sharp relief. She looks so solid, the most solid I've seen since she died. I can't help myself. I reach out and cup her cheek. It's smooth as polished stone. Her cool hand folds over mine.

"I can feel you," I say, joy rising up in me. *I can finally get that hug.*

"I'm so sorry," my mother says, pressing my hand to her cheek with her own. "I'm so sorry I wasn't able to stay any longer."

"What do you mean?" I croak. "Stay, Mom, you can always stay."

"No, sweetie. It's time for me to go."

"Go? Go where?"

"Pumpkin."

I begin to cry. *Really* cry. "No, Mom. Please. Please don't go."

I'm trying to sit up. I'm trying to take hold of her with

both arms. If I can hold on to her then she can't go. She can't leave without me.

"It's going to be okay, Laurie. You're going to be okay."

"I'm not. I'm *not*. I haven't made it yet. You were supposed to see me—you were—we don't have the movie yet. We're supposed to watch the movie together and—I can't do this without you. I can't keep trying without—"

I choke on the words. It feels impossible to breathe. My heartbeat is pounding throughout my entire body.

"I want you to be proud of me," I say with what little air I have left. Squeezing those words out of my mouth takes tremendous effort.

"Oh darling." My mom smiles down on me. When she speaks her voice is full of heartbreak. "I'm already proud of you. You were the best part of my life. The *very* best. A hundred movie credits or red-carpet premieres will *never* change that." Mom presses a kiss into my palm one last time. "You made it worth it. Don't *ever* forget that. You made it all worth it."

She releases me, withdrawing into the darkness.

"Mom, no. Please. Mom, *please*." My teeth are chattering. "Mom! Come back! Mom!"

"I think she's going into shock."

I don't know who says this. It's not Mom. It's not Kaitlyn. I realize then there are other voices in the room. I don't even care.

It doesn't matter how much I scream or cry, she's going. She's fading. She's leaving me. Mom is *really* leaving me this time. And no amount of tears is going to bring her back.

I reach for her one last time. "No. *No*. Please. *Please*."

But the hand that takes mine is very human, very alive.

Kaitlyn's face looms above mine. Tears are bright in the corners of her eyes.

"Laurie, stay with me. Stay with me."

But it's so hard to hold on when my heart is breaking.

"Please," she says again. She says it over and over again like a prayer. Or maybe an incantation. "Stay with me. Stay with me. They're almost here."

The last thing I hear is the sirens growing louder in the distance.

Good luck, I think. *Godspeed.*

11

When I wake in the hospital, I'm so drugged that I can't keep my eyes open. Mostly I experience the world in a blur of colors, sounds. The occasional question like *How are you feeling, Laurie?* floats toward me, but if I give any articulate answer to this inquiry, I've no idea.

Slowly, the world takes shape again.

I become aware of my body first. Pain is *very* centering that way.

Then the bed, the room, the—flowers?

My eyes struggle to focus. I pull myself up to sitting, trying to squint at the splash of color to my left, hoping to make some sense of it.

Finally my head stops swimming and my vision sharpens.

Flowers, yes. Several bouquets. A pile of cards. A cluster of balloons. A Chucky doll.

"Jesus," I say. "Who brought that in here?"

"You're awake." I turn in time to see Kaitlyn closing the door behind her. "How do you feel?"

I point at the Chucky doll. "Did you do that?"

"No. One of your students brought it. Why?"

I shake my head. I don't have the bandwidth to even *consider* a possessed doll right now. "Steiner didn't touch that before he died, did he?"

She's looking at me like I'm nuts. "I don't think so."

I brace myself. Because if this were a scary movie, she'd tell me he was missing. That he was taken to the police station but has since escaped after killing all the officers. Cue the screaming in the hallway and nurse blood spraying the walls.

"He's dead," she says.

"They always *seem* dead. But then they come back."

Kaitlyn takes a seat at my bedside. "I scrubbed his brains off your floor. I'm fairly certain he's dead."

"Oh." I mean, that is very convincing. "Wow. You killed a killer."

She doesn't smile. "I have a lot more to tell you and a lot of questions for you, too, but now probably isn't the best time. And here might not be the best place."

"Why do I feel like I'm in trouble?"

"You're not in trouble. You have some explaining to do. But you should rest."

She puts her cup of coffee on the table clotted with cards and leans across my bed, tucking me in. I'm very aware of the breasts in my face.

"Stop being a pervert," she says.

"I didn't say anything."

"I see what you're looking at." At least she's smiling now. She's still smiling when she draws back. "Did you mean what you said?"

"I didn't say—"

"Not about my tits," she says. "In the house. You said I was beautiful."

I can't say it was the death talking. Because it wasn't. "I mean, you are."

"Then when this is over, let's meet for breakfast in the diner. We can talk some things over. It seems like we have a lot to talk about. Am I wrong?"

"Depends. Did you see—"

"An elephant-sized *specter* attack Dennis and drive him away from you? Why yes. Yes, I did."

"Then I suppose there are a few things I could explain."

"I thought so." She gives my covered foot a squeeze. "Rest. You're safe. I'll keep watch over you."

I lie back against the pillows. "You know in the movies, a promise like that would *definitely* get you killed."

"In a movie, I'd be the killer all along," she counters with a wicked grin and a wag of her eyebrows.

After she's gone, I think about this for a long time.

But you'd be a hot killer.

It's two weeks before I'm up and moving enough to meet Kaitlyn at the diner. I'm there first, and I ask for the booth in the far corner, away from prying ears.

Because I'm early I have the pleasure of watching her drive up, park, and walk the full length of the diner to our booth.

She's got a stack of papers in her hands which she slides across the table to me as she takes her seat.

"Hey," she says.

Of course I'm grinning like a fool. "Hey. Fancy meeting you here."

"Were you waiting long?" She shrugs out of her coat.

"No, I haven't even gotten my coff—Here it is." The waitress grabs my mug, turns it over, and fills it.

As she does, she speaks to Kaitlyn. "What can I get you, sweetie?"

"The hippie hash with a side of sausage, please. I'd also love a coffee. And a water."

When she leaves, I take the first paper and look at it more closely.

It's not hard to find the relevant article since Kaitlyn circled it with a marker.

I read aloud, "Dennis Smart was killed during an altercation with police in Michigan last week. He was the suspect in two unsolved murder cases in Pennsylvania and the person of interest in six other unsolved cases across the Northeast."

"They've got enough evidence to convict him of four of those murders," Kaitlyn says. "But it's likely he killed a lot more than that."

"All women?"

"Yeah." She taps her nails on the tabletop. "He had a type."

The waitress comes back with Kaitlyn's water.

Unspoken words hang in the air between us. I realize for the first time that she's wearing a little bit of mascara and lip tint. And I'm pretty sure I also smell a bit of perfume or something.

Did she doll herself up for breakfast? Or am I making this about me again?

When the waitress walks away, I ask, "Why did he stick around? If he's from the Northeast, why the hell was he here? Did you ever figure that out?"

She shuffles the papers until she finds what she's looking for.

In the photo, the police chief is giving a statement to a crowd. The caption reads *Police Chief McAdams briefs reporters.* My eyes slide over the adjacent article. I have to get through the whole first paragraph before I find anything relevant

"Hester Nelson testifies that she saw Dennis Smart kill a woman four months ago in New Jersey. Afraid for her life, she fled to Michigan, where her mother and brother live, while collaborating with the police to identify the killer. It is believed that Smart came to Michigan to track down Nelson and kill her before she could testify."

"That's why he was here? He was trying to kill another witness?"

I remember the look in Smart's eyes when he said, *I can't go to jail if there are no witnesses.*

Which now that I think about it is horrible logic. Plenty of people go to jail when there are no witnesses.

"They were going to catch him sooner or later," Kaitlyn says. "I wish they would've done it before he hit your mom."

Mom.

I haven't seen her since Halloween. She probably saved my life that night. I still don't fully understand what was up with the shadowy thing, but I know how it felt when it was close.

It felt like I was supposed to go. Everything in me wanted to go.

Is that how Mom had felt this whole time? Had she had to fight that feeling just to stay behind with me?

"Are we going to talk about the *other* crazy thing that happened that night?" Kaitlyn asks.

"The mattress?" I ask. "I mean, I was surprised it worked too. What would've happened if I'd tried to flip it and it just didn't go up? Or what if he'd tried to climb on the bed. God, can you imagine? Because it's pretty much *all* I've been imagining since I woke up."

I can tell by her face this isn't at all what she meant.

"Laurie, I saw her. It was your mom, right? She looked like you. Well, not at first, obviously. But there at the end."

I sit there holding my cup of hot coffee, letting it warm

my chilled hands. Do I really want to tell her? If I do, I'm going to start crying again. I was hoping maybe we could get through a meal without crying.

"You don't seem surprised to see a ghost," I say.

"Oh, I was surprised," she says, jaw hanging open. She leans forward, her elbows on the table. "But there was also a psycho with a knife. You have to pick your battles."

"Why did you come to my house? Were you the one who called?" Because the killer cracked the display on my phone either on purpose or during the scuffle. Either way, I was never able to confirm that it had been Kaitlyn who'd called twice in a row that night.

"I *might* have been circling your neighborhood, checking on you." Kaitlyn looks shy all of a sudden, pushing a strand of hair behind her ears. "I just wanted to make sure he wasn't lurking, and lo and behold, I spotted the stolen Mustang two blocks over from your house. I called you. You didn't answer. Then I called the police. The line was actually busy. Busy!"

"Halloween," I say simply.

"I kept calling till I got through to dispatch. I was still on the phone with them when I got to your house."

"I saw that part." I fill her in on my hiding behind the shed and my absolutely stupid plan to lure him outside. "He called my bluff, I guess."

"You were behind the shed."

I can't tell if she's proud or disappointed.

The waitress brings the food. It smells amazing. But before I can take a bite, Kaitlyn says, "I got the impression that your mom had been around for a while. The way you talked to her—"

"Begged her to stay, you mean."

Kaitlyn's face is soft with concern. "How long had you been seeing her like that?"

My throat is tightening. It hurts to think about Mom. To

talk about her. I feel like I've lost her all over again now that I know she's really gone and is never coming back.

"Do you remember the movie *Beetlejuice?*" I ask.

Kaitlyn snorts. "My brothers loved it. I can't count how many times I've had to watch it."

"The first time that Mom came back, she came back like that. Like a ghost wearing a sheet. There was no real sheet. She can't—couldn't—touch stuff. She was all visuals and air, but she made it look like she was a ghost in a sheet."

"Got it."

"*Beetlejuice* was my first horror comedy. I watched it on repeat every day for like a year. Anyway, now that I think about it, I'm sure that's why she did it. She didn't want to scare me. She knew if she came back—came back like that—I wouldn't be afraid."

And here we are. The tears are filling my eyes, spilling over my cheeks again.

"I think she came back because of me. She said she heard me crying and couldn't leave me behind like that."

"She sounds like a good mom." Kaitlyn offers me a tissue.

I'm not too proud to take it. "She was. But she also pretty much spent the next few months scaring the hell out of me. You saw how she took the shape of—"

"That giant freaking monster," she hisses across the table. "It was terrifying."

"It's from the movie *Poltergeist*. She could do that, look like other things. Sometimes she became movie monsters and other times—" I remember that Kaitlyn liked *Silence of the Lambs*. "You know, she was Hannibal Lecter a few times. I'd look in a mirror and there she was, standing behind me in that muzzle mask. I had to banish her from the bathroom. Anyway, I think she did it to cheer me up. She said once that you can't be sad and scared at the same time."

"She sounds fun." Kaitlyn takes my hand and squeezes it.

"You're so lucky that you had her as a mom. I think it's sweet that she stayed to comfort you."

I look at our clasped hands. I'm torn between the wonderfulness of a cute girl holding my hand and being horrified because I just used that hand to hold my snotty tissue.

"My hands are dirty."

"There's a thing called soap," she says simply. "We'll wash up before we eat."

And we do.

When we return to the table, she says, "You've given this atheist a lot to think about."

I'm halfway through my short stack and scrambled eggs when I ask, "Do you think she'll be at peace now? I think, if I can't have her with me, all I really want is for her to be at peace."

Kaitlyn doesn't give me platitudes. None of that *Oh poor baby, of course. She's in a better place.*

Instead, she looks up and considers for a moment before putting down her fork.

"You know, it sucks that she died like that. She was only fifty-eight. She should've had more time."

My heart sinks. But before it gets too low, Kaitlyn grins.

"*But*, that said, she didn't get run over by just anyone. She got run over by a serial killer. A *serial killer*. And her death set off a chain of events that not only got him killed, but it's going to bring justice to those families."

She's searching my face.

"Your mom's death brought down a serial killer." She picks up her fork again. "You gotta admit, she would've *loved* that."

I laugh despite myself. I laugh because she's right. That level of morbidity would've been right up Mom's alley.

Kaitlyn looks pleased with herself, probably because she got a laugh out of me.

"Now that's settled, there's only one piece of business left between us," she says.

"Oh, I sent the final check to your receptionist—"

"Good," she interrupts. "Because I do hope our professional relationship is over."

"Jesus. A little blunt, but okay. Was it something I said or—?"

"Oh it was something you said all right."

I sit up taller. I'm rapidly trying to recover the ground I've lost, with no idea what I did to upset her. "I'm sorry if—"

"You said I was beautiful." She's smiling. No, *grinning*. "Isn't that what you said?"

I consider lying, but where would that get me. Besides, that smile is very inviting. "I mean, I was dying."

"Is that all it was?" She looks ready to roll her eyes.

"No. Dying just meant I was brave enough to be honest."

She leans back against the booth. "That's what I thought. Tell me about your last relationship."

And just like that, I find myself in an interview.

"She was an actress in Hollywood, trying to break into the movies. I was a screenwriter also trying to break into the movies. I guess she got tired of her friends telling her the joke about the starlet who sleeps with the screenwriter. She dumped me for her tennis instructor. I failed to get any of my work optioned, ran out of money, and had no choice but to move back home."

I used to hate that things had gone that way. But now I'm grateful.

If Mom had died while I was in LA, I don't think I could've ever forgiven myself, even if we did talk for an hour every day while I was away.

I'm glad I got to spend the last years of her life with her. More than glad.

"Do you want to move back to LA?" Kaitlyn asks.

"It was a fun way to spend my twenties, but I like it here. I like teaching. I like being able to write on my own terms without the pressure of trying to pay the bills with it."

"So you think you'll stick around Michigan?" she asks.

"Yeah," I say, now that I know where this is going. "Would you like that?"

"I think you know the answer."

I wrinkle my nose. "I don't know. I'm pretty thick. I don't have any of your detective skills. You've really got to spell things out for me."

"Sign the termination contract ending our professional relationship and then I'll spell whatever you want me to."

This brings many, many thoughts to my dark mind.

"You really are a pervert," she says.

I laugh. "Wow. I don't know if I like how easily you can read me."

"You'll grow to like it," she says. She slides the termination contract across the table with a pen. "Just you wait."

EPILOGUE

Five years later

The movie set is everything I thought it would be. Chaotic, mostly. Actors running around, half covered in blood and shredded clothes. The lead is getting her split-lip makeup retouched between takes as I lean against a pole on the edge of the set, where the studio lights meet that edge of darkness. I've been invited to come and see my story come to life, but I'm not taking it for granted. I'm sure the only way to ever get invited back is to stay the hell out of everyone's way.

Even so, I can't stay here much longer. Tonight is our anniversary and I promised to take Kaitlyn to my favorite sushi restaurant while we're in town, before we return to Michigan next week. She's back in the hotel getting ready. I saw the new dress she bought for the occasion hanging on the bathroom door, and let me just say, I'm really looking forward to dinner *and* dessert.

Until then, I try to make the most of the little time I have left here. Take everything in.

Savor and appreciate the moment. It was so hard getting here, and I may never get another chance.

But try as I might, I can't quite shake the weight of my disappointment.

Mom should be here. Mom should be sharing this moment with me. My biggest supporter for all of my life should—A pain shoots across the top of my skull.

"Ow!"

My cry makes everyone turn my way.

"Sorry," I say, rubbing the top of my skull.

I flash apologetic smiles until the attention returns to the set and the actors get back into their places, ready to start the next scene. The moment when our heroine becomes the final girl.

Before she does, I bend down, looking to see what the hell hit me on the top of the head. I find it between my feet. A small chunk of colorful stone.

I try to hold it up in the light to inspect it, but it's too dark in here. I've no choice but to pocket it and save the inspection for later.

I forget all about the rock until I'm back in the hotel room. Kaitlyn is in the bathroom getting ready when I come in. I throw my keycard on the desk and dig the contents out of my pocket.

That's when I remember the rock that struck me on top of the head just as I was starting to miss my mom.

I sink into the desk chair, holding the rock up into the light. It's pretty.

The bathroom door opens and Kaitlyn emerges.

She's every bit as gorgeous as I knew she'd be, with her dark hair falling in curls over her shoulder.

"Hurry up and get ready. I'm starving." Her eyes fall on the stone. "Is that from your office?"

I frown, confused. "No. I found this on set. It hit me on top of the head."

"Oh, it looks like one of the rocks on your desk."

Now that she mentions it, it does look exactly like the kind of rock that Mom would have given me.

"That reminds me. Look what I found when I went out to get another coffee." She digs her wallet out of her purse and roots around in it for a moment. Then she pulls out a red feather. "It just rolled right up to me on the sidewalk."

She takes it and places it on the tabletop beside the rock.

"Pretty." I pull her into my lap and press a kiss to her bare shoulder. "But not as pretty as you."

Kaitlyn wraps her arms around me. "How was it today?"

"Good, but I miss her. She should be here."

Kaitlyn kisses the top of my head. "I'm sure she is. She might not be able to talk to you the way she did before, but she sees your dreams coming true. And I'm sure she's so proud."

A hundred movie credits or red-carpet premieres will never change that.

I lift the rock, holding it up in the light with my free hand, the other still tight around Kaitlyn's waist.

THE LAST WINTER BEFORE SUMMER

Author's Note

*While I believe that our hero's story ends on a happy and hopeful note,
I wanted to provide a trigger warning here given the story's themes of
suicide and depression.*

*If you are feeling vulnerable at this time, maybe come back to this one
later.*

THE LAST WINTER BEFORE SUMMER

Now

A sound wakes me. I come up onto my elbows, straining to hear it again. The dog lifts his head. His ears twitch, soft black snout turning in the direction of the window.

I follow his gaze but see nothing. In part because we're in the third-floor attic of this old farmhouse, and in part because more snow fell during the night, painting icy fractals across the glass.

The pane creaks as the wind presses against it.

The dog, sensing no threat, puts his head on his white paws and closes his eyes again.

It takes me a moment to realize that the wind, at a certain pitch, sounds like *they* do—when they release one of their terrible, frustrated screams.

That must have been what woke me, the sound of the wind bleeding into my dream.

I lay my own head back on the pillow and curl deeper under the mound of thick blankets.

I slow my breath in an effort to ease the wiry tension and dose of adrenaline pulsing beneath my skin.

I try to remember what I had been dreaming about before the wind woke me but can't. Only a sense of unease remains. I was probably dreaming of Greta.

It must not have been a good dream. Or if it was, it must have soured at the end, perhaps due to the sounds of the wind pulling at the house.

I don't begin to truly relax until the dog rolls over onto his back, his paws in the air, exposing his belly.

He always hears *them* before I do. If we were in danger, he would know. He would tell me in his way.

It's a comforting thought. So is his warmth. Beneath the covers I pull him closer. He doesn't protest. In fact, his bobbed tail thumps against my leg as I hold him, as I bury my face in the soft fur of his neck.

In return, he presses his warm forehead to the side of my cheek, and only then am I able to slide into sleep again, no matter how many monsters may be waiting for us outside.

WHEN WE WAKE AGAIN, THE FROST IS STARTING TO MELT. It runs in rivulets down the windowpane. Blessedly, the wind has stopped its tantrum, though the house remains cold.

Nothing to do about that.

The electricity has been out in most of the country for the last eight months. Perhaps if I had been an electrician in my previous life rather than a writer, I would have known how to install a generator, but I would be too scared to run it anyway given how loud they are. And the lights might draw unwanted attention.

Better to shuffle around in the dark. I give myself a hard time about all those years spent bent over a keyboard, pounding out twelve novels, twenty-three short stories, and a handful of poems.

I hit a couple of lists and earned a modest collection of awards for my work, of which I had been ridiculously proud. They're probably still hanging on the wall over my desk back home.

Home.

A little bungalow with a backyard that I shared with my wife before the world went to shit. Before we had to make a terrible choice between staying at 301 Chestnut Street for better or worse, or taking our chances on the road.

That was before we knew even worse choices would follow.

That I was going to lose everything anyway—no matter how careful I was.

There's no such thing as doing everything right in a world like this.

The dog stretches at the end of the bed, his rump high in the air.

He looks to me expectantly.

"All right," I say. "Breakfast it is."

Reluctantly, I pull away from the warmth of the bed and cross to the low table against the far wall.

In my mind I refer to this corner of the attic as the kitchen. In truth, it's simply where I put the dining table from downstairs and the mini fridge from the basement. It had been hell getting everything up here, and that was even before I took a sledgehammer to the stairs.

But the mini fridge, even without its power, was the closest thing I could find to a cooler, and I needed something to pack with ice to store the meat in.

It had felt like Christmas when I'd found the battery-powered hot plate in the basement. Considering that it was on a shelf with some sleeping bags, a lantern, flashlights, and bottled water, I suspect it was once used for camping.

We're all camping now, I think bitterly as I put the last of the rabbit I caught two days ago in the warming pan. The dog is already drooling. I eat half of a stale granola bar while we wait and think about how this time last year, I was vegan.

How the cashiers at the bougie grocery store a mile from my house would greet me by name whenever I came in to buy useless shit like fair trade chocolate and organic pretzels. Or soda made from leaves.

"Now look at me," I say to no one, and close the box of stale granola bars.

The dog, assuming I must be speaking to him, does look at me.

I give him the last bite of the granola bar.

Wiping my hands of crumbs, I do a count of the nonperishables I have left: three jars of peanut butter, five more granola bars, six cans of tuna, four cans of green beans, a can of carrots, three cans of peaches in light syrup, two cans of baked beans, two and a half sleeves of saltine crackers, and a box of mac and cheese—I'm saving the mac and cheese for a special occasion.

I would shoot someone for some coffee.

But I haven't found any coffee since we ran out in the first week. The headache that followed had me in bed for almost two days. Let me just say that getting a caffeine-withdrawal migraine while the world falls apart is its own kind of hell.

I count the food again and figure this stash will probably last about ten days. Maybe two weeks if I'm careful. Gone are the days when I can sit down with a bag of chips and finish them just because I can.

At least I don't need bullets. The previous owner of this house had a stockpile for the Marlin 1894 I found propped by the kitchen door. The ammo was in the basement, stacked in neat rows not far from the camping supplies. Nearly forty bulk boxes with one hundred rounds each. Wild. I wonder sometimes what the hell he was preparing for.

I should start planning another trip into town. It's been about a month since I made the five-mile trek down the main road—ten miles if I count the return.

Last time wasn't the best of experiences, considering I had to shoot a dead girl between the eyes before she ripped my arm off. She couldn't have been more than seven years old. But I have to admit that the walk to town is less dreadful with Priest for company.

That's what I call the dog. He answers to the name and seems to like it.

Priest knows when they're close before I do. I think he smells them.

I don't envy him that.

On one hand, I'm glad that they're slow and awkward. If they really could run and climb like in the movies, I would have been dead ages ago. But what I hadn't expected is that they're so damn *quiet*. I thought I'd hear the shuffling, or moaning. Anything. The only time I can really hear them is when they throw their heads back and scream at the sky.

Not that I'd want them to do that either. But the creeping—

I shiver and stir the browning rabbit meat with a wooden spoon. It's because of the dog that I started eating rabbit. I knew he needed meat to be healthy. I was happy to eat peanut butter and stale oats for the rest of my life. But one morning, out of either boredom or curiosity, I ate a piece myself, plucking it out of the pan as I was plating it for him. It wasn't too bad. So now sometimes I eat it too. It's true that I always overcook it, practically burning it. But I'd rather that than contract some disease or parasite.

I put most of the meat on a plate for Priest, which he

inhales in record time. Then I add a can of baked beans to the pan and stir until they're warm.

I eat this sugary bean stew with its few chunks of rabbit by the small attic window, looking out on the snowy field.

I can't see much from here. Just an endless field of white, punctuated by patches of brown. I can also see part of the wooden fence, marking where the fields start.

When I arrived here in November, a little over three months ago, there was already snow on the ground. It will be May before I have any idea what might be waiting under the snow.

I kinda hope that the trees on the east side of the property are peaches. And the ones at the northern border are cherries. They're only bare brown branches now.

It's strange, after all that's happened, to find myself looking forward to something.

I RELOAD THE MARLIN, PULL ON MY SNOW BOOTS AND coat. I fill one pocket with extra bullets and the other with a granola bar, in case I don't make it home in time for lunch.

The attic door is pinned in place by a slab of wood that I wedged there for extra measure of protection. I slide the brace away, placing it to one side, and listen.

Nothing.

I lower the attic door only a third of the way down and wait again.

I hold it suspended by the string for several moments, straining to hear anything.

Still nothing. The house remains silent.

I lock the stairs in place and descend to the second floor. Once there, I grab the plank propped against the wall and lay it over the stairs. Priest descends the ramp, leaping from the platform to the carpet before bowing deep in a stretch. He only needs this ramp to come down the stairs, not go up them.

The first time I saw Priest bolt up into the attic, I was surprised. He's a clever, agile boy.

As I return the plank to its resting place and push the stairs back up into the ceiling, I turn to find him looking up at me, ears up. I relax a little more then. Not that one of them could be up here anyway.

There are only four doors on the second level, and I've shut, locked, and boarded up three of them. I took out the stairs with a sledgehammer, making entry from the first floor to the second impossible. Now I look down into the gap where the stairs used to be. I nearly threw out my shoulder demolishing that staircase, but it was very therapeutic.

It had helped distract me when I was still pretty raw about what happened to Greta.

I'm still raw, honestly.

Nothing moves below. And Priest remains unperturbed. He's already at the room at the end of the hallway, waiting for me to catch up.

It was a bedroom once, but I've pushed the mattress and furniture up against the far wall, leaving only a clear path to the window overlooking the roof of the garage. I pick up the binoculars and scan the area well. I know that they can't possibly scale a garage and crawl through this window, but they're not the only ones I have to worry about.

I am all too aware that I am a woman on my own out here. A tall, muscular woman, true, but still a woman. I do feel safer with a gun, and with Priest, but a bit of caution couldn't possibly hurt.

But I see no one. Only the freshly fallen snow sparking orange with the morning light.

I open the window and step out onto the roof. The snow offers a bit of traction for my boots. If it were really icy, I'd probably go back to bed. No such luck, so I guess it's a hunting day after all. Priest jumps out after me, his stub of a tail flicking back and forth as he keeps his balance.

I dust the snow off the folded ladder and lower it into position.

I do one more scan once on the ground because nothing will ruin my day faster than one of those fuckers popping up around the side of the garage while I'm trying to get my dog off the roof.

But it's all clear. There aren't even any tracks in the snow.

I grab the second slab of wood resting against the side of the house and push it against the top rung of the ladder.

Displaying enormous trust that I don't feel I've remotely earned, Priest jumps from the roof onto the makeshift wooden ramp. He bounds down it with far too much faith in my upper-body strength.

Or maybe he just thinks this is good fun given how he turns a happy little circle at the bottom.

I imagine trying to navigate this maze with anything less than a farm dog who looks like he should be running an agility course or herding sheep and can't picture it.

Greta and I used to have a bulldog, Rex, who died two years before all hell broke loose. I don't know what I'd do if I had Rex now.

Carry him in a backpack, maybe. All fifty-five pounds of him. Assuming he'd made it this far.

No reason to believe he would have.

After all, Greta hasn't.

WE WALK FOR TEN MINUTES BEFORE WE REACH THE WOODS, across the white fields beneath the brightening sky. I stop only to watch a hawk sail overhead.

I never hunt birds.

I don't have the heart to shoot them, not after all those years I spent as a backyard birder, watching them from my desk as I worked. Killing them now seems like a shitty way to repay them for their good company.

Priest and I walk the woods, checking the snare traps one by one. I'm hit with a mix of relief and sadness when I spot a rabbit struggling in a snare up ahead. Priest gallops over to it and traps it under his paws. I grab a sturdy branch as I approach. As I get closer, it's wet black eyes dart around, its nose twitching. I place the branch on the back of its neck, just behind the skull.

"Let go," I tell Priest.

He does.

I take a slow breath as I grab the rabbit's back legs firmly, holding tight in spite of the kicking.

"I'm sorry," I say to the rabbit, that pit in my stomach hard again. I step on the branch the same moment I pull the legs upward in a quick motion.

The neck snaps instantly.

I remove the branch and lift the limp, warm body.

"Thank you," I say, my throat tight.

My indulgent moment of guilt is ruined when Priest bolts forward suddenly.

I missed one.

I lift the gun and aim without thinking. My heart is pounding in my temples. Adrenaline hits my veins like ice water.

But it isn't one of them. Priest pounces on something and it screams. He stands, legs firmly planted, bobbed tail flicking as he proudly presents his catch. The rabbit hangs from his mouth the way a mother might carry her pup. It twists itself uselessly, unable to free itself from his grip.

Relief crawls down my spine, my head light with it.

Not a monster.

"Good boy," I say weakly, lowering the rifle. "You're such a good hunter."

Now with two dead rabbits in my fist, and all the snares back in place, I rise, adjusting the gun across my back. We follow our usual route, traversing this copse of woods to circle back toward the house. We reach the southernmost edge of the woods, the farthest patch from the house, to find no more snares have been triggered. I am just beginning to think that's it for today, that two rabbits are a decent haul, when Priest freezes, his body going rigid.

I grab the gun without question.

But he isn't listening to something or looking around.

His nose is pressed to the ground.

I ease closer, stooping to see what has concerned him.

There's a footprint in the snow.

A human footprint.

A bare footprint.

There's a little bit of snow in the crevice of the heel, either kicked into the print by Priest or because the print was made sometime in the night before the snow had quit falling. In either case, it isn't enough to erase the clear outline of the bare foot, from heel to toes.

Only one kind of person would be walking around out here without shoes on.

Yes, some of them still have their shoes. Though I've found that, strangely, almost the way toddlers can't keep their socks and shoes on, neither can they.

My heart is pounding so hard I feel faint. I try to pull myself together, taking deep breaths as I look in every direction for the smallest twitch of movement.

One good thing about winter is that the branches are bare. I can see through the neighboring copse of trees. Of course, I'm staring so hard, waiting for some dark shape to separate from a tree trunk, that water begins to leak from my eyes.

I finally accept that there's nothing.

Still holding my gun in the ready position, I follow the footsteps across the gap between two copses. They grow faint and disappear completely in the underbrush of the neighboring patch of woods.

That isn't exactly the direction of the house. If it keeps moving south or southwest, it will pass well enough away from our place.

Priest isn't having fun anymore.

He whines and turns back toward the house.

I agree it's time to go home. There are many hours before sundown, but even beneath a cheerful blue sky, it's dangerous to be out here with one of them.

Then

"You were in the middle of the highway," Greta scolded me.

I had no choice but to listen. First of all, because I was strapped to the hospital bed and the restraints made it impossible to escape or even cover my ears to block out the lecture. Second of all, because she was crying, tears streaming down her face, her voice breaking with emotion, and I knew completely that it was my own fault that she was devastated.

"You could have been killed," she cried, throwing up her hands.

"That was sort of the point," I said. I wish I could say that I regretted letting my inside thoughts become outside thoughts, but the truth is that at this point I was so tired and so numb that I simply didn't have the will to protect anyone anymore, not even myself. It would be over a year before I found the strength to hide my misery from her.

"Don't say that," she said. She came to the side of the bed. She took my face in her hands. Her fingers were freezing, and her eyes were so full of desperation that it hurt to look at her.

"Annie, I mean it. Don't ever say that."

She was the only one who ever called me that.

Annie.

Because it hurt to look at her, I turned my face away.

She seemed to realize then that I was in restraints and backed up, touching them as if seeing them for the first time.

"My god," she whispered, her voice hoarse. "How did we get to this? Just look at you."

"I'd rather not." I was using the same flat humor I always relied on. A tone that said, *I'm joking. Or am I?*

I wasn't joking.

It wouldn't take a genius to see that I was most definitely sick of looking at myself. So much so that I had consumed an entire bottle of pills, one by one. Then, when I still found myself not an inch closer to death an hour later, I chased it with an entire bottle of gin.

I was convinced that the pills and booze wouldn't be enough to kill me. The sudden terror of that realization had spurred me to run barefoot from our home, sixteen blocks to the railroad tracks. My plan was to jump in front of the next train when it came—just to be sure.

Only the train never came because it was too late at night.

I waited by the tracks without a coat or shoes for almost an hour. I tried not to vomit but still did, twice. Someone stopped and asked me if I needed help. I responded by running across the tracks to the next busy intersection.

I walked into traffic and threw my arms wide.

I may have even screamed *come on* at the car rapidly approaching.

The only regret I have from that whole experience is that I likely became nightmare fuel for the poor woman driving the red Ford Taurus who swerved but not far enough. She still clipped my hip and knocked me down with her car. It was her swearing that filled my ears the moment before I passed out.

I think about her a lot. Especially the wide whites of her eyes as her mouth opened in surprise. The dramatic way she jerked the wheel, but a second too late. The sound of wheels screeching across wet pavement and the sense of my body spinning, tumbling. The streetlights becoming a kaleidoscope of color the second before I struck the pavement.

Or maybe the driver is dead, like everyone else, and in a funny twist of fate it's only me left, dreaming of her.

Of everyone.

"We'll get you help," Greta had said. Her eyes were puffy with dark circles beneath. It occurred to me then that she likely hadn't slept at all since getting the call that I'd been scraped off the road and driven to Memorial Hospital. That she had likely been in this sterile place for hours and hours, waiting to find out if I would live or die.

Wondering which one of us would get our wish.

"Whatever it takes," she said. "I *will* find someone who can help you."

I said nothing. I said nothing because I didn't know how to tell her that I didn't think there was a single person in the world who was going to change my mind.

Now

MY NERVES VIBRATE LIKE LIVE WIRES ON THE WALK BACK. I turn and look over my shoulder at least a thousand times, as if I'm going to see it behind me, running full tilt through the snow to catch me. But I see no one. And I'm not just searching the area, I'm also scanning the ground for signs of more tracks.

But the hair on Priest's scruff is flat again, and he hasn't stopped to sniff or alert me to anything.

The house comes into view, and irrationally, I expect to see it surrounded by some relentless horde.

It's not.

I walk the entire perimeter, searching for footprints or any sign of disturbance, but we're all clear.

I return to where I left the ladder and plank leaning against the house and put the plank in place.

Priest gallops up the slope, doing a little spin on the roof once he leaps clear.

I unfold the ladder, climb it, and pull it up after me. I fold it in half again and tuck it up against the house to protect it from the weather a bit. It's not much protection, but I'm less worried about rust than I am other things.

Once secured, we climb back through the bedroom window and lock it behind us.

The bedroom is clear.

The second-floor landing is clear.

The whole house is quiet.

All the windows are boarded up down there, and the doors locked and boarded too. That has never stopped me from searching for moving shadows, just to be sure. Even if everything looks secure from the outside when I do my walkaround, I still must complete this part of the security ritual in order to relax.

In my old life, I compulsively checked my oven. Now, it's this.

"What do you think?" I whisper to Priest once finished.

His tail wags as he noses the two dead rabbits in my grip.

His thoughts are on dinner. He's forgotten all about the monsters. If only my nervous system were as easy to regulate.

I pull the string hanging from the ceiling and the attic stairs lower. Priest doesn't wait for the board. He climbs them easily.

With the gun over my shoulder and the rabbits in one fist, I climb up after him with far less grace.

It isn't until I have the stairs locked in place with the two-by-four and have looked into every corner of the attic that I'm able to take a full breath.

I know it doesn't make sense that someone—or something—would sneak in here while we were gone. But that doesn't stop my mind from gnawing on the possibility.

Since we are home a few hours early, I now have the challenge of filling the rest of the day.

I turn immediately to the business of dressing the rabbits. They haven't begun to smell yet, and if I'm lucky, I can keep it that way.

I take off all my outerwear first. The boots go in a bin meant to catch the water as the snow melts. My gloves, scarf, hat, and coat go on the hooks I installed on a sleepy December afternoon when I was feeling especially bored.

I think of this particular corner of the attic as my office. It has my work bench, my cleaning supplies and kitchen gloves. I can prep the meat in this corner, but this is also where I do my laundry, in the big tub under the bench. The bench is really just a slab of wood resting on four overturned five-gallon buckets—I found ten stacked inside of each other in the garage. And my seat is nothing more than an upholstered footstool which I took from the living room.

I like doing my dirty work in this little corner since I don't like dressing the meat at the same table where I write, eat, and draw. It just feels—unsanitary. I also like being far enough away from my clothes and bed that I don't have to scrape wayward guts or blood off anything.

I lay the rabbits on the table and pull the first of six buckets toward me. This one is empty, and I use it to collect the parts of the rabbit we don't eat.

I skin the rabbits over the bucket, letting the slop fall in, and being careful not to puncture the guts. I did that the first time, and the smell was so bad that I vomited until my ribs hurt. If I think too hard about it, I can still smell it.

Once the rabbits are skinned and gutted—setting aside the hearts, livers, and kidneys, which I know Priest will love—I close the lid tightly to keep the smell in. I'll bury that in the woods later, terrified the smell might attract them if I don't.

Now I open the second five-gallon bucket. I packed this one, and the remaining two, with snow yesterday and brought them up before sundown. I'm pleased to see that the snow has melted into water. There's an old-fashioned mercury thermometer affixed to the garage outside which read twenty-eight degrees when I passed it this morning. I'd say the attic is about twenty degrees warmer. Not the most comfortable, but it's not intolerable either.

My fingers do get cold as I rinse my knife and the meat and organs until everything is clean.

The snow water is a reddish pink when I'm finished. I double-rinse in the third bucket to be sure.

Satisfied that I've made the meat as clean as I can, I lean over the table, cubing it. I wrap it all in a cloth before packing it into the snow-stuffed mini fridge. We will still need to eat that in the next few days. The meat will keep up to five days in the cloth at the back of the fridge, especially if I pack the snow on top of it, but the organs will have to be eaten tonight and tomorrow morning.

I still have a clean bucket of snow water, which means I

can bathe later if I want. I do feel better when I bathe, but it's also so cold I hate it. Unless I take the time to warm some of it on the hot plate to raise the temperature a bit.

You want to die anyway, I think. *What's a freezing-cold whore bath to you?*

I snort to myself. "Fair enough."

Fortunately, I don't have to drink the snow. I've still got plenty of bottled water that I found in the basement. I put most of it in the garage for easier access but brought about thirty cases up into the attic with me.

It took me two days, but what else was I going to do?

Watch television? Call my friends?

Go to *brunch*?

Beneath my workstation is my stash of cleaning supplies. A bottle of disinfectant and some clean rags to wipe down my worktable. I use soap—I've still got six bars—and a bit of snow water to wash my hands well and dry them using a rag which I hang on a little makeshift clothesline overhead when I'm done.

Then I move on to the next chore.

I check the gun, make sure it's loaded and propped by the bed for easy access. I count the water. I've still got eleven cases with twenty-four bottles each. A twelfth case has six left—five after I open a bottle up and begin to drink it. I pour another bottle into Priest's dish because it's low. He drinks it happily.

The agony I felt trying to get the cases just right over a support beam—my head full of horrifying scenarios where the roof of the attic caves in and we—and all our supplies— fall down into a ravenous horde below.

Fortunately, that hasn't happened.

I count every battery. I've got eighteen AAs, an unopened twelve-pack of D-cells for the camping lantern. Five C batteries, for a flashlight that I never use because no one could pay me to go outside at night for any reason. And three lithium-ion battery packs for the hot plate. Hopefully that's enough to get me through winter. Cooking outside won't be an issue once the weather warms up—assuming I can get over my fear that smoke might attract unwanted attention.

Without thinking, I take half the snow water out of the bucket and warm it on the hot plate. Once boiling, I add it back to the bucket, strip down, and use the soapy washrag to get clean. I stick my head in the bucket to wash my hair and I even have some conditioner left.

I add *conditioner* to my mental grocery list which I've started writing in preparation for my impending trip into town. The thought fills me with dread, but considering the footprints in the snow today, maybe I'll get lucky, and the stragglers I had to navigate last month have wandered off.

Or maybe the cold will slow them down. January was bitter, but February is always worse.

I pull on a couple of sweaters, long-johns and fingerless gloves. Two pairs of thick socks that must have once belonged to a man given their enormous size—whoever lived here.

Not for the first time, I wonder what he must have been like, and what had happened to him in the final days of the chaos. His house was really well stocked. Not just with the gun ammo but also all that water, the camping supplies, batteries.

He didn't have a ton of food, that's true. I ate through his pantry in the first two days after taking up residence.

And I don't think he was here alone because this place wasn't a true bachelor pad. One of the bedrooms was a little girl's room. Pretty and pink.

The towels I took from the closet had a feminine touch in their decorativeness.

While I was able to get four big comforters from the beds

and closet, all the clothes I found belonged to him. Big jackets and sweaters. Flannel. Warm things. Useful things.

I'd only found one pair of boots in a women's size 8 ½.

Something terrible—or at least very urgent—must have happened to make him leave this fortress and venture out.

Maybe he was trying to get to someone.

Or maybe he wasn't even home when it happened, and he hadn't been able to get back.

The outbreak had been out of control for almost a year before I stumbled upon this place. If he'd been able to come back, I think he would have done it by now.

I grab a spoon, the jar of peanut butter, and a packet of saltines before climbing under the covers with Priest. I find a half-read paperback under my pillow. The cover has a woman in an off-shoulder dress in the arms of a man.

A Bride for the Sheriff.

Western romances weren't a genre I would have ever considered in my previous life. Westerns of any kind, really, but let's just say my access to books has been limited. There were the few I'd taken from town on my last trip in—my choices were Stephen King and Western romance. And while I do love a good horror story, I feel a little saturated with horror at the moment.

There weren't many books in the house either. A couple copies of the Bible downstairs, three Judy Blume books and four Nancy Drews in the kid's room, along with about five hundred issues of National Geographic from 1989 to 1993.

I also dumped all the DVDs and VHS tapes into the living room and brought up the little shelves to serve as a bookcase.

I now call this my library, as pathetic as it is.

It isn't quite as extensive as the independent bookstore in my hometown where I used to give readings whenever I had a release, but it does its job.

Maybe I can improve it.

I was in a hurry the last time I went into town. I had gone to the gas station to look for supplies and then snuck across the street to the drug store. I'd only been in the drugstore for five minutes tops when the little girl popped up out of nowhere and tried to tear my arm off, which of course spooked me and sent me running home half stocked.

Maybe I would have had more time to pick something nice if that girl hadn't showed up.

It's a nice thought. The idea that I can get more books. Maybe that would make the trip—the risk—worth it.

It's getting nice and warm under the blankets with Priest snuggled so close, heat radiating from his soft body.

I smear peanut butter on a saltine and give it to him before shoveling one in my own mouth.

My mind wanders as I eat. It replays the last time I was in town. What I did right, what I screwed up. Who I saw shambling in the streets. The bodies that weren't moving at all. The signs warning of contagion flapping off light posts and store windows.

The little girl.

I think again of the pink bedroom, locked and boarded beneath me. Cold and forgotten for months.

God.

I hope the bedroom below me hadn't belonged to her— the little girl whose brains I sprayed across the drugstore tile.

Then

"Are you seeing this?" Greta asked.

I wasn't. I was on a book deadline and twelve thousand words short on my promised draft that I had exactly thirty-six hours to deliver to my editor. Worse than that, the words I did have were shit.

I knew Evelyn would give me more time if I asked, but I hated the feeling I got when I had to ask—like I was screwing it up again. That I was making a mess of everything.

That was one of the feelings I'd been trying to avoid since promising my wife I wouldn't kill myself.

"Annie, look at this."

I was more than a little irritated, but I did look up from the laptop and pushed my blue-light glasses up onto my head.

"What?"

She pointed at the television as if this answered my question. I searched the screen, but it didn't mean much to me. Mostly I just saw the red. There were red circles on the map.

"It's eating through Japan like wildfire," she said. "They had only a level-two threat yesterday and now it's a five. How is it moving so quickly?"

I had no idea why she was asking me. I wasn't some infectious disease specialist. More importantly, I thought the dissenters on social media were probably right, that the story was being blown out of proportion and not nearly as bad as the fear-mongering was making it out to be all in the name of television ratings and advertising dollars.

I just wasn't going to say that aloud because I hated agreeing with people as a rule.

"What are the symptoms again?" I asked. I didn't care. My mind was still on the deadline. I just knew I had to ask a certain number of questions before I would be allowed to return to my work.

"Fever, delirium, aggression."

"Awesome," I said. "Can't wait to be attacked by strangers in the street."

At the time I thought I was making a great joke.

"*Babe.* This is serious. I think it's going to get worse." She turned and frowned at me.

I needed to speed this along. I closed the laptop, stood up, and went to her. I wrapped my arms around her waist and rested my chin on her shoulder.

"How many cases are in the US?" I asked her.

"Not many yet." She softened in my arms, which was a good sign. "It's in Atlanta, LA, and Chicago. Felipe said the schools closed two days ago."

Felipe was her brother, and I really liked him. He was less fond of me after the suicide attempt, probably feeling like I was putting his older sister through unnecessary heartbreak. I couldn't blame him there.

"If this goes on, maybe he'll have a longer summer vacation this year. That'd be cool."

"Maybe," Greta said. But her voice was distant now and her body was tensing again, no doubt as she thought about what kind of risk her brother was facing as a public school teacher in a major metropolitan hub during some sort of fast-spreading pandemic.

"Tell him to come stay with us," I told her. "If it will make you feel better to have him here, ask him to come."

This earned me a smile.

"Good idea. He'll probably say no, but it can't hurt to ask."

Felipe wouldn't make it to Michigan. He wouldn't make it anywhere because he would stop answering his phone three days later.

If I had known then what I know now, I wouldn't have wasted that weekend on making a book deadline that wouldn't even matter in a few days.

My editor would stop answering her phone ten days later. New York would go dark three weeks after that. The rest of the country would be plunged into total radio silence within another three months.

But I *had* wasted the weekend writing a book that I didn't love and that would never get published.

I don't know exactly when I began lying to my wife, but my writing projects were part of the lie.

When she saw me working, she thought I was safe.

I don't know where she got this idea. Perhaps because my first attempt had come days after I finished a book. Maybe from that she developed an irrational fear of me being between projects.

Even with her attention glued to the news as the infection spread itself across the globe, she still expressed concern after I emailed the book to Evelyn late Monday night.

We lay beneath the covers together. She was wearing a sheet mask, her hair clipped up so that it would curl as she slept.

"What are you going to write next?" she asked.

"A love story, maybe," I said.

She nudged me. "Be serious. You don't write romance."

She was always telling me to be serious even though we both knew that was probably the last thing I should be. Clearly I took myself way too fucking seriously.

"I'm serious," I said. "It'll be dark, but ultimately it's a romance."

"Happy ending or sad ending?"

I said, "I'm not sure. Tragic, probably. It's early days."

"It can't be romance without a happily ever after."

"The best I can promise is an optimistic ever after. Maybe our hero will find someone who understands her, and accepts her as she is. Darkness and all," I said. "That's romantic, isn't it?"

She curled up against me, tucking herself into my side. "I can't wait to read it. When will you start?"

"Tomorrow."

Once I'd started lying, it was easy to keep doing it.

GRETA DIDN'T HAVE TO GO TO WORK THE NEXT DAY. WE had our first confirmed case of the HNV-3 in Michigan that morning. Someone had boarded a plane from Chicago and flown into Lansing—just down the road from us. The passenger felt fine when she boarded—with only fatigue and a headache—but was quite sick by the time they landed. By the time she was carried off the plane, she was bleeding from her ears and nose and her fingertips had turned black.

Greta's boss had thought it was safest to let everyone work from home rather than get exposed to anything.

"We have more important things to do," Greta told me as soon as she hung up with her boss.

I had hoped for a leisurely breakfast and day of reading— I always liked to lounge around after the rush of a deadline— but Greta had other plans.

"After breakfast, we need to go to the store. We'll stock up and then hunker down until this all passes," she said.

I gave some sort of vague agreement while simultaneously trying to tamp down my irritation.

She was making this declaration at seven in the morning, and I hadn't yet had coffee.

Within the hour I was dressed, caffeinated, and in the Jeep driving us to the bigger grocery store across town, rather than the bougie one around the corner.

The store was packed when we got there.

"I didn't realize that nine a.m. on a Tuesday morning is peak shopping time," I said, pulling a cart from the rack.

"It's not," she said. "It's usually only seniors."

There were seniors, most of whom looked quite pissed to

share the aisles with the panic-buyers, rushing past snatching bread and toilet paper off the shelves.

I never liked crowds, not even on my best days, so finding myself in a crush of bodies in a store at an hour where I was most definitely supposed to still be in bed with a book wasn't improving my mood.

What made it even worse was the frenetic way Greta kept circling back to aisles we'd already covered in order to grab more of what we already had in the cart.

"I think we need more sanitizer. And gloves. More gloves."

I looked at the six gallon-sized bottles of hand sanitizer in the cart. "I can't imagine we'll use all of this. Besides, we're not going to have any room in the cart for food."

Of which we have none, I did *not* say. I had just now managed to get her over to the bakery section. Though our options for bread weren't looking promising.

"Andrea DeMonte, do you want to bleed from your eyes and have your fingers turn black and fall off?"

An old woman holding a four-pack of muffins regarded me over the rim of her glasses. She raised her brows and gave a small shake of her head as if warding me off from disaster.

"No," I said cautiously. "I guess not."

"Then I'm going back to get more sanitizer. Pick out some bread but get extras. We can freeze the rest."

She bolted through the crush of bodies out of sight, leaving me alone with the old woman.

"You have your hands full," the woman said, putting the muffins in her cart.

"I'm the troublemaker usually," I admit. I don't know if I wanted to protect Greta from this woman's judgment or if I wanted to be honest. In either case, I didn't want to talk about me. "What do you think about this virus stuff?"

The woman shrugged, pushing her black-rimmed glasses up on her head. "Maybe it'll kill me, maybe it won't."

"You're not worried?" I don't know if I was surprised or skeptical.

"At my age, there's not much to worry about. What's the point in worrying about the inevitable anyway?"

It's hard to describe what a profound statement this was to someone who, two years ago, had waited in the blistering cold for a train to come and end it all.

"Death comes for us all in the end?" I asked.

"Yes, darling. So why worry about it? We'll each get our turn."

I think about this conversation a lot and wonder what happened to her. For her sake, I hope she's dead.

Now

SOMETHING IS ON THE ROOF. I LIE IN THE DARK, HEART pounding, and strain to hear it. My mind, being the drama queen it is, has imagined a half-dead person who has grown wings and can now land on roofs. That any minute now one is going to burst through one of the two small attic windows and attack.

But then I hear the scratch and the unmistakable chirp of a squirrel. My heart falls down into my stomach. It must have climbed up the adjacent oak tree, whose large branches hang over the roof of the house. It's possible that its nest was blown down in the storm and it's looking for a new home, somewhere warm.

"Don't come in here," I mumble. "Priest would like nothing more than to eat you up."

The dog's tail thumps under the covers in agreement.

The squirrel stops scratching and with one last little chirp goes silent.

When I wake again, sunlight is streaming through the window.

I check my watch, which sooner or later is going to give out on me, and see that it's almost nine. Priest is ready for breakfast. I know this because he's out of the covers and standing on my chest.

"All right, all *right*."

With much effort, I rise and put the pan on the hotplate so it can start to warm up. I dip a rag in snow water and wash my face, my hands. I brush my teeth. I am very aware that dentist appointments are no longer a thing, and learning how to pull my own rotted teeth is not a skill I want to hone.

I change my clothes quickly, re-wearing everything except for the innermost layer, which smells faintly of sweat. The only thing that's still cold is my nose and cheeks, which are exposed. I wrap a blanket around Priest's shoulders and then another around my own while I cook breakfast.

Rabbit for him.

A can of peaches and another stale granola bar for me. I do my counts. Batteries, water, food.

Five days. I have five days of supplies left.

I should go before I get hungry because I will need my full faculties to navigate town.

That means I should go tomorrow or the day after.

Why not today? a little voice asks.

Immediately my mind makes up all kinds of excuses. I need to finish my shopping list. I need to check the snares. I need to clean the buckets and bury the slop. I need to repack the minifridge with fresh snow. I need to take the remainder of the mostly clean bucket water down to the bathroom for the toilets—that's how I flush.

Which reminds me that I need to let Priest out. He's very good about only needing to do his business three or four times a day. And if he really needs to go but it's after dark, then we go down to the second-floor bathroom.

I'd rather clean up the bathroom than take our chances in the dark. He seems to agree.

It's already almost ten by the time we're done with break-fast. That means I've got eight hours of daylight at best. It's not enough time to go to town and back.

I'd want to leave at first light to give myself as much time as possible to make it back before dark.

"I'll prepare today," I tell him, already feeling sick to my stomach. "I'll head out tomorrow."

He cocks his head as if trying to understand.

That makes both of us.

Why am I trying so hard to stay alive now when before—before—

Then

"Come on," she said. "It's our best option."

"I don't see how driving to the cabin can possibly be our best option," I said. I was aware of the bitchiness in my voice. I had been fighting hard against it since shit had gone from bad to worse to terrifying. Mostly because I was used to terrible things happening. The first twenty years of my life had been one catastrophe after another. My family wasn't—ideal. Greta hadn't had a perfect childhood, but she also wasn't used to the level of destruction we were experiencing now. Her fear was wearing her down. All of this to say I was still trying to be considerate and felt like I was failing at every turn.

"We can't stay in the city. It's getting too bad here. There are too many people."

I agreed and disagreed.

If we went into town, if we tried to get supplies, yes. There were too many people. Too many of *them*. But in our neighborhood, it wasn't so bad.

Back in April the city had been blockaded. No one in, no one out. By June the blockades had been abandoned, and no one knew why. There was no explanation, no big announcement. Because the power grid was down, we hadn't gotten news in ages.

It was impossible to know what was going on in the rest of the country—hell, in the world. We only heard rumors. Someone had a kid in the military. Someone else had a cousin in the government, in the CDC. All the so-called reports were the same: things were shit everywhere and would be shit until someone figured it out. That's what I had gathered from the hushed conversations I had on the sidewalks with neighbors over the following weeks.

By August, it had been two months since we'd lost contact with Greta's family—I'd stopped talking to mine about fifteen years earlier. Then we lost touch with our friends, anyone who was farther away than walking distance, which just left my friend Deidra, who lived a block away.

She was about six years older than me and whip-smart. She'd come to one of my readings and we struck up a conversation after.

It was weird, making friends as an adult, but when she

found out I lived around the corner, she invited me and Greta over for dinner. Greta hadn't liked her.

She's too crass.

I loved her bluntness and no-bullshit attitude. In those first days while the world fell apart, Deidra and I drank or smoked weed—when she still had it—on her back deck and talked. We talked about everything. About nothing.

She was the only one I'd tried explaining my suicide attempt to.

You're an artist, she'd said. *You have all the raw, mad power and pain of creation inside you. Keep writing or that power will tear you apart.*

I remember thinking that Greta would have agreed with that. I hadn't been able to deny that I felt steadier—more stable—when I was working on something. I just had doubts that the work was really going to be enough to carry me through this whole terrible experience called life.

One day in July I went over to Deidra's only to find a note on the door and the house locked up tight.

Don't come in. I'm sick.

I read it twice. A third time. I stared at it, uncomprehending.

I went up to the living room window and pressed my face against the dark glass.

I saw a shadow moving inside the house, but before I could confirm it was her, I turned and left, heart heavy.

I never saw her again.

Then Greta got it into her head that if we didn't leave the city now, we were going to end up just like her.

"It's in the neighborhood now. The further we are from people, the safer we'll be," she said, words I never thought I'd hear my extroverted wife say. Me? Yes. I thought people were the worst. But Greta? She loved everyone. Everyone but Deidra.

"The cabin is over a hundred miles away," I said. "How the hell are we going to get up there?"

"The Jeep still has half a tank. I turned it on yesterday just to see if it would run, and it does. And the barricades are open. We just put everything we can in the car and we *go*."

I'd bought the cabin and its twenty-one acres just three months before the outbreak started. Greta had agreed that having a writing retreat, somewhere saturated in nature, would be good for me—as long as I promised not to go out there and kill myself.

We shook on it. Oh, the fucking irony.

I'd only had one writing weekend there, in which I did very little writing. Mostly I'd listened to the birds and lain in the sun. It might not have been the most productive weekend, but it had been good.

"It's going to get cold soon," I told her. "It's got heaters, but they're electric. How the hell are we going to stay warm?"

"It's got the woodburning stove, doesn't it? We'll chop wood and burn it."

"And what about food? The nearest store to the cabin is fifteen miles away."

This was an exaggeration. It was probably closer to twelve, but I didn't want to go. I had a terrible feeling going to the cabin would be a mistake, even though I knew she was right about the neighborhood not being a safe haven anymore.

"Why are you fighting me on this?" she said.

"Because we could get hurt. We could get stuck out there and not be able to make it to the cabin or back home. Then what?"

"You don't even care if you live or die," she spat. "Why does it fucking matter?"

I knew she regretted the words as soon as they left her lips. I could see it on her face. In the way her mouth came open in a surprised little *O*, as if it had been someone else who'd said it.

"I'm sorry," she said. "I'm so sorry. I don't know why I said that."

I did. She was tired. She was scared. She'd lost touch with everyone she loved and was grieving. And because, unlike me, she *did* want to live. She was just trying to figure out how.

"You're right," I said, taking hold of her hand. "I don't care what happens to me. But I do care about what happens to you."

We didn't say anything for a long time.

"If you really think we should go, we'll go," I finally said, kissing her shoulder.

At least she paused. At least she gave it a moment's consideration. I only wish she'd reached a different conclusion.

"I can't stay here." Her breath was hot on my neck. She pulled back, wiping at her nose with the sleeve of her flannel shirt. Mine, actually. She'd always loved wearing my clothes, which were a little bigger. "If I stay here any longer, I feel like I'll go crazy just sitting here, letting it creep up on me. You know what I mean?"

"Yes," I said.

Because I did. I *really* did.

I held her. Then the tears came. I knew her well enough to know she was beating herself up for what she'd said to me and no amount of reassurance from me was going to ease that guilt even though I really didn't give a shit.

The truth was I found her anger refreshing. Her admitting out loud that she knew how I felt was infinitely better than all those times that she told me to cheer up. Every way she'd tried to make me deny how low I was, how miserable.

Things were shit, but at least now she was admitting it. I

found a weird comfort in that—that she wasn't asking me to play pretend anymore.

It was the pretending that had been killing me from the inside out.

Now

I CAN'T PUT IT OFF ANY LONGER. TODAY I *HAVE* TO DO THE supplies run.

The attic is cleaned, my buckets replenished.

Last night I gave Priest a whole rabbit and the leftover organs so that if something happens to me, he won't go hungry right away. Hell, who am I kidding? He was on his own before we met, and he'll be all right if I never come back.

I think it's clear I need him a lot more than he needs me.

In my old life, I fought my depression with sunlamps and long, hot showers. There were also my anti-depressants. I haven't had any of those luxuries for months now. Oddly, I miss the showers more than the pills.

Now all I have for comfort is this sweet farm dog. He's been the best part of all of this.

I'm stalling. I don't want to get up. I want to stay curled under the blankets as if I can simply will more food to appear in the attic. But I'm down to a jar of peanut butter and half a sleeve of crackers. And, of course, the box of mac and cheese. That's it.

I've always found Februarys in Michigan brutal. The endless gray skies and frigid temperatures. February has a way of wearing a person down. If I were going to kill myself, it would be in February. I have a feeling that the person who made the month shorter knew that if it were even a few days longer, some of us wouldn't make it.

Priest rolls onto his back and sighs loudly.

"I know," I tell him. "But we have to get up."

The sun rose ten minutes ago.

I've been awake since before dark, hunkered under the covers, heart racing and mind full of dread for the day ahead. When I'm here on the farm, or even in the woods surrounding the property, my chances of running into one of them is low. My safety isn't guaranteed anywhere, but I'm much safer here.

In town, I *will* encounter them. Several.

It's unavoidable. The only objective in that situation is to avoid a horde. Squaring off against more than two or three of them at a time becomes a big problem and fast.

That was the mistake I made the first time I went into town.

That first time, I counted forty-two of them, wandering the streets and parking lots. Fortunately, they don't open doors, so there were only a couple inside the stores. I was searching for painkillers, trying to find something for the headache I'd had for a week—probably caused by the caffeine withdrawal—when I heard the crunch of glass.

Three of them had bumped into each other outside and had fallen through the partially broken window into the store. I'm guessing looters had broken the window, trying to get to the medicine they thought might help—but obviously hadn't.

I hadn't had much time to wonder how this had happened because they were now in the store. While they don't open doors or climb, they *can* get up if they are knocked down. It's freaky when they do it since they just sort of rise.

But what I hate most about them is that while they are usually slow moving, they will speed up if their target speeds up. That's exactly what they did once they spotted me. I can't call what they did running. It wasn't. Let's just say they didn't leave me much time for decision-making. Before I could really think about what I was doing, I vaulted over the checkout counter. I quickly checked the little room that I suspected was used as an office for a pharmacist to make sure there wasn't one waiting for me. There wasn't, only the ancient PC sitting on the desk, its screen dark.

I had two options. Run into the room and lock it behind me, risking that somehow they'd get over the counter—either by sheer dumb luck or my own misfortune—or take them out now.

I whirled and aimed, blowing the head off the one leaning over the counter, his arms outstretched toward me, his blackened fingers groping. The second flinched—I don't know what it means either, if it's just a reflex or something more telling. But I blew this one's head off too. When the gun clicked, telling me I was out, I turned the Marlin in my hand and struck the third just above the bridge of its nose, knocking it back. This gave me the time I needed to reload.

Once all three were dead, I stood there in the little alcove, chest heaving.

I wasn't sure if more would get inside like these three had. I suspected I was right about the window, though, since now that I could see them, one of them had a large shard of glass protruding from the front of his thigh.

The quiet stretched long. I heard no more crunching glass. Saw no movement. I did a sweep of the store and found it empty. I'd forgotten all about the batteries and left once the coast was clear. Fortunately, I'd already collected my food before I got spooked.

The second time I went into town, I'd counted twenty-nine of them. Some looked familiar. That woman with the sunflower apron. The guy in the backward hat, the name of a car dealership printed in white letters on its navy-blue fabric.

Most of them I hadn't recognized. That meant that either some of them had wandered in or out of town—hopefully in the opposite direction of the farm—or that others had come through on their own supply runs and killed some—or had become them.

There were more bodies in the streets, so I remember thinking it was a possibility.

The only dangerous encounter during the second supplies run had been with the girl who'd tried to take my arm off, her little hands fisting my jacket with inhuman strength as she pulled my forearm toward her mouth. I had been so scared by the encounter I went back to the farm only half stocked.

Still, I'd gotten lucky that time. And the first.

Third time's a charm.

"Don't think that way," I say aloud. "We have to stay positive."

Priest's ears twitch.

Like I said, February has a way of wearing a person down and making the cold and gray skies feel especially brutal. It's easy to push my usual glumness to new lengths when it's like this.

"Let's get it over with." I throw back the covers and force myself onto my feet. But my stomach refuses to settle, twisting in on itself while I get dressed, wash up, feed Priest, and force down the remaining saltines with peanut butter spread across their flaky surface.

I dream of the possibility of finding something delicious today and ask the powers that be to have mercy on me. Surely more stale oatmeal is not what I need right now.

Outside, on the roof of the garage, I search the area for trouble. Fresh footprints, anything, but I see only my tracks leading from the woods back to the house, with Priest's cheerful pawprints running alongside them.

On the ground, I do a sweep just to be sure, then secure the ladder and Priest's ramp. He descends without a hitch.

So far so good.

The garage door is too loud when I open it. I stand in the driveway, wincing, heart pounding, for a long time until I'm certain no one is coming. The oil slick in the center of the cement floor was still semi-fresh when I arrived, but now it's nearly gone. There's only a hint of its shadow left on the concrete.

A gardening cart with a flat tire sits against one wall.

I had the brilliant—and yes, very delayed—idea last night that there must be a way to inflate the tire. If I can inflate it, then I can take the cart to town and fill it with supplies.

More supplies gathered means fewer trips to town. Hell, maybe I'll even be able to get two or three months' worth of stuff. Then the rabbits and the fruit trees will carry me through summer.

"If I can inflate the tire, I will. If I can't, we'll ditch it," I tell Priest, who has started to sniff the old oil stain.

Priest wags his stub in approval.

After a ten-minute search, I do find an air pump, and I'm able to inflate the tire. I put my ear close to it to listen for any whistling air or seepage but hear none. If it *is* losing air, I'll know by the time I walk the five miles to the edge of town.

I test it by pushing on it to see if it feels stable. I put it against the garage, and holding on to the side of the garage, step up into it. I jump. Once. Twice.

Nothing.

I pull it up and down the driveway. There's a squeak in a wheel, and I use the WD-40 on a top shelf to take care of that.

Now it makes no sound at all.

Cart it is.

I just have to hope my luck will hold and I'll get it all the way back to the house still full of supplies without any emergencies that will make me ditch it.

I check my watch. I've got nine hours before sunset. I'll spend at least three and a half hours just walking there and back. That leaves me only five hours to get what I need in town and get out.

It's time to get moving.

I check one more time that the Marlin is fully loaded. Then I count the cartridges in my pocket.

I've got twelve in the left pocket. Thirteen in the right. And twenty more in the big pocket on the inside of the coat. I'm feeling the extra weight on my left side, but I don't care about that. I'm only praying that I won't find myself in a situation where I will need to use forty-five shots to keep myself alive.

The sky is a clear shade of blue. The fluffy white clouds rolling by are deceptively cheerful-looking, like couples hand in hand on a quaint stroll. It's making me nervous as hell. Leave it to me to get eaten alive on a day like this. When everything looks perfect, when all is supposed to be bright, only to watch it take a massive, twisted turn on itself.

Priest's happy trot at my side only compacts this feeling that things are too good. He's always had an adventurous spirit, since the first moment I turned up in view of the farmhouse. I must have looked like one of them—like hell walking.

He hadn't even pulled away when I collapsed on my knees and began sobbing into his fur. He just took it like a champ.

But now his ears are up, his tongue hanging from his mouth, as he scans the clear road ahead.

There are only three houses in the whole five-mile stretch

between the farm and town, and they're set back from the road by long driveways. A quarter-mile each at least.

I suppose if things get really tough and there are no supplies in town, I could check out these houses for anything useful. It's unlikely that I'll need to. At the rate I'm going through rations, even considering the downtown's small size, it would still take me years to pick it clean.

I could never live in those other houses though. Two of them are ranch-style. It would be impossible for me to feel safe on the ground level. The third house does have two stories, but there's something about it that strikes me as uninviting. Like when I look at its big windows, it starts looking back at me.

Besides, I like the farmhouse. It's not the easiest to crawl in and out of, but Priest makes it cozy.

We're about a mile from town when Priest's trot slows and his ears flick. He lifts his nose slightly.

I see the problem immediately. Two figures are in the road. They're so far away that they're just dark shapes on the horizon. Once I get close enough, I know they can't be survivors. It's how they move. They don't walk in a straight line like people. They're just sort of meandering in the middle of the road, their heads resting on their shoulders.

The distance between us and the slowness of their approach give me plenty of time to consider how I want to play this. Not that it stops me from looking around suspiciously several times in all directions as if I expect them to have friends that will jump out at us.

But no. It's just me, Priest, and these two.

I decide to use the butt of my gun rather than shoot them. Not just because I want to save my ammo should I get in a tight spot in town, but because I don't want the noise to draw attention if I can help it. We're definitely close enough to town to be heard.

One of them is the woman in the sunflower apron.

Stupidly, I say, "Oh, hey," as if I've just recognized a friend.

I don't recognize the other guy, though, with the black blood crusted over his face, so he gets no hello from me. As soon as they're in range, Priest sprints right and the woman follows.

I push the cart forward and it hits the man in his knees. He stumbles, and as he falls, I sidestep him and drive the butt of the gun into the back of his skull. It goes right through and strikes the concrete road. I hit him again until the skull actually detaches from the neck.

He's been dead a long time then. His body is already disintegrating like an overripe tomato. Gross.

If they don't eat us—or, hell, maybe even if they do—the virus keeps eating the body.

Greta's voice fills my mind, and I see a flash of her face in my head on the day she burst into my office, about two months into the lockdown.

They're saying that we just have to wait it out. That as long as we don't get infected, the virus will destroy the host without being passed on. There's a way out—there's—

The woman in the sunflower apron lunges for Priest.

"No!" My mind snaps back to the present moment.

I swing the gun and strike her shoulder, knocking her off balance. Priest is able to get out of range, doing another half-turn as if to remind me that he should be herding sheep but the world has left him only these monsters instead.

Drawn by the movement, the woman—or what's left of a woman—turns toward me. I strike her in the side of the skull as her mouth opens, her jaw elongating.

I can tell by the resistance that meets the end of my gun that she's not as far along as the other one. The hit knocks her back, but her head doesn't go soft like overripe fruit. There's still solid bone under there.

I strike her again until I'm sure she won't be getting up. When she goes motionless on the ground, I step back, shaking out my hands as I do. They're sore from the repeated impact.

Priest rushes to my side as I put distance between us and the remains.

I go down onto my knees to check him over. But there's no blood or scratches on either of us.

"We're okay," I tell him. "It's okay."

His happy demeanor suggests that he agrees. Of course, he keeps a distance between us and the bodies, but his attention is already on the town ahead.

I follow his gaze up the road, the outline of the buildings small on the horizon. It's less than a mile between here and the thick of it.

I don't want to but I grab the handle of my cart and start walking.

At the edge of town, I stop.

I turn to Priest and kneel down in front of him. I place one hand on his warm, dark head. "This is as far as you go, buddy."

He whines.

"I know. But it's not safe for you in there. You know that."

I stop short of saying, *Stay.* I want him to have the freedom to leave if he wants.

Or if I don't come back.

I've had nightmares about becoming infected and trying to hurt him, unable to stop myself. If that happens, I'll finally have a reason to break my promise to Greta.

"I'll be back," I say. And it's a promise I hope to keep.

I kiss the end of his nose and look into his big brown eyes. "The garage is still open if I don't make it back before dark."

Then, because daylight is a resource I can't waste, I leave

him there, in the middle of the road, halfway between the dead monsters and a city haunted.

I look back only twice. Both times he is sitting where I left him, waiting. His ears are pinned back, tail down.

It's his worried face.

Then

WE PACKED UP THE JEEP WITH THE FOOD AND SUPPLIES WE had left. I poured the rest of the gas from the lawn mower canister into the car. Even before we decided to leave town and try to get to the writing cabin, periodically we'd turn on the car to charge our phones.

The electricity grid had gone out months ago, but even with a charged phone we weren't able to reach anyone. That hadn't stopped Greta from trying.

The last time a national news station updated was six weeks before, and the message felt recycled. "Stay inside. Wait it out. Avoid others."

As I navigated the narrow streets of our neighborhood, out onto the main roads leading toward the highway, Greta attempted, yet again, to call her family and friends from the passenger seat. Her brother. Her mom. But every call responded with the same busy tone that we'd received for months telling us that the network was down.

The internet was no more useful. *Network Unavailable* stared back at us from the screen.

It wasn't until we reached the main road that we realized just how dire things were. There were bodies in the streets. More than a few of the infected were wandering around.

As soon as they caught sight of our moving car, their unfocused stumbling changed.

They lumbered toward us.

"Go faster," Greta said, her fingers turning white on the arm rest. "Faster, Annie."

I did. I managed to get through the maze of abandoned cars, bodies, and lunging monsters, only clipping one of them when the space between two cars was too narrow to move over any further.

We'd decided even before we abandoned our home that we would take the back roads rather than the interstate. We had heard about the traffic on the interstate. How it had come to a standstill for days. We hoped we'd have better luck going the long way, even if it extended our travel time.

We seemed to be right, at least at first.

There were plenty of abandoned cars. Some of them rested in the middle of the road as if they'd simply rolled to a stop there. Usually when we slid past these, we found one of them still in the vehicle, strapped into the driver's seat.

Their blood-crusted faces would pivot toward us as we slid past.

There were also cars overturned in the ditch, windows busted.

Whoever had been in those vehicles was long gone. I hoped they were somewhere safe but knew they probably weren't. There was too much blood on the windows. On the ground.

At one point, it looked like someone had tried to clear a path of blocked cars.

A mass of vehicles had been shoved to each side of the road, with enormous scratches on the paint.

"Did someone push these off the road with a snowplow?" Greta asked, leaning out the window. She'd pulled her dark hair up off her neck in the heat. The sun was starting to turn the tops of her shoulders red, but when I'd told her to put on sunscreen, she told me she had bigger problems than a sunburn.

I let it go because I didn't want to argue.

And she'd been right, since forty-eight hours later she was dead.

We were still thirty miles from the cabin when she'd said, "I want to stop here."

"Here *where?*" Because from where I sat, we were at a four-way stop in the middle of nowhere. There was a gas station off to the right with two abandoned cars parked at the pumps, and there was one of those kitschy garden centers off to the left. The kind that promises to sell everything from plants to souvenirs, in-season produce to homemade jam and quilts.

She pointed in the direction of the gas station. "There. We could get gas."

"I doubt it." Because as much research as I did as a writer, I knew that pumps had to be turned on. "They need electricity to work, and there's none. I'm pretty sure that's why those cars were abandoned."

I was pissing her off and I knew it. We'd been together too long for me not to know when my wife was mad at me.

"I still want to get out. I need to use the bathroom and we need water."

"Can't it wait? I really want to get to the cabin before sunset."

"We'll still get there before dark, and we need water. Pull over."

I swung the car into the lot, driving slowly past the parked cars to make sure there was nothing in them, then cruised slowly past the large glass front windows, but we saw no movement inside.

With great reluctance, I parked just to the right of the entrance—less distance to cover should we need to run—and took the gun off the dashboard. It was warm in my hand, and I had a moment to wonder if it had been stupid to keep it on the dashboard in the sunlight. But I'd wanted it within reach considering that Greta had even less experience with firearms than I did.

I'd taken a course while writing a book in which the main character was a retired agent haunted by the killer that had gotten away. The premise was borderline clichéd, but for me, I'd needed an outlet for my feelings of hopelessness and regret.

It had worked well enough.

While writing the book, I'd gone to the range almost every day for the eight months it had taken me to complete the first draft. By the end, the instructor had called me a hell of a shot.

I'd been strangely proud of that even though I'd never owned a gun in my life and had never wanted one.

It was Deidra who had forced me to take the 9 mm pistol.

She'd insisted one night after we'd had a few drinks. "It's getting rough out here. It'll make me feel better knowing you have it," she'd said.

"What about you?"

"I have others."

"And what if I use it to kill myself?" I'd asked her, because at that point I'd already told her every secret I had.

About wanting to die.

About the childhood that had broken something inside me. How for many years, the writing, the storytelling, had been the only thing stitching my soul together, and some-times even that couldn't do it. So I drank and took pills and wished I was dead.

"I might just put it in my mouth and blow my brains out," I'd said.

"You won't." She'd been so confident when she'd said it. "It's not your style."

I'd laughed at that. Because she'd been right and because there was something nice about having someone see me for exactly who I was and not who they thought I could be if they just loved me enough to keep the demons away.

So that night I'd walked home with the 9 mm in one pocket and the box of ammo she'd also given me swinging loosely in my grip. By the time I'd arrived, Greta had fallen asleep in front of the TV, the static racing across the screen, volume off. I carried her to bed so I could lock the bedroom door behind us. I loaded the gun and put it on the bedside table, and that was that.

Greta never asked about the gun.

She'd simply accepted its appearance as the necessity it was.

When Greta reached for the handle of the gas station's main door, I threw my hand out, stopping her.

"Let me, please." I lifted the gun, as if that was all the explanation I needed.

She stepped aside.

I checked each of the aisles first. Nothing.

I found the dead man behind the counter, black blood crusting his ears and eyes. Flies swarmed his face, but he didn't move when I kicked his foot. That was enough to tell me he was *dead* dead.

"Someone's shot him in the side of the head," Greta said.

My insides had clenched at the sound of her voice, but I'd managed not to jump.

She was right. Now that she'd pointed it out, I saw the wound.

A bullet had passed cleanly through one temple and out the other.

I didn't know if the killing blow had come from his own hand or someone else's. I could imagine both scenarios. One in which he knew he was getting sick and ended it himself, perhaps with a gun kept in the register. Then another passerby found the gun on a supply run just like ours and decided to take it.

Or a second scenario within which a traveler had stopped, had seen him stumbling around behind the counter, and had decided—either out of fear or empathy—to end his half-life.

No matter the case, he wasn't a problem, which was all I cared about.

"I have to pee," she said.

"Let me check the bathrooms." Because I'd seen enough horror movies to know that bathrooms were the worst kind of risk.

But as nerve-wracking as going into the dimly lit, window-less rooms proved to be, how hard my heart had hammered as I bent down to look for feet under each of the stalls before pushing the doors open one by one, the bathroom was empty.

The real threat—the room I'd missed—had been the storeroom.

Its swinging door had been closed when I first passed it, but when I'd yanked open the bathroom door, it must have caused enough of a shift in the air pressure to create a crack or movement.

I'll never know if it had been standing on the other side of the door waiting to be set free.

If it had been the sounds of me checking out the bath-room, the stall doors swinging open and shut, that had alerted it to our presence—or our voices—it didn't matter.

What mattered was that when I came out of the bathroom to tell Greta she had the all clear, it pushed itself through the storeroom door and launched itself at my turned back.

I saw her fear first.

Greta's mouth coming open in a scream. Her eyes doubling in size. "No!"

I only managed a small pivot before she threw herself forward, shoving me out of the way. I hit the bathroom door and it fell open.

The air left my lungs when my ribs connected with the tiled floor.

The gun slid against the adjacent wall, stopping beneath the hand dryers.

Greta had her forearm braced against the throat of a boy no older than sixteen or seventeen. He wore a neon safety vest, and the hands he tried to grab her with were black up to the wrist. One of the fingers was bent at an unnatural angle.

"Shoot him!" Greta screamed. "Shoot him!"

I shouldn't have listened to her.

But I did. I recovered the gun and pulled the trigger. My ears rang, the world spinning.

I staggered to my feet and went to her.

"Fucking hell. Are you okay?"

I reached for her.

"Don't!" she said. "Don't touch me."

I thought she was pissed at me for what had happened. But as she pushed past me to the sink, as she began furiously washing her hands and face, I realized that the brains and blood that had sprayed across the adjacent wall had also gotten on Greta's face.

"Don't touch me," she said again as I reached for her once more.

"You don't have any cuts on your face," I said calmly. "I don't see anything in your eyes."

"It went in my mouth. I *tasted* it." Her voice traced the edge of hysteria.

"We don't know if it's transmitted that way," I told her. But I had doubts even as I said it. "You might not have—"

"It tastes like fucking brains, Andrea!"

She filled her mouth with water from the sink, swished, and spat several times.

I lowered my hands.

There was no point in saying that there was no way she knew what brains tasted like. That anything could have gone into her mouth, or nothing at all, for that matter. That if blood—or brains—*had* gotten in her mouth, it would have been only a drop or two.

Had there been blood on her face, yes. But most of it had been on her cheek, where she had turned her face away to keep herself out of reach. How could she have caught it?

Her face was red, scrubbed clean, but she kept scrubbing frantically.

"Stop," I said. "Stop, you're going to hurt yourself."

"Don't—" She pulled away again, but I didn't let her this time. I took hold of her and pulled her to me.

"I might infect you," she said.

"You're not infected," I said.

"I am, and I'm going to get you sick."

"I don't care," I said.

"Annie—"

I tilted her head up, forcing her to look at me. I kissed her.

When I pulled back, I said, "*I don't care.*"

I'd meant it.

The truth was I knew how contagious this was. I was as convinced as she was that she was infected.

When I kissed her, my only hope in that moment was that she would take me with her.

But she didn't.

Now

I'M NOT SURE WHAT I EXPECTED WALKING INTO TOWN. More bodies? A horde, hungry and waiting? What I did not expect was the silence. Maybe because two of them met me on the road coming into town, I had expected a welcome party.

But the streets are empty, and for some reason, that's worse.

The hair on the back of my neck rises and a cold sweat breaks out at my temples. I'm so scared I could throw up. It's reminding me of all those years ago when I had to give a talk about my new book on stage, in front of an audience. I'd peeked out from behind the curtain to see almost two thousand people talking, laughing, waiting for *me*. My adrenaline had spiked so high I'd felt like fainting.

The fear raking its nails down my spine now is only slightly worse than that.

I leave the cart the at the edge of the first parking lot. I don't see anyone, but I also don't want to take the chance that the sound of its wheels across cement or gravel will attract unwanted attention.

I look around at the patches of slushy gray ice. What's left has almost melted completely away. I suppose I should be grateful for that. It will help me move more quietly.

I creep forward, heading in the direction of the grocery store.

I'll get the food first. If I have time to hunt for books, paper, pens, clothes, especially anything warm, great. But food is what I need most, and if the suspiciously absent horde decides to show itself, then I want to know I didn't waste this chance to grab as much of it as I can.

I look into the storefronts that I pass, but they are mostly dark inside, no movement. I keep the rifle up, half aimed, as I sidestep a patch of glittering glass so that my boots don't crunch against it.

I'm struggling to keep my breath steady. The last thing I need to do is have a panic attack. Somehow, I keep moving forward.

Storefront after storefront.

Liquor store. Hardware store. Thrift store. An artsy boutique with a few seascape paintings in the window. A bullet has torn a hole in the corner of one of the canvases and the window is broken, but otherwise, it looks mostly intact.

A ransacked bank. Beside a ransacked electronics store.

Looters probably tore each apart back when we still had reason to believe that money and electricity would be a part of this newfound reality.

There's the pharmacy I stopped at last time for tampons and painkillers.

Where I'd been looking at the small rack of paperbacks before the girl had found me.

I can't see the rack of books from here. Or her.

I keep moving.

The grocery store comes into view. Still nothing. The streets are completely clear.

"The fuck is going on," I whisper.

I look around, expecting to see at least one of them. If

not shuffling toward me, at least standing somewhere, waiting to catch sight of movement.

But there's nothing.

In its former life, the grocery store had one of those sliding glass doors that opened when someone approached. Someone had turned that feature off, possibly even before the power went out, and barred the front of the store with shopping carts to prevent intruders.

I doubt the barricade worked, given that the glass was busted out even before I made my first supply run.

The overturned shopping carts are still here.

I step around them carefully, doing my best not to make any noises as I clear the threshold. It's impossible not to step on glass this time, but I still move slowly, cautiously.

My coat catches on the edge of a metal shelf, but I'm able to pull it free without tearing it or cutting myself, and that proves to be the last of the entryway obstacles.

The store is darker inside than outside, but there's still enough gray light filtering in to see by.

I do a walkthrough first, just to make sure there aren't any of them lurking. The last thing I want is to have one creep up on me like before while my arms are full of canned goods.

But the store is empty. There is, however, a horrible splash of blood on the floor that looks new. Or at least I don't remember that being there before. I feel like I would have remembered that much blood. That and the boot prints trailing through it. Hard to say when it happened, but given the amount of blood, I don't think anyone walked away from that all right. No one alive, anyway.

More than a little uneasy, I head for the aisle of canned goods. I stick to the middle of the aisle, so that I have a clear view of both sides.

I'm pretty sure there is less stock now than when I came a month ago. Even so, there is still a lot to choose from.

Slowly, I unzip my backpack and start stuffing it with canned baked beans, corn, green beans, peas, carrots. There are only two cans of potatoes left, and I take those. There's an abundance of Vienna sausages and Spam left, and even some canned chicken and tuna. I throw them in on top of the canned peaches, pears, and that weird fruit cocktail in heavy syrup. I grab another two big jars of peanut butter, a bag of nearly expired ramen, and a box of apple and cinnamon oatmeal.

When my backpack is too full to stuff even one more can in there, I decide to head back to the cart.

I don't want to fill up my arms in case I need to pull the gun.

Magically, I make it all the way back to the cart, empty the backpack into it—and I'm thrilled to find this doesn't even fill it halfway. *Maybe* a quarter. I've got so much room left.

Practically bouncing with excitement, I return to the store without seeing a soul.

This can't be possible.

Have they all wandered out of town like those two I saw on the road? Like the one whose footprints I found in the woods near the farm? Or maybe they're all decomposing somewhere? Those two I'd just killed were pretty soft. Could I be so lucky that they've all just gone off to die somewhere?

Whatever the reason for their absence, I'm able to make two more trips to the cart without incident. During these runs I collect two boxes of add-water pancake mix and a bottle of *real* maple syrup. More noodles, stew, canned chili, crackers, and even a box of Lucky Charms and three cans of evaporated milk—it feels like Christmas. Then, when I think it can't get any better, I find a box of dog treats. The little biscuits that look like bones. Of course, I take that too. That and a bag of fake dog bacon that won't expire for another two months.

"Oh my *god*. He'll *love* these," I say to no one.

The hardware store is also empty.

I grab a pack of glowsticks that I can use as bookmarks for reading after dark. I take a pack of super glue—never know when I might need that. There are also two snares and a machete, all of which fit in the cart well. I take a mylar blanket, another manual can opener, and on a whim, a bunch of seed packets. Green beans, carrots, greens—spinach, lettuce, and kale of all things—tomatoes, cucumbers, squash. And there are herbs, basil, parsley, cilantro, and dill. I also take a packet of sunflower seeds and marigolds—two flowers that Greta had always loved. I have no idea how to grow any of this shit, but I foresee a long and boring summer ahead of me with little else to do.

I put the seeds in my backpack in hopes of keeping them dry and then collect more batteries. And a giant roll of duct tape—though the farm's previous owner had a decent supply too. I just personally feel like I can never have too much duct tape.

The cart holds a lot more than I thought it would, which means I *still* have room in my backpack for books and journals. I decide to press my luck and stop in the pharmacy one last time before I head back. Even though I know going to the book section means I'll see the girl's body.

I steady myself and do it anyway.

Just like with the grocery store and the hardware store, I check everything first, but no one is here. No one is moving.

The little girl's body isn't even where I left it.

I'm not sure if that makes me feel better or worse.

There is blood on the ground where she fell. A big smear of it. But the corpse is gone.

"What the fuck," I whisper.

Did she get up? Is it possible that I didn't get a clean shot and she survived—if I can call *that* surviving?

All the good feelings of luck leave me. Because either she got up and walked off on her own, and I didn't notice because I was too busy running away like a coward, or someone—or something—took her.

Neither possibility feels good.

A new wave of dreadful paranoia sinks its teeth into my spine as I cram six composition notebooks, a pack of new black ink pens, and thirteen paperbacks—four space operas, seven mysteries, and two Amish romance novels—into my backpack.

My hand hovers over a fourteenth: *The Last Night in Harrow House*.

It's my book. The last one that got released.

On the back is a photo of me taken about six years ago. I'm sitting in the armchair in my office, one leg crossed over the other, wearing a dark pantsuit open at the collar. My forearm tattoo peeks out from underneath the cuff.

Big shadow daddy energy, Greta had teased once. *Your eyes look so dark*. The night that the first batch of books had arrived at the house and we'd opened the box together.

That office. That suit. That life—it feels like a dream. Even that person—me before I tried to die—feels like someone else.

I look at the cover for a long time. At Harrow House in flames, fire dancing in its windows. I flip back and forth between the author photo and the cover. Front. Back. Front.

I almost put the book back on the shelf, then, for some reason, take it at the last second.

Impulsively, I also grab a fistful of candy bars on my way out.

It's lucky that the streets are still empty given how my mind wanders. It would be so easy for one of them to creep up on me with my thoughts swimming as they are. I'm lost in thoughts of Greta, my old life, the story of Harrow House.

I make it all the way back to the filled cart and put my backpack full of books and pens on top. I grab the handle, pull the cart out into the road that will take me back to the farm—to Priest. I only manage a few steps before a scream cuts through everything.

All thought, all distraction, evaporates.

First I believe it's one of them. I've heard their frustrated, ear-splitting screams before, the sound that rips from their throats when they throw their heads back and curse the sky.

But then a second scream splits the day in half, and this one is far too desperate to mistake for anything except human.

There's real fear in that scream.

There's someone here. A living someone. And by the sound of it, they need help.

I drop the handle of the cart and run toward the screams, taking only the rifle with me.

I cover ten blocks to the opposite side of downtown before I hear it again. Three more blocks, around a corner, and there they are.

A throbbing mass of tangled bodies.

What they're swarming I can't see. I need to get higher. I search for a better vantage point and spot a ladder running up the side of a brick building. I climb to the roof and run to the far edge.

From up here I can see the horde is surrounding a car. They are throwing their bodies against it, rocking it back and forth with the weight of their efforts. I count eighteen, nineteen—twenty-one of them.

The glass on the passenger-side window is splintered like a spider web, starting to give.

I lift the rifle and train it on a rotting face pressed against the glass.

I hesitate. I'm a good shot, but if I miss, I'll shatter the window. The bullet could hit the person inside, or it could simply open the flood gates on them. Fuck.

Instead, I shoot one of the bumbling bodies in the back. The bullet takes off the top of its head and it falls to the pavement.

I take out two more. Then three more. I weed out the pack until the rifle clicks empty and I have to reload.

I need something that will draw them away from the car and give me a better shot.

I sure as hell am not going down there and drawing them to *me*, but I also feel like I can't *not* help this person. Not now that I realize this is why I've had such a pleasant fucking shopping day. Because the horde was over here trying to eat someone else.

On the roof I find a brick broken into four pieces. I gather each piece and return to the edge of the roof. I throw one chunk of brick at the nearest storefront window while screaming, "Oh no. Don't eat me. *No.*"

I see those on the outer edge turn toward the sound of my voice. A few in the back move toward the window, and I manage to take out three more before their attention returns to the car.

I throw the second chunk of brick, and this gets me a clear shot of four more before I lose their attention. The third chunk gets me another three, and the last piece gets me only one.

That leaves two of them, the ones closest to the car still frantically trying to get in.

I realize they must be able to see the person inside, and that's why they're not giving up.

I have to take the shot even though they're so close to the car the chance of striking it is very high.

"Can you hear me?" I scream.

Nothing.

I try again. "Hey, you! Person in the car trying not to die, can you hear me?"

"Yes!" a voice calls out.

"I need you to get down so I don't shoot you. Get down onto the floorboard as low as you can so—"

Before I can line up the shot, the passenger door flies open, knocking the closest one back. A girl with tight black curls bolts from the car. She trips over one of the ones I shot and hits the pavement hard.

"Ouch, shit."

The one she knocked over is on its feet, stumbling toward her, but I shoot it before it reaches her. She raises a small pistol and pulls the trigger, but the shot goes wide.

She turns and runs toward the opposite edge of town, northeast. Maybe that's where she's camped, or maybe she's just running scared.

Whatever the case, I shoot the last one as it shuffles after her.

She doesn't stop. She doesn't even look back.

I watch her run down the main street, black hair streaming behind her, until she cuts a corner out of sight.

"Thanks," I say. I'm not sure if I'm thanking her for keeping them busy while I gathered supplies or if I'm thanking her for not dying in front of me. Both, probably.

I turn toward the sky and see the sun is lowering itself toward the horizon. I probably have two hours before dark at best. I need to get moving. It'll take me all of an hour and a half to get home, and that's if I hurry.

Fortunately, the streets are quiet as I retrace my steps to the empty parking lot on my side of town.

The cart is where I left it. Full and ready.

I grab the handle and start the trek home.

About a mile outside town, a small dark shape comes into view. I have a second to worry about whether or not it's one of them and do a mental calculation to make sure the rifle is still loaded.

Until the little dark shape does a happy spin that I recognize so well.

Not one of them then.

Just my dog, happy to see me, and ready to go home.

Then

BY THE TIME WE REACHED THE CABIN, GRETA'S NOSE WAS bleeding. She said she felt fine, but a pallor had crept into her face and the sweat across her brow and temples was visible. She was squinting, and when I asked why, she said the light hurt her eyes. And she kept doing this—somewhat terrifying —thing where she was licking her lips and pressing them together, almost as if she were tasting the air. I thought maybe her mouth was dry, but she refused the water I offered, saying she wasn't thirsty.

It was still light outside when we found the turn-off for the cabin, but it was darker beneath the shade of the trees. I followed the twisting driveway to the tune of, "We're almost there. You can lay down in a minute. Just hold on a little while longer."

After I parked and ran around to open her door, she insisted she was still strong enough to walk inside herself.

With the pistol in hand, I checked all the rooms and the area around the cabin but found no signs of trouble.

Part of the reason why I'd bought this place was because it was truly secluded. We were far more likely to get harassed by raccoons than by any people here.

Except that I had the growing feeling we weren't going to be here long enough to worry about people. Or raccoons.

"I want to lie down," she said.

So I took her to the bedroom. Not the master bedroom I preferred upstairs but the second, smaller one on the main floor. I don't even think she noticed. At the time I was thinking that I was saving her the trouble of trying to get up those stairs. But later, I would question if I already knew then what was about to happen, and if I was just getting ahead of it.

I tried again to get her to drink water and take some pills for the headache she'd begun to complain about, but she refused. She did let me pull off her shoes and tuck her under the covers. She also let me wet two wash rags. One to clean the blood off her face. Another to place on her forehead.

Once that task was done, I bent down and kissed the back of her hand.

"Don't," she said. "You'll get sick."

"I don't care," I said.

I'd meant it, even though later I decided the only thing more terrifying than attempting to kill myself and failing was the possibility of becoming something that couldn't die—that was stuck in some sort of endless limbo, hungry and furious. Forever.

I stayed by Greta's side until she dropped into sleep, then I slipped out, closing the door behind me. I stood in the darkening living room for a long time, pistol in hand, considering what the hell I was going to do. And because I had no idea what I was going to do, I did a bunch of shit that didn't matter.

I took a shower and changed my clothes. I grabbed firewood from the covered rack outside and built a fire. I made sandwiches from the supplies we took from the gas station and ate mine before carrying the other into the bedroom.

I half expected Greta to spring up and attack me like the kid at the gas station had.

But she was still in the bed, bathed in the moonlight pouring through the window.

"Are you hungry?" I asked.

No answer.

I went to the side of the bed, sandwich plate in one hand and another bottle of water in the other.

"Baby?" I asked softly. "Do you want to eat something?"

Nothing. She was still on her side in her favorite sleeping position, one leg drawn up higher than the other, almost to her chest. Her face was still pinched and agitated. Her breathing was congested.

I put the sandwich plate and water on the side table.

Then, without thinking, I reached out and touched her cheek.

It was hot to the touch, and only when I pulled my hand away did I see the blood seeping out of her ears.

She's infected, I thought. *And her sweat is all over my hand.*

Nonsensically, I checked that all the windows were locked, and then I shut the door behind me.

In the kitchen I washed my hands. I grabbed a bottle of red wine stored for some future celebration that would never come and took it over to the couch with the corkscrew. I drank it straight from the bottle, staring into the fire. As I drank, I looked from the fire to the pistol on the coffee table.

Pistol.

Fire.

Pistol.

When the wine was gone, I put the empty bottle on the table, the firelight dancing hypnotically in the dark glass.

I picked up the pistol.

I thumbed off the safety. I pressed it to the side of my head. I put it under my chin. In my mouth. Nothing felt right.

Deidra had been right. Guns weren't my style.

I put the pistol on the table in front of me and pulled the quilt off the back of the couch. I fell asleep like that, in front of the fire, the wine making the world soft at its edges.

When I woke, sunlight was streaming through the window.

My head hurt like hell.

I went to the bathroom and expected to see blood crusted to my face, or coming out of my ears, but I just looked like shit.

The kind of shit that results from falling asleep on the couch after drinking a bottle of wine—not the sick kind of shit that came from being infected with a virus that liquefied someone's humanity from the inside out.

I washed my face, took another shower.

I drank a lot of water and took some aspirin.

Then I went to the bedroom door and knocked after only a moment's hesitation. "Babe? You up?"

A groan.

My heart kicked at the base of my throat at the sound of it.

"Greta?"

I didn't bother to get the pistol. I couldn't even shoot myself. I knew I'd never be able to shoot my wife.

Instead, I cracked open the door slowly.

I wasn't greeted with gnashing teeth. She was sitting up in bed, holding her head like it hurt.

"How do you feel?" I asked from the doorway.

"Very sick," she said, her throat a dry rasp.

When she lifted her head, I flinched.

Her fingers were black at their tips. One of her eyes was full of blood.

"Christ."

"That bad, huh?"

Everything that I should have said died on my lips.

I'll get help. I'll call the doctor. Just lay down and rest, you'll feel better soon. You can ride this out.

None of that was possible now. Still, I should have expected what she said next.

"Bring me the gun."

It felt like the ocean was rolling through my ears.

"W-what?" My voice broke.

"Bring it to me while I still have the strength to do it."

"Do *what?*"

"You know what. Give me the gun."

"No."

"What did you expect? I'm not getting better."

Those words struck a chord. They were too close to the words I'd said to her after I woke up in the hospital. After the pills couldn't do it, after the train never came, after even the fucking car couldn't take me out.

I'd said, *What did you expect? I'm not getting better.*

That meant it was my turn to say her line. "I don't need you better. I just need you here with me."

She was still enough of herself then to know exactly what those words meant. I caught the flicker of recognition in her eyes.

"This isn't the same," she said.

"I wanted to die, and you told me no. How is it not the same?"

"Because you weren't going to turn into a fucking—"

Anger strained her voice. She fell into a coughing fit, unable to go on.

I pushed off the doorway and went to her side, easing her into a position that I thought would make it easier to breathe.

She pulled away from me. And I could see why. Each cough sprayed blood. Into her hands. Across the coverlet.

"Get away from me."

"I don't care if I catch it," I told her.

"I fucking *know* you don't care," she said, gasping. Her words were sharp, but the anger was gone. In its place was only heartbreaking sadness. "But *I* do. I care. Get me the gun."

"I can't. Greta, I can't." I sank to my knees beside the bed and began crying. "I'm sorry, but you can't ask me to do that."

I thought that was how we might end. She would get too sick and become whatever the hell those people were and then I would be next.

I didn't want that for us. But I also wasn't convinced it could be any worse than this going-through-the-motions purgatory I'd been wading through for years. A half-life is a half-life.

She placed a hand on my head, her fingers in my hair. I waited for the bite. I prayed, silently, that she would kill me rather than turn me.

But she said, "Do you remember the night we broke up, before we got back together?"

I raised my head to look at her. "At your old apartment?"

She gave a small nod, keeping her voice low. Probably trying not to trigger another coughing fit.

"Do you remember why you broke up with me?" she asked.

"Because you deserved better."

It had been like a movie. I'd come over late and thought

I'd just leave a note in her mailbox, but she'd been taking out the trash and caught me in the parking lot on the way to her door.

So I'd been trapped there, in the orange halo of the street-lamps. I couldn't just leave and pretend I wasn't there. She invited me up and I refused, so I had no choice but to tell her the truth to her face instead of in a letter like a coward as planned.

I gave her a million bullshit reasons to cut and run. I hadn't tried suicide yet, but I was self-destructing in every other way. Drinking. Pills. I was trying to create a pain bigger than the one I'd been born with, as if it would somehow cancel it out.

I confessed every wrongdoing to her, hoping it would push her away. Before I could even finish my list, it started to rain. I thought she would go inside, but she didn't.

She just stood there, with lightning cracking across the sky, rain falling, and listened to me.

Even as I begged her to leave me, I knew deep down I was just terrified to be loved by someone. I also knew it was too late. Love already had its teeth in the back of my neck.

From day one, Greta was so kind. So gentle and forgiving.

"You said I deserve someone who won't hurt me." Greta licked the blood from her lips. "*I* said, 'I think we both know the only person you're trying to hurt here is yourself.'"

Had she said that?

I had had a few drinks to settle my nerves before I went over to see her. I couldn't remember exactly what had been said.

"On our wedding day, I promised I would love you until you loved yourself. But you never learned how, did you?"

"I'm sorry." I took her hand and squeezed it. It was so cold. I covered my face with the other. "I'm sorry."

You're not going to cut and run on me, are you?

We'd been standing on the balcony alone, overlooking the garden below. Our friends rushed around, trying to get the last of the preparations ready for the ceremony that would make Greta my wife.

The photographer had just gotten our first-look photos and disappeared to find the bridal party, giving us a minute alone. That's when she'd asked, *You're not going to cut and run on me, are you?*

I'm not going anywhere, I'd said. *I just think you can do better.*

I know you do, and that's a real shame.

The smell of roses wafted from the pink bouquet in her other hand.

She came up onto her toes and kissed me. Then, with her head on my shoulder, she said, *I guess I'll just have to love you twice as much until you realize how great you are.*

"I promised," she said. "And I'm keeping that promise, Annie. I won't be the one who hurts you. And I won't let you use me to hurt you either. Now go get me the gun. It's the least you can do."

I refused until she tried to get up. Her trying to get out of the bed caused a coughing fit so terrible—and my god, the *blood*—I thought she was going to die right in front of my eyes. But she held on.

Held on long enough for me to get the pistol. Long enough for me to check that it was loaded. Long enough for me to turn off the safety and return to the bedroom and put it in her hand.

"I love you. I love you more than anything," she rasped, her chin soaked in blood. "Now get out."

I hesitated in the doorway.

"And wash your hands."

I didn't wash my hands. I ran from the cabin as fast as I could. I was trying to outrun the sound of the gun going off, but I didn't make it. It fired at the same moment I reached the car. I staggered against it as if I'd been struck.

For a moment the world was off-center on its axis. I don't know how I got the door open and climbed behind the steering wheel. How I started it or made it down that long, narrow driveway.

Blindly, I drove north.

I drove so fast that anything—a deer, a dead person, anything—could have sent me careening off the road if it had simply stepped out in front of me.

Nothing did.

I drove until the car ran out of gas.

It rolled to a stop in the middle of an empty road. At first I did nothing. I sat behind the wheel, hands at ten and two.

To the left was a large field that connected the road with woods in the distance. To the right, flat farmland as far as the eye could see.

I chose left. I ran across the field, which ended in a patch of thick woods. I kept running. My lungs burned, feeling as if they would burst. My legs ached and threatened to buckle.

I kept running.

When the woods finally broke open, the farmhouse came into view. On the horizon, it was the size of a dollhouse.

My cheeks were freezing and my lips cracked, but I stumbled toward it. I'd grabbed my jacket when I abandoned the car, but I'd never put it on. I held it against my chest like a shield, for all the good that would do me.

I collapsed a hundred yards from the farmhouse's backdoor. I probably would have just lain down and died of hypothermia on that very spot if not for Priest.

He came from the garage. Maybe he had been sleeping in there.

When he saw me, he approached slowly, ears up, alert.

He looked suspicious. So I said, almost reflexively, "It's okay. It's okay, boy."

Then I burst into tears because nothing was okay. And it hadn't been okay for a very long time.

He ran to me then, his bobbed tail wagging as if he'd been waiting all this time for me to come home.

I threw my arms around him and sobbed into his fur. I held on to him as if it were only the two of us adrift at sea.

I can't say how long I stayed like that, kneeling in the snow, holding Priest and crying. And I have no idea why he let me, but he never tried to move away.

As the tears dried, slowly I came back to myself, about the same time the sun fell below the horizon. I could feel the cold of night approaching from the forest, as if the darkness I'd run from was catching up.

I looked back, realizing that a part of me was hoping Greta would walk out of those woods. That she would say she was feeling better. That everything was going to be okay.

"Come on," I told him, pulling myself up to standing on my trembling legs. "We need to get inside before dark."

Now

IT TAKES ME THREE TRIPS TO GET ALL THE SUPPLIES UP TO our attic. What a *haul*. As I make pancakes for dinner, I wrestle with mixed feelings. On one hand, I'm relieved the run into town was a breeze. On the other hand, I feel bad that my luck came at the expense of the girl. I was perusing paperbacks while she was fighting for her life.

There's also a third, less clear feeling.

I'm not sure what the emotion is, exactly, only that it's strange, knowing someone else is alive out there and not that far away.

Am I happy about that? Annoyed?

I eat my pancakes drenched in syrup in front of the battery-powered lantern and consider the possibilities. When I reach no conclusions, I move on to the books. I read chapter one of a new romance until I fall asleep. I don't dream.

When I wake, I start sorting the seed packets.

I read the instructions on the back about when to plant the seeds indoors. How much light they need. Water. According to the packets, I need to start the seedlings as early as March.

This house isn't heated, so I'm not sure how that will work. Maybe I've no choice but to wait for the weather to warm up outside before I can begin, even if that will delay any possible harvest.

"You can help with the digging, right?" I ask, letting Priest sniff a packet of green bean seeds.

I can use my notebook to sketch out where to plant what. It will be quite the project. But it will be nice to have fresh produce after all this canned and boxed food. If those really are fruit trees like I suspect they are, when they bloom it's going to feel like Christmas around here.

A strange feeling washes over me again. A distant recognition that I am...not sad.

I don't know if I can call this happy, exactly. But I'm moving in that direction.

Something in me is shifting. Something I carried long before the world fell apart, before Greta died, is melting away.

Or maybe it's *because* the world ended that something is changing within me.

With just me and the dog—and them—I don't have to pretend that everything is okay. And when I'm not being forced to pretend, it's easier to live.

I wake to the walls shaking. A pack of water bottles slides to the floor. Books fall off the shelves of my little library. A spoon clatters in an unwashed bowl.

Priest barks, and that startles me even more.

I didn't even know he could bark. He is so good at being quiet—presumably because of them—that I just assumed he wasn't a barker.

It takes me a minute to realize what's happening—what I'm hearing.

A helicopter.

A fucking helicopter.

That means there are people out there. People who might be looking for survivors like me.

For a reason I can't possibly explain, I throw the covers over my head as if this will hide me. I pop out only long enough to grab Priest and pull him under with me.

We stay like that until the whirring sound fades into the distance and the house is still again.

It isn't until I'm certain they're not coming back—that and a desperate need to piss—that I peek my head out from under the covers.

Priest's wagging, bobbed tail taps my leg.

"I think they're gone," I say. "Let's eat then go check the snares."

NOTHING HAPPENS FOR DAYS. WE EAT, WE HUNT. I READ and dream of the garden. By the fourth day my sense of unease recedes. I convince myself that the helicopter was just passing through. Maybe it belongs to the military and they're on their way to a base where they will keep working to solve the collapse of the world. As if it can be solved.

Or maybe it's a private helicopter, and some surviving millionaire is making his own supply run.

I almost convince myself that everything is fine until the fifth morning.

It isn't the helicopter. No. It's a brand-new problem. A problem that almost kills me.

After we eat, I pull on my boots, coat, and fingerless gloves. Priest and I climb carefully out of the attic, listen for trouble, and hear nothing.

Everything is fine until the moment I climb out of the second-story bedroom onto the roof. Priest goes rigid beside me. The hair on the back of his scruff rises, standing at attention.

I take him at his word. Priest can smell things, hear things, I can't.

And something is clearly wrong in his book.

My hand goes to the rifle instinctually, but I don't see anything. Instead, I open the bedroom window and call Priest back inside.

He doesn't have to be told twice and leaps back into the bedroom.

"Stay," I whisper.

He does, his big, soulful brown eyes watching me over the lip of the windowsill.

I walk the entire perimeter of the roof, scanning as far as the eye can see.

Nothing.

Not so much as a smudge on the horizon.

A terrifying thought occurs to me, that maybe it—whatever the danger is—is very close to the house. Like right up against it.

I walk the perimeter of the roof again, slowly, looking for any signs of danger.

That's when I spot them.

Prints in the snow.

My first thought goes to the girl in town. Maybe she's circled back, looking for rations or maybe even me.

Except it definitely isn't her.

I don't know anything about the girl, really, but I can be sure that she didn't walk five-plus miles out here with no shoes on.

I see the footprints, but I don't see their owner.

Maybe it's moved on, and Priest is just reacting to its lingering scent.

I grab the ladder and move to lower it.

I freeze, ladder hanging in the air.

On the far side of the house—the part I can't see well—there's a shadow darkening the snow.

I could blame that shadow on anything. The side of the house itself. Maybe the tree.

Except it's moving. Slightly. Back and forth.

"Shit."

What a terrible place for one of them to hide. I run the timing calculations for all possible scenarios, and none of them are in my favor.

Descend the ladder. Too noisy, slow, and there's a chance I won't get the rifle shot lined up by the time it's on top of me.

Jump off the roof. A decent drop. It's faster, but the possibility of hurting myself or dropping my gun is high. In horrors, someone often limps away with danger on their heels all the time.

I will not be that person.

I yank the ladder up and put it back on the roof. Once it's in place, I look to see if the clattering has provoked it from its hiding place.

The shadow is gone. Fuck. Now I don't know where it is.

I need to lure it into view so I can shoot it with the rifle.

Priest is still watching me.

I climb back through the window and begin the search for what I need to lay a trap.

Fifteen minutes later, I'm on the roof again, but this time I have a babydoll with some fishing wire tied around its neck.

"Stay inside," I tell the dog, who remains dutifully beside the window, his jaw resting on the sill. I would find that incredibly cute if not for the horror of the situation.

After double-checking that the line is tight, I throw the doll, the fishing line unspooling as it sails twenty yards and hits the ground with an audible *plop*.

Slowly, I begin to reel the doll toward me.

I see the shadow first. It stretches itself long across the snow. Longer and longer until it finally staggers into view.

Long dark hair.

From behind, she looks just like Greta.

Heart thrashing in my ears, I keep reeling the doll, and as it passes her, she lunges, falling as she misses.

As soon as I see her face, I release a breath I hadn't realized I'd been holding.

It's not Greta. Even with the blood and gore on her face, I can see that. They don't look anything alike. Also, Greta had a tattoo of an arctic fox in a wizard's hat on her right arm. This woman's arm is bare, unmarked.

And yet my heart keeps knocking wildly in my chest as I put the fishing rod down and lift the rifle.

It's not hard to line up the shot now.

I pull the trigger and the bullet hits home. The monster's head knocks back as if punched and blood sprays across the snow. As soon as it's done, Priest hops through the window, tail wagging.

It's the closest to a *good job* I'm going to get from anyone.

For a long time, I only sit there, watching it bleed out as blood darkens the snow. Slowly, I note that I'm vaguely glad that the body is off to one side, and therefore it will be easy to avoid. And of all the thoughts I could have had, what comes to me is, *I'm glad it didn't die anywhere near the garden.*

"We can't leave it there," I tell Priest. "It'll attract animals."

Or attention.

With a sigh far more dramatic than the chore requires, I push myself to standing.

"Come on then. This body ain't going to bury itself."

AFTER I DIG A HOLE WITH A RUSTY SHOVEL AND WRAP THE body in a tarp that I find in the garage, I'm ready to heave the corpse into the ground. Once the body is gone, there's only the matter of all the blood. I try to cover it with snow, but that just dilutes it from red to pink. Once I realize I'm just spreading it around, I give up.

Priest is giving the ring of red a wide berth, and I do too.

I'm out of breath by the end of it all. Burying bodies is hard work.

Afterward, I check my clothes, my hands, everything, for any sign that I've come into contact with blood, but there's none. The back of my knuckles are red from the cold, nothing more. No fluids of any kind got on me, as far as I can tell. It probably helps that I never touched the body—just rolled it onto the tarp with the end of the shovel before dragging it to the hole.

I pick up the rifle and give the sky an appraising look.

It feels like spring. The sky is robin's-egg blue and nearly cloudless. The air is warm. It would be a beautiful day if not for the blood-soaked snow staining it.

"Should we go check the snares?" I ask Priest. His bobbed tail wiggles back and forth and he does a happy half-turn.

We only make it fifty yards from the house before I hear it.

The distant whirring of blades.

My heart leaps into my throat at the same time my stomach is drop-kicked.

"Priest, *come*!"

I turn and bolt back to the house. I get Priest onto the roof first and clamber up after him. I'm already in the attic before I realize that in my rush I forgot to pull the ladder onto the roof or lock the bedroom window behind us.

Priest is standing on the bed, tail wagging. He doesn't know what's going on, but he seems to think this is some kind of game.

I double-check the two-by-four keeping the attic door locked into place. I pull it a second and third time just to be sure, but it doesn't budge.

The house begins vibrating.

The highest stack of water bottles falls again, and the windows rattle in their frames.

At least I don't climb under the covers like a child this time. But I am hiding. I sit in the corner nearest the door, my back pressed against the wall, to make sure I can't be seen through any of the windows. I've got my rifle in my hands, butt resting against the wood.

The helicopter passes overhead, but before I can register relief, I hear it coming back.

When the vibrating reaches a fever pitch and I'm expecting the roof to come down on top of me, the engine cuts suddenly. The rapid *tuk-tuk-tuk-tuk* of its blades slows down with a laborious whine.

"Shit."

Priest's ears twitch at my tone.

The helicopter doesn't fly away. It's landed.

Before I can fully unpack the implications of this, the ladder rattles against the roof.

"Oh shit, oh shit, oh shit."

Now I do hide under the covers.

Priest, not understanding the gravity of the situation, has begun pouncing on top of me.

"No!" I hiss. "Get under here."

To his credit, he does, wiggling under the comforter with me, his tail still wagging. He can't possibly understand the danger we're in.

I lie perfectly still, heart pounding, straining to hear.

Voices.

Muffled, but they waft up from the second floor. So they *did* climb through the fucking window. I can hear them in the house, moving slowly from the room into the hallway below us. Someone whistles, long and low. A voice says, "Look at that."

"Thorough," someone replies.

I have no idea what they're talking about, but I can admit my curiosity is piqued.

When the attic door rattles, the curiosity is gone. The air sticks in my throat. I don't dare breathe.

Then it rattles again.

It's okay it's okay it's okay. They can't get through the two-by-four. I put the rifle on my lap. *And if they try to break in, I have a solution for that, too.*

"Are you in there?" a voice calls. Soft, feminine.

My hand covers my mouth as if I don't trust myself not to speak.

"Maybe they're out."

"The door is locked from the inside. They have to be in there."

"If it's a girl, she might be scared to let us in. We could be murdering rapists for all she knows."

"If I were alone in the middle of the apocalypse, I wouldn't open the door for fucking strangers either," agrees another. "And we don't have doorbell cams and peepholes anymore."

I like that one. Whoever they are.

A moment of silence hangs in the air.

"I'm sorry if we scared you, coming into your, uh, place like this." The voice is clearly pitched loud enough for me to hear. They're practically shouting up through the floorboards. "We're going to wait outside by the helicopter for a while, and if you want to come down and talk, please do. You can bring your gun if that makes you feel safer."

There is a soft thump.

"What?" someone hisses. "We know she has one. Kenya said so."

Kenya. Who the hell is Kenya?

Then it occurs to me that the only person who has ever seen me with a gun is the girl whose life I saved back in town.

Did she send friends? Is this really some sort of post-apocalypse wellness check?

"Can you, like, acknowledge that you heard us at least?" the same voice calls up through the floorboard.

I hesitate. For a moment, I sit there, mouth pursed, unsure of how to respond.

Then I take the butt of the rifle and tap it twice on the floor.

"Thank you! We'll get out of your house now and wait outside. If you don't come out, we'll assume you don't want to talk and we'll just go, okay?"

To my surprise, as if possessed, I tap the floor again twice.

"Great! Bye for now!"

They make good on their word. Their footsteps trail away. The ladder rattles as they, presumably, climb off the roof to return to their helicopter.

Once I'm sure they're out of the house, I go to one of the little attic windows. The one overlooking the backyard. Sure enough, there's the helicopter. It's hard to see from this distance, but it looks like two people are standing beside it, talking.

Priest whines, and I turn and see that he's standing by the door. He paws it the way he sometimes does when he needs to relieve himself.

"Are you sure?" I ask him. "They might kill us for our rations. Even if they don't, they're still people."

But his tail is wagging.

I look from Priest to the people outside to Priest again.

"If you're sure," I say. He does a little happy pounce as if to insist he is.

I pull on my coat, grab the rifle, and unlock the attic, sliding the two-by-four away.

They didn't leave someone behind to grab me. The bottom of the stairs, bathroom, and bedroom are all clear. They even closed the bedroom window behind them, which I find strangely considerate. They also left the stairs in place for me.

After Priest runs down the little ramp, someone claps. He

doesn't even wait for me. He runs straight to one of the girls standing beside the helicopter.

"A dog!" she cries. She falls to her knees in front of him and Priest offers his belly. "Oh my *goodness*. Such a handsome *boy*."

I watch this scene unfold as I approach.

The woman standing offers a hand. Her face is both hard and inviting at the same time. A strange combination. Kind of like she's happy to meet me but also has no qualms about putting me in my place if that's what needs doing. She has long dark blonde hair pulled up in a ponytail. High cheek-bones, hazel-green eyes.

"Summer." Her shake is firm but not overpowering.

"An-Andy." I don't feel like Andrea anymore, and I can't introduce myself as Annie to these people. Annie died with Greta.

"Thank you for coming down to talk to us, Andy."

"And for letting us meet your *dog*," the girl on the ground exclaims in the baby voice that most dog-lovers have. When she looks up at me, she's still smiling. "I'm Erin. What's this good boy's name?"

"I call him Priest, but I don't know what it was before."

"Priest!" she cries. "I get it! Because he's black with the white collar."

Sure. Let's go with that. Not because I expected him to be the last person on Earth that I spoke to before I died.

Summer's watching me with those hazel-green eyes. "You found him?"

"He came with the house," I say.

"Where were you before?" she asks.

"Haslett." Neither of them seems to know where that is, so I add, "The Lansing area."

"How the hell did you end up here?"

"I have a cabin outside Grayling. We went there first,

but..." I don't know how to finish. Also, I've just used the word *we*, and I don't want them to ask about Greta, so here I am with a mouthful of a half-finished conversation that I don't know what to do with. Eventually, I decide on, "When I left, I drove until the car ran out of gas then just walked until I found this place."

And by walked I mean ran like a demon.

"That sucks," Erin says. "It was the same with me too. I had two brothers, but they only made it to Charlevoix, then I was on my own until Summer picked me up."

"Do you like being on your own?" Summer asks. She's still watching me carefully, and I have the distinct impression that she's assessing me.

I don't know how to answer her.

Erin pauses in her frantic kissing of the top of Priest's head—which he seems to love—to say, "We're asking because we thought you might want to come with us. Not everyone does, but some do."

"How did you know I was here?"

"We picked up a woman a week ago named Kenya. She said you saved her life up the road in town. We searched the area for you. On this second sweep I noticed the ladder had moved. Figured this might be your place."

That fucking ladder. If I hadn't panicked and had put it back properly, maybe they would have passed by without stopping.

"You sound like a damn action hero," Erin adds. "Did you really kill like forty of them in a couple of minutes?"

"Twenty-one," I say. "I was on a roof. It was a good vantage point."

Sunlight brightens Summer's eyes, giving them a hint of gold amongst the green. "Are you the one who took out the staircase and proofed the inside of the house?"

This is definitely some kind of interview.

"They can't really climb," I say. "I didn't want anything sneaking up on me."

"Can you hunt with that rifle?" Erin nods at the Marlin.

"I hunt rabbits for Priest, but I don't shoot them. It's a waste of ammo. I use snares. I should go check them, actually, before it gets dark."

"Can we come with you?" Erin stands up, knocking snow off her knees. I realize now that she was just letting her legs get wet and cold so that she could pour all her love onto Priest. "Come on, Priest. Show us where the rabbits are."

I hadn't expected them to invite themselves along, and I don't know why I take them with me, but the four of us go into the woods together. I check all the snares and collect two rabbits. They watch silently as I break their necks.

"It's enough to make a girl go vegetarian," Erin says before looking away.

"I was vegan," I say. "Before all this."

"*Vegan*. Girl, that's what we call *growth*."

There is a strange intimacy, talking to strangers in the woods like this. I'm surprised to find I like it. And I like listening to Erin chatter as we walk back to the house together.

Before I know it, I'm standing outside the helicopter with Priest and two dead rabbits in my grip.

Summer's face is softer now. "We need to head back. The helicopter is in decent shape, but one of its headlights is out and I haven't found a replacement yet, so I don't like flying her after dark."

"You're the pilot?" I say, and immediately feel stupid. Of course she is.

Erin scoffs. "You bet she is. You don't want *me* to drive anything. Plane, train, or automobile."

Erin takes a seat on the lip of the helicopter's open door.

With both doors open like this, I can see straight through to the other side.

Of course, I immediately imagine the terrible scenario in which one of them comes out of the woods and grabs Erin from behind.

"You can come with us if you want," Summer says, her gaze fixed on me again. "We have a compound about sixty miles north, on an island. We need more capable people like you."

I snort without meaning to. It's a bitter, almost derisive sound.

Capable. Tell that to my dead wife.

"It's true," Erin says with so much earnestness it hurts. "You can hunt, you can make places secure, and you can kill the hell out of those things. You're *amazing*."

Summer is watching me.

"Erin, why don't you take Priest for a lap around the house."

Erin doesn't even protest. She just calls Priest, who doesn't obey her until I say, "It's okay."

Then he bounds after her as if I just acquitted him of homework so he could go outside and play with his friends.

Once we're alone, Summer says, "Are you infected? I saw the blood in the snow."

"No. I'm not infected." I have a second to worry that maybe she's about to shoot me and that's why she sent Erin away.

"If you want to stay on your own, it's okay. We'll understand," she says.

I still can't seem to find my voice. I look up as if my future is written up there somewhere. I see nothing but a clear, cloudless blue sky.

"We only brought good people back with us. We don't have the supplies or time for assholes who—"

"I don't know if I can go on like this." I can't bear to have her guess anymore. It's easier just to spit out the truth.

I search her face to see if she understands.

I'm not sure she does, and so I add, "Even before this happened, I was looking for a way out, you know? I tried—I tried to—but it didn't work. And then this happened and my wife—"

It's suddenly very hard to breathe.

"My wife died—and she wanted me to keep going, but I don't know if—I feel like I have to because she's—but I—"

Summer squeezes my shoulder with a steady hand. "Take a breath. Breathe."

I bite down on the words, bracing myself. I expect her to tell me to suck it up. That it's not all bad. Or maybe she'll use any of the thousand platitudes that Greta always threw at me every time I tried to tell her about the void in my chest, devouring me from the inside out.

But Summer doesn't do that. Instead, she says, "You see this gun?"

She points at the pistol on her hip. I nod.

"I've put this barrel in my mouth *twice*. Don't ask me why I didn't pull the trigger. I don't know. I had a million reasons to do it, but I didn't."

The honesty hits me like a slug to the chest.

"I don't *know* if I can go on like this either," she says. "But what I *do* know is that there are a lot of scared people left in this world. None of us know what's going on. None of us know what's going to happen. So I figured the best thing I can do with my time here is to help out. You may not want to be here, but it's still true that a lot of people would benefit from you sticking around."

I don't know why, but I start crying.

I take one more look at the frozen wasteland around me.

Looking specifically in the direction of the cabin where I left Greta months before.

When I meet Summer's eyes again, she's blurry through my tears.

"It's your choice. It'll always be your choice." She squeezes my shoulder again. I resist the urge to collapse into her. I'm worried I'll fall apart if I do that.

After a moment, she says, "I hope you'll choose to stay. With us. We really do need you."

I wipe at my nose. "You sure about that?"

"Yeah, I'm sure." She's smiling when I dare to look at her again. "You can bring the dog too. He'll fly okay. We'll close both doors so he can't fall out."

"I can bring Priest?" I ask.

She laughs, short and sharp in the back of her throat. "That's all it took? Yeah. Bring the dog. It'll make Erin's day. They're immune, you know."

"Are they really?"

"We found out through the bulletin." When I only blink at her, she adds, "We get a weekly broadcast from a channel in Canada. Do you have a radio?"

"I do, but I've kept it turned off."

"You're going to feel like a king with all your new amenities. Tank even got the water line working last week. We have *showers* now."

I don't have time to ask who Tank is before Erin runs up to us with Priest bounding at her heels.

Erin's face is bright from laughter and red from exertion. "So? Are you coming with us? Because if you're not, can I stay with you? I'm in love with Priest! You can't separate us."

"I'll come."

Erin whoops, actually jumping up in the air. "Hot damn! This may be the best day I've had all year."

"Just pack what you need for the night. Toiletries,

clothes," Summer says, adjusting the gun across her back. "We'll come back tomorrow with a moving crew for the rest."

Erin takes the rabbits—Priest's dinner—and tosses them into the helicopter. "You'll have your own rooms, so don't worry about privacy."

It doesn't take long to pack an overnight bag for me and Priest. I grab clothes, a book, my journal, a couple of pens. And the box of mac and cheese, which for some reason I've decided I'll eat tonight.

Before I know it, I'm back at the helicopter with my backpack slung over my shoulder, wondering what the hell I'm doing. If really, just like that, I'm going to walk away from this place.

Priest leaps up into the helicopter after Erin. He turns back to me, his little tail wagging.

"Somebody is ready to go home." Erin pats him on his rump and climbs into one of the seats. Summer steps up into the helicopter too, extending her hand toward me.

I take it and she pulls me in. She holds my hand a little longer than necessary. Maybe she's scared I'll take off running, but the expression on her face is warm.

"It's good to have you with us, Andy," she says. "Let's go introduce you to everyone else."

"And just in time for dinner!" Erin straps herself in. "I'm starving. I hope Grace made more of her eggplant parm and mash. That shit's delicious."

"I brought macaroni and cheese, actually."

"Mac and cheese! Oh my god. I haven't had that in forever. Oh no, you look sad already. Summer, what did you tell her?"

"Nothing." Summer looks back at me questioningly as she straps herself into the pilot seat.

"I was thinking about the fruit trees. I guess I won't get to see them bloom after all. I was looking forward to having a garden this summer."

They exchange a sly look.

Then Erin bursts into laughter. "You didn't tell her, did you?"

Summer is smiling too. "We're beside an orchard. Apples mostly. But I think there are cherries and peaches too."

"And blueberries! There's an abandoned u-pick farm up the road. And Jenna grew up on a pumpkin farm. If you want to talk gardening with someone, she's the one. She hasn't shut up about it for weeks. Apparently, we have to start planting our seeds in the greenhouse next week."

"You have a greenhouse?" I ask.

"You really didn't tell her anything!" Erin cries, scandalized. "What the hell were you guys talking about for so long?"

Neither Summer nor I offers details.

Erin prattles on. "Well, all I can say is that if you're half as capable with garden tools as you are with a rifle, Jenna is going to love you. I think she's been looking for someone to spoil since her daughter—"

I don't hear the rest. The helicopter's blades kick to life.

I hold tight to Priest, my fingers in his soft black fur, as the helicopter lifts into the sky. I can feel his stub of a tail hitting my shin happily as I lean over to peer out the small window at the icy world below.

I still don't know what I'm looking for.

But for the first time in forever, I'm looking ahead instead of behind me.

ABOUT EMILY

1

———

I can't be sure the exact moment I knew Tiffany's new friend would be a problem—no, that's not true. By the time I'd gotten the call from Principal Granger, I had a pretty good idea that the situation with Emily was escalating.

But I can't begin there.

If I begin the day I was called down to Harbor Elementary and asked to account for all the blood, tears, and fistfuls of hair, you won't understand why I made the decision I made.

Why, later, I lied to the police. Why I was ready to bury a body and more than a few secrets as if this were a perfectly sane thing to do.

As if a mother's love could ever be considered logical or sane.

In my defense, at the time, I didn't realize the full gravity of my decision. I wondered if I was making a mistake, sure. But how *big* of a mistake—no clue.

We go through our lives making a hundred decisions a day: what to wear, whether or not to drink that second cup of coffee, which road to take to work in the morning.

Ninety-nine percent of our decisions are meaningless.

Rarely do we realize that what we thought was a very simple decision would irrevocably alter the course of our lives until after the fact.

That's why I assured the principal that everything was fine. Why I walked my seven-year-old out of the school and back to the car. Why I helped her into the backseat before fastening the seatbelt across her lap. Why I climbed behind the wheel and reversed out of Harbor Elementary's parking lot, putting the whole incident in the rearview as if my daughter's troublesome friend was only a phase that Tiffany would outgrow.

I wouldn't realize the magnitude of that decision until I was standing in the rain on a cold, dark night in April fourteen years later, as I stared down at the mangled body of a man while Tiffany sobbed, her body trembling in my arms, her wet hair plastered to her skull, our faces bathed red in the car's taillights.

Then and only then would I realize just how badly I'd fucked up.

2

———

Transcript of Police Interview
Date: November 9, 2006
Time: 3:13 a.m.
Location: Harbor Bay County Sheriff's Office
Interviewing Officer: Detective Daniel Monroe
Secondary Officer: Detective Lisa Carter
Interviewee: Diane Yates

BEGIN TRANSCRIPT:

Detective Carter: Do you need another towel? More hot tea?

Diane Yates: No, thank you. Let's just get this over with. It's late.

Detective Monroe: It is. Thank you for agreeing to come down to the station with us. We appreciate your cooperation. Can you please state your full name and relation to Tiffany Yates for the record?

Diane Yates: My name is Diane Marie Yates. I'm Tiffany's mother.

Detective Monroe: I understand this is a difficult situation, and we want to get a clear understanding of the events leading up to your arrival here tonight. When was the last time you spoke with your daughter?

Diane Yates: This afternoon. I mean, yesterday afternoon. She called me when she got out of class. I believe it ends at 1:50 or 2:00.

Detective Carter: Did she say what she was doing?

Diane Yates: She was going to lunch with a friend.

Detective Carter: Which friend?

Diane Yates: She didn't say. I assumed it was a friend from class. She's twenty years old. She comes and goes as she pleases.

Detective Monroe: And did she seem upset when you spoke to her? Nervous? Anything out of the ordinary?

Diane Yates: No, she was fine. Normal. She said she'd call me later when she got home after work.

Detective Monroe: Where does your daughter work?

Diane Yates: In one of the laboratories on campus. She has to check on all the lab animals before they close up for the night.

Detective Monroe: Strange job, and it has your daughter running around on campus at all hours of the night.

Diane Yates: She isn't running around campus at all hours of the night. The schedule is very specific. It has to be because of the experiments. It's her job as part of her financial aid. She's a premed student.

Detective Carter: Did she call you like she said she would?
Diane Yates: No. I figured she fell asleep. Until you showed up on my doorstep.

Detective Monroe: Mrs. Yates, your daughter was found covered in blood near a body. You understand that we have some questions.

Diane Yates: I know that you're treating my daughter like a suspect instead of a victim, which is fucked up, if you ask me.

Detective Carter: No one is saying your daughter is a suspect. We're just trying to understand what happened.

Detective Carter: Ms. Yates, do you know who Aaron Whitaker is?

Diane Yates: No. Am I supposed to?

Detective Carter: What about Tiffany? Did she ever mention him?

Diane Yates: No, never. Are we supposed to know that name?

Detective Carter: Did she mention anyone new? Like a

new boyfriend or someone from work? Anyone hanging around?

Diane Yates: No. Are you going to keep ignoring my question? Is this some kind of test?

Detective Carter: The man in the trunk was identified as Aaron Whitaker.

Diane Yates: Oh. I see.

Detective Monroe: Do you? Whitaker was found in the trunk of his car, Mrs. Yates. And the state of his body was brutal. We need to determine whether Tiffany was involved or if there was someone else at that scene, and right now, she isn't speaking.

Detective Carter: Monroe, he clocks in at two-eighty, three hundred pounds. Surely you're not implying that Tiffany could have done this?

Detective Monroe: Tiffany's school records show that she got into fights. She has a history of violence.

Diane Yates: She got into one fight. When she stood up to her bullies in the second grade. If you think that means she is capable of murdering a man twice her size and stuffing him in the trunk of a car, you're crazy. You said yourself that the body is brutalized. Did you even find a weapon?

Detective Monroe: No. But maybe there was someone else there. Someone who took it with them. And now she's not talking to protect them.

Diane Yates: Christ.

Detective Carter: I'm sorry, Ms. Yates, but we have to consider all possibilities. Tiffany's car was broken down right next to his. It looks like he may have pulled over to help her. And now he's dead.

Detective Monroe: Does Tiffany have any questionable friends? Roommates? Jealous boyfriends?

Diane Yates: No. She doesn't have many friends. She's a shy girl. Smart and hardworking but shy.

Detective Carter: What about her mental state? Any history of psychiatric conditions? Blackouts?

Diane Yates: She had some trouble during the divorce, but that was ages ago.

Detective Monroe: What about drug use? Alcohol? Any reason she might have been impaired last night?

Diane Yates: Don't you test for those things when you bring someone in?

Detective Monroe: We do.

Diane Yates: Did her results show anything?

Detective Carter: Both her breathalyzer and urine test were clear.

Diane Yates: Then you have your answer.

Detective Monroe: So you're saying you can't think of a single reason she would be covered in someone else's blood?

Diane Yates: The only thing that makes sense is that she was in the wrong place at the wrong time. Maybe she saw something she shouldn't have. Maybe she was attacked and now she doesn't want to speak up because she's scared they'll come back and kill her. You know she's autistic. When she's overwhelmed, she can shut down like this. She just needs time, then she can tell us what happened. Hell, maybe the guy was already dead on the side of the road and she pulled over to help him, not the other way around.

Detective Monroe: She doesn't have any injuries, Mrs. Yates. Apart from a bruise on her forearm, there are no signs of a struggle.

Diane Yates: So not only did she murder a three-hundred-pound man and stuff him in a trunk, she did it effortlessly? That's your theory?

Detective Carter: Ms. Yates.

Diane Yates: I don't know what happened, but I do know that Tiffany isn't a killer. She's my daughter.

Detective Monroe: Do you know if Tiffany carries any weapons? A knife, perhaps?

Diane Yates: No, why would she? Wait. I gave her pepper spray when she moved to campus. It's possible she still has that. Any sign that she used pepper spray on Aaron What-shisname?

Detective Monroe: No. We found deep lacerations on the victim, Mrs. Yates. Do you understand what that suggests?

Diane Yates: Ms. Yates. Yates is my maiden name. I never took my husband's last name. And no, I don't know what you're suggesting.

Detective Monroe: Whitaker was mauled. Almost torn apart.

Diane Yates: Again, why you think my daughter is capable of that, I have no idea.

Detective Carter: Only Tiffany knows what happened. Even if she was late to the scene, she may have valuable information we can use to find the killer. We need Tiffany to speak to us, Ms. Yates. If she's innocent, she needs to tell us what happened. We want you to talk to her. See what you can find out.

Diane Yates: And if she won't speak to me either?

Detective Monroe: Until we get some answers, she'll remain in our custody, Ms. Yates. It's in your best interests that you get her to talk.

END TRANSCRIPT.

Rereading the interviews now, I can spot the moments where I lied. Intentionally, anyway. I say intentionally because it's possible I was lying a lot more than that—but mostly to myself.

Does it matter if I looked right into those detectives' eyes and misled them?

I can't be the first mother who has lied to the police to protect her child.

But I do think that's why Monroe was such a bitch.

He took one look at me and knew I was hiding something.

And he was right.

3

———————

I closed on this house July 31, 1993. I wanted Tiffany to have at least a month to adjust to the new place before school started in August, but with all the bank's bullshit and the back and forth with Paul on the child support and alimony, we were left with only about two weeks before the onslaught of the school year began.

It was already going to be hard on her, starting a new school. She was such a shy kid, and she'd had a hard time making friends in kindergarten and again in first grade. Paul wanted to get her evaluated for autism and I told him to fuck himself whenever he found a free moment from fucking the coworker he left us for.

I had read that a diagnosis could be helpful—*affirming* was the word the literature used—but I didn't want anyone using that as an excuse to treat Tiffany differently. If she'd needed special accommodations for her schoolwork, I would have changed my tune, but her grades were never a problem, just her social skills, and frankly I didn't think she was the problem. I still don't.

People are a fucking nightmare.

Eventually we did get the diagnosis, but only after she asked to be tested.

I scheduled the appointment as soon as she asked, and they confirmed her Asperger's.

She was relieved, and that made me happy.

The diagnosis didn't matter to me. I've loved Tiffany with my whole being from the moment I realized she was growing inside me.

I'm not big on the over-romanticized bullshit version of motherhood we see everywhere.

Motherhood is dirty, ugly, and hard.

But it's true all the same that I was ready to put a body in the ground if that's what it took to keep my kid safe.

All of this is to say that by the time we moved into the new house, I was worried about her. About her new school. About her ability to make friends. About whether or not Paul's bullshit would make things harder for her now that she would see him every other weekend without me running interference against his stupid fucking ideas about how she *should* be.

So imagine my surprise when, one week after arriving in Harbor Bay, Tiffany informed me that she'd made a friend.

We were at the dining room table, our dinner of Chinese takeout spread out before us. Tiffany could be fussy about food, but she loved noodles of all kinds.

She'd never say no to good noodles. I'm with her on that.

And fortune cookies. I always had to ask for extras so that she could open them all up and line up the little slips of paper in rows how she likes. Sometimes she even liked to cut up the words and rearrange them to make poems. She was good at that.

On this particular night I'm thinking of, I was working my way through a box of orange chicken and lo mein when I noticed that she seemed ready to burst.

Sometimes she got like that. It would be clear that she wanted to talk about something, but she was unsure of how to start the conversation. I found that by asking a question first, it gave her some sort of permission to speak.

"What do you think of the new room?" I asked. A shot in the dark but an educated one.

I knew she'd spent the afternoon organizing her art supplies and the bookshelves that stood on either side of the desk. She had a thing for color, so it wasn't enough to simply stick everything on the shelves like I did. She liked to organize every book by color and size. It was beautiful, but I don't have the patience to do something like that for myself.

"There's a girl in there. I love it."

My hand froze, my chopsticks stuck in the box of lo mein. "A girl?"

"Yeah. I like her."

When I didn't understand Tiffany, I had this bad habit of repeating what she said. "What do you mean, there's a girl in there?"

"There's a girl. She's funny. You have to turn your head just right to see her. I think she's shy like me."

I can still remember the effort it took to not panic. I was also trying not to say anything that might sound bitchy or dismissive. I knew my tone could be blunt—how many times had Paul complained about it in the thirteen years we were together?

I put the carton down. "Do you mean you saw someone outside? Like through the window?"

Her bedroom had a beautiful bay window overlooking the backyard.

"No. She was in my bedroom with me. We talked for a long time. Her name is Emily. She said she would be my friend."

"Oh, well, that's nice of her," I said. I had no idea what the proper response was.

"I like her, but she's funny."

"Funny how?" I asked, my heart racing.

"Her voice. And her face. The way I have to look at her."

Tiffany demonstrated this by tilting her head to one side. It made me think of a bird.

I wasn't oblivious to the idea of an imaginary friend. My sister, Melissa, had gone through this phase with both of her daughters. Sitting across the table from Tiffany, her head cocked bird-like, I tried to remember what the doctors had told them.

That having an imaginary friend was normal. That it was a healthy part of childhood and the product of their developing brains. That it was even a great way for kids to practice social skills—and I sure as hell couldn't argue that Tiffany needed all the practice she could get.

The doctor had advised Melissa to play along until the kids outgrew it.

And that's what I decided to do. I played along.

"I'm glad you made a friend, honey," I said, slowly sliding more noodles out of the box and onto my plate even as my stomach soured. "Your first friend in Harbor Bay. How *exciting*."

She lined up her fortune cookie pieces in a straight line around the top edge of her plate.

"Yes," she said. "And I like her so much."

"I'm thrilled to hear it. Tell her I can't wait to meet her."

4

———

Of course there were warning signs, but almost everything aligned with the idea of an imaginary friend. All the times I followed my daughter's voice to her bedroom, only to open the door to find her alone. But then there were the times when I would walk into the kitchen and find all the cabinet doors all open—even the ones Tiffany couldn't reach. Or all the taps in the house would be running at the same time and I had to go from room to room, turning them all off.

Sometimes children are forgetful. I have memories of my own mother lecturing me: *Diane, for the love of God, please turn off the light when you leave a room. And close the door behind you!*

You have to remember that Tiffany was only seven then. A very cute, very sweet seven-year-old. When she looked up at me with those big doe eyes and said it wasn't her who hid the keys, making us late for the handoff with Paul, that it was *Emily*, I couldn't be mad at her for it.

I just thought it was her way of telling me she didn't want to spend the weekend with her father, and I could hardly blame her.

But there were other things I couldn't pin on my daughter's eccentricities.

Lights flickering. Chairs moving on their own. Cold spots. Shadows in the corner of my eyes that always disappeared when I turned my head and looked in that direction. The grotesque death of Mrs. Schmitt's cat, Muffin, after it made the fatal mistake of scratching Tiffany's face.

Immediately upon seeing the mangled remains of Aaron Whitaker's body, my first thought had been of Muffin. Followed by, *What did you do to deserve this?*

In the beginning, I simply thought something was wrong with the house. I didn't assume straightaway that Emily and the weird events were one and the same. I thought it more likely that Tiffany was making sense of the strangeness of her new life and circumstances by blaming the events on her *friend*.

My sister even suggested it was Tiffany doing it, but I didn't think so.

I know you'll say that's a mother's delusions, but it's true.

Not once did I believe my daughter responsible for anything that happened.

It never *felt* like her. Which, yes, I understand is a very vague and likely unsatisfying explanation.

I also considered the possibility that it was me. That because I was pissed off, I was making bad things happen.

Our lives in Grendall had been more comfortable. More sorted.

I'd liked our neighborhood, our friends, and the house itself was nicer. It was more modern in its amenities and design. My routine, after years of trial and error, had been perfected.

I'd loved the life I'd built until Paul had tossed a bomb into it because he had failed, *again*, to keep his dick in his pants.

If we're being honest, and I think it's clear we are, I would have kept ignoring his infidelity. I'd done it before. I could have done it again. For better or worse, I liked Paul. I thought he was funny, most of the time, and he was great in bed. Spending time with him was never a chore—unless he'd had one or two too many beers and was being a dick. So yes, as pathetic as it might sound, I could have seen me sticking it out for another ten years until Tiffany went off to school just to make her life easier.

But what I have no tolerance for is humiliation.

When a very drunk Christina stood up at our Christmas party and started bragging about fucking my husband in *my* upstairs bathroom, outlining all the ways he was too hot for *me*, in front of all *my* family and friends—let's just say I was done. I sent everyone home with their white elephant gifts as my sister, Melissa, dragged Christina out by the back of her neck as if she were a stray dog.

But no.

I would learn later that the bad vibes I felt in the house had nothing to do with me or Tiffany, or even Paul.

The malignancy was old, and well rooted even before we moved in. And it intensified after we found Emily's things under the floorboard.

It was January. I'd waited until after Christmas—the first on our own—to start the remodel on the floors. First and foremost because we were still being careful with our money then. Secondly because I wanted to make sure my new job would stick and that I could give Tiffany a good Christmas. Also because Melissa, Ryan, and the kids came up for the holidays.

I wanted the house to be in order, the decorations put away for the year, and the guests gone before contractors came in and started ripping up the place.

I'd been in the kitchen making a chicken risotto—one of

Tiffany's six approved dishes I could reliably get her to eat—when the contractor called my name.

Wiping my hands on a dish towel, I followed their voices to the spare room, the one adjacent to Tiffany's bedroom.

"I'm sorry to bother you, Ms. Yates, but we just wanted to know what you wanted to do about these boxes?"

I had no idea what they were talking about. "What boxes?"

Unhelpfully, they pointed at the hole in the floor where they'd begun removing some of the flooring as if that answered my question. I went over and peered into the gap. I had to lie down on my stomach in a room full of men and grope in the darkness before I found them.

There were three dust-covered boxes in that hole.

"I have no idea what these are," I admitted. "Maybe they belonged to the previous owners."

One of the contractors hopped down into the hole and began hauling the boxes up.

"You could try contacting the previous owners," one of the men suggested.

I didn't waste my breath explaining that the previous owners were living out in Seattle. As far as I knew, they had inherited the house from an uncle when he died. They had never actually lived here themselves. The house had been cleaned up, put on the market, and sold by a property management company on their behalf.

"Just put the boxes in my bedroom for now, thanks." I needed to get back to the risotto.

I forgot all about the boxes even before the risotto was plated. I remembered them only around midnight, when weary from the day, I crawled into bed and saw them stacked in the corner of my bedroom accusingly.

"Fuck." I hated getting up after getting comfortable.

But there was something about the way the boxes stood there, as if daring me to look inside them. So I did.

The contents were—unsettling.

It wasn't that it was a box of girl's clothing. We had plenty such boxes in the attic, mostly outfits that Tiffany had outgrown or refused to wear anymore due to one offense or another. She had a strong boycott against tags and certain fibers. And both of my nieces were younger, so it wasn't quite time to hand them down, and in the attic they waited.

What unsettled me about *these* clothes was the state of them. Every outfit was torn or muddy. Some grass-stained. This also could be explained away as belonging to a rough and rowdy tomboy. If not for the blood.

The tears at the shoulders, elbows, waist gave the impression that the children who'd worn them had been grabbed by rough and unforgiving hands.

There was a smell to them.

I couldn't have told you what the smell was exactly, only that it activated some primal part of my brain. For reasons I didn't understand, terror shot through me when I pulled each shirt, each pair of pants from the box.

Later I would read a study about how humans can smell fear in the sweat of other humans. I didn't know it at the time, but I believe now that's what I smelled.

The fear of those little girls—the terror they felt before whatever happened to them happened.

Based on the size of the clothing, I would have guessed they belonged to girls between the ages of eight and twelve. But who they belonged to—no clue.

It would be years before I started looking for those answers.

5

———

Transcript of Police Interview
Date: November 10, 2006
Time: 5:42 p.m.
Location: Harbor Bay County Sheriff's Office
Interviewing Officer: Detective Daniel Monroe
Secondary Officer: Detective Lisa Carter
Interviewee: Diane Yates

BEGIN TRANSCRIPT:

Detective Monroe: Ms. Yates, thanks again for coming in. We just have a few follow-up questions to clarify some things from our last conversation.

Diane Yates: You people sure have a funny way of saying thank you.

Detective Carter: We understand it's been difficult. We just need to go over the details one more time. Can you tell

us again where you were between 8 p.m. and midnight the
night Tiffany was found?

Diane Yates: I told you already I was at home. I made tea, I
watched some mindless cooking show, and then I went
to bed.

Detective Monroe: Alone?

Diane Yates: Yes, alone. I am a divorced middle-aged
woman. I don't need a chaperone.

Detective Carter: Do you have any neighbors who might
have seen you? Anyone you spoke with during that time?

Diane Yates: I live alone on a half-acre lot. None of my
neighbors can see me coming and going. My closest neighbor,
Mrs. Schmitt, died eight months ago. Her house has sat
vacant since.

Detective Monroe: Ms. Yates, I'll cut to the chase. Our
records show a call between you and Tiffany at 11:07 p.m.
That call lasted for twelve seconds.

Diane Yates: I wouldn't consider that a call, but yes, technically my phone did ring.

Detective Carter: Earlier you told us that you didn't hear
from her the night of the incident.

Diane Yates: I didn't. When I answered the call, no one was
there. I assumed it was a butt dial. It certainly wasn't the first
butt dial I've ever received from her.

Detective Monroe: Did you leave the house after that call?

Diane Yates: No.

Detective Monroe: When our officers arrived at your residence around 2:30, your hair was wet. It had been raining heavily for over four hours by that point.

Diane Yates: I took a shower. I told you that when I followed you to the station last time. If you recall, you gave me a towel.

Detective Carter: You took a shower. At 2 a.m.?

Diane Yates: I couldn't sleep. That's why I made tea and was watching cooking shows. I didn't realize my insomnia made me a suspect. You know that lots of people have trouble sleeping during storms.

Detective Monroe: So you didn't leave the house at any point after eleven?

Diane Yates: No.

Detective Carter: Because here's what we're trying to figure out. You say you stayed home. But Tiffany made a call. Short, vague. Then when we came to your door, you were dripping wet. And when asked directly about that night, you never mentioned a phone call.

Diane Yates: You got me there. I didn't think a twelve-second butt dial was relevant, no.

Detective Monroe: It matters if you went to see her. If you were at that scene. If there's anything you're not telling us.

Diane Yates: So you think that I'm the one who killed the guy and stuffed his mangled body in the trunk of a car now?

Detective Monroe: It seems more physically plausible than your daughter, yes.

Diane Yates: How would I know where Tiffany was from a twelve-second phone call?

Detective Monroe: We reviewed your daughter's cell phone. Yes, with a warrant, and have confirmed that your phones' locations are linked. You could have assumed the call was a distress call. Maybe she was crying or screaming, and like any good mom, you got in the car and drove to the location your phone provided, no questions.

Diane Yates: I will agree that yes, that does sound like something I would do. But I already told you I didn't leave the house.

Detective Carter: Even though your hair was wet. And if we got a warrant, what else would we find, Ms. Yates? Muddy shoes? Tread marks from the scene matching your car?

Diane Yates: You're grasping at straws. But sure, come check out the house and my car if you need to. Whatever makes you stop harassing my traumatized daughter. I'd rather your bullshit be directed at me than at her.

Detective Monroe: We just want to know the truth, Ms.

Yates. If you were there, even just to check on her, it changes the timeline. It could clear things up.

Diane Yates: I understand, but the fact remains that I wasn't there.

Detective Carter: Not even for a moment?

Diane Yates: Not even for a moment.

Detective Monroe: All right. But if anything comes back that contradicts your statement, we'll be having another conversation. Under very different circumstances.

END TRANSCRIPT.

6

———————

You know, I actually got the house blessed, if you can believe it.

I know.

I didn't want to call a priest to the house. My relationship with God is more complicated than my relationship with Paul, but Melissa had convinced me to do it, saying that it couldn't hurt to have someone come in and clear the place of any *negative energy*.

I had told her the stories of the moving chairs, open cabinets, and Tiffany's imaginary friend. She told me that I was a stone's throw from demonic possession, or Tiffany being sucked into an alternate dimension by a poltergeist.

I admit her fear was contagious, and before I knew it, there was a priest on my doorstep in the full garb, holy water and Bible in hand.

I asked him if it mattered that I wasn't a Christian.

"Not as long as you're willing to risk being cast out of the house yourself," he rasped.

A sense of humor. That was enough for me. I said, "Come on in."

The cleansing itself was uneventful. There was no demonic screaming or bleeding walls. No apparitions or bursting mirrors. No invisible entity tried to choke me or bite me or pull my hair. I simply walked silently from room to room, giving the priest a wide berth so he could work in peace.

When he was done, he accepted my offer to fix him a cup of tea and we sat at the dining room table together for a few minutes.

I asked, "Well? Sense anything dark or devilish?"

I was relieved when he replied, "No, not at all."

I was less relieved when he added, "Some anger though. There was some anger in the little girl's room. And more in the basement. That was perhaps the heaviest place. I'm not sure what happened down there, but it wasn't pleasant. It's lucky that you don't use that part of the house."

I never would.

I've always hated basements. The relief I felt when I discovered that the house's fuse box was in the garage and the laundry was on the first floor was immense.

"Are you saying my daughter is angry with me?" I asked.

"I don't know," he said. "Maybe the anger doesn't belong to her. But that's the only part of the house where I sensed a presence."

Those words stayed with me long after the priest left, giving a final blessing in the sign of a cross on the porch before he sauntered, hunched, back to his boat of a car.

I was still thinking about his words that night when it came time to tuck Tiffany in for bed.

She read me a chapter from her book—yes, she preferred to read to me rather than the other way around. Then I did the pillow and blanket check to her specifications. Before I gave her the customary three kisses—one on her forehead, one on each cheek, in a counterclockwise motion—I asked, "Honey, are you mad at me?"

"No."

I knew immediately that something was wrong.

Tiffany is like me. Blunt, honest. She doesn't mince words. Her reply was far too polite.

"No? If you're mad at me, you can tell me. I won't be upset."

Still she hesitated, her chin hidden under the edge of her blanket.

"If you don't tell me, how will I fix it?" I asked, really worried now. "You have to tell people when you're upset with them so they can apologize or make amends, remember?"

I waited in silence for an uncomfortable amount of time.

Finally, she said, "I'm not mad at you, but Emily is."

"Emily?" For a moment I wondered if she was projecting her feelings onto Emily but decided I didn't care. I wanted to get to the bottom of this. "Why is Emily mad at me?"

"She says that you don't want her here. That you're trying to get rid of her."

Now I was confused, because I definitely did *not* send any signals to my daughter suggesting I didn't want her here.

"What do you mean, sweetie? I don't want anyone to leave. We live here."

"She said you brought a man to the house to water the rooms. That you were trying to get rid of her."

"She's mad about the priest? It was just a house blessing, honey. Lots of people get them when they move into new houses. Aunt Missy gave it to us as a gift."

This was technically true. I told her that if she was so worried about ghost people and demonic possession that she could pay for this house cleansing, and she had.

"So you're not mad at Emily? You're not trying to make her go away?"

"No, baby. Emily is your friend. If you care about her and she's important to you, then she's important to me too."

I did feel something then. Later I would convince myself it was the mere power of suggestion. That the room hadn't actually gotten lighter, as if it were now easier to breathe.

"You tell Emily that any friend of yours is a friend of mine. And that in this house, we look out for our friends."

Tiffany's big blue eyes were visibly relieved.

It must have been April by then, maybe almost May, because the magnolia blossoms were shining in the moonlight outside the big window.

I was starting to believe we were going to get through the whole school year without incident.

I was wrong about that.

It wouldn't be until later, when I was lying alone in my bedroom down the hallway, that I realized I'd never told Tiffany about the priest. That I hadn't even reported back to Melissa yet to let her know how it had gone. He'd come and gone while Tiffany was at school and she'd seen no one else from the moment I'd brought her home throughout the evening.

There was no way for her to know that anyone had come unless there was someone *in* the house who'd seen the whole thing.

As I was lying in the dark, trying to puzzle out this equation, my daughter's giggles and soft voice began echoing through the wall.

Transcript of Police Interview
Date: November 14, 2006
Time: 10:42 a.m.
Location: Harbor Bay County Sheriff's Office Interview
Room 2
Interviewing Officer: Detective Daniel Monroe
Secondary Officer: Detective Lisa Carter
Interviewee: Tiffany Yates
Legal Representation: Celeste Warren, Esq.

BEGIN TRANSCRIPT:

Detective Carter: Good morning, Tiffany. Ms. Warren.
Thank you both for coming in today.

Ms. Warren: You requested this meeting. We're here. Let's
keep it brief and respectful.

Detective Monroe: Understood. Tiffany, we know it's been a difficult few days. We're hoping you're ready to tell us what happened that night on State Route 14.

Tiffany Yates: I already said everything I could.

Detective Monroe: Please speak up for the transcript, Tiffany, if you can.

Tiffany Yates: I already said everything I could.

Detective Carter: We've reviewed the initial statement. We'd like to go over it again with you directly. Walk us through what happened, from the beginning. Take your time.

Ms. Warren: Tiffany, you can answer if you feel comfortable. If not, I'll advise you accordingly.

Detective Carter: Tiffany, instead of nodding, I'll need you to verbalize your answers so that we can get them on record, all right?

Tiffany Yates: Yes.

Detective Monroe: All right. Take it from the beginning. What happened? Why were you on Route 14 that late at night?

Tiffany Yates: I was driving back to my apartment from campus after work. Something hit my car. I pulled over.

Detective Monroe: What kind of something? Like an animal? A person?

Tiffany Yates: No, like a bullet or a rock. It scared me. I don't like loud sounds. I pulled over to make sure it was okay. The car.

Detective Monroe: Was it still light out when you pulled over?

Tiffany Yates: No, it was very dark.

Detective Carter: What time was this approximately?

Tiffany Yates: The dashboard clock said 10:59 before I turned off the car.

Detective Carter: Turned off the car? Why would you turn off the car?

Tiffany Yates: You should always turn off your car before you get **out.** So it doesn't roll. It's safety.

Detective Monroe: You care a lot about safety?

Celeste Warren: Watch your tone with my client, please, Detective.

Detective Monroe: No harm meant. It was a compliment. We love safety here at the precinct.

Detective Carter: Tiffany, how did Aaron Whitaker come to be there that night?

Tiffany Yates: Who?

Detective Monroe: The bloody guy in the trunk. You didn't know his name?

Celeste Warren: Detective. I hardly think that is a professional description.

Detective Monroe: No, but it's certainly a clear one, isn't it?

Tiffany Yates: I didn't know his name.

Detective Carter: Had you seen him before?

Tiffany Yates: No. I mean, yes. I don't know.

Detective Monroe: You don't know? What, does he look different stuffed in a trunk?

Celeste Warren: My client has explained in her written statement that she thought she may have seen Aaron Whitaker on campus before the night in question, but can't be sure.

Detective Carter: Is that what you're trying to say now, Tiffany?

Tiffany Yates: Yes. I thought I saw him on campus one night after I left the labs. I can't be sure.

Detective Carter: And if it was him, what was he doing the night you think you saw him?

Tiffany Yates: He was in the parking lot. He was watching me walk to my car.

Detective Monroe: Got it. So this man you may or may not know came to be there that night with you on the side of the road? How?

Tiffany Yates: He parked behind me on the side of the road. I thought he was stopping to help. He got out of his car and came to my window. He asked if I needed a ride. I said no. I told him help was coming.

Detective Carter: What did he do next?

Tiffany Yates: He told me to get out of the car. He pulled open my door and grabbed me. Hard. Tried to pull me to his car.

Detective Monroe: How did he get into your car if you were inside it?

Tiffany Yates: It was unlocked. I was about to get out to check if the car was okay, but when I saw headlights, I waited for the car to pass. But it didn't pass.

Detective Carter: Did he say anything else?

Tiffany Yates: He said, "Don't be a bitch. Just let me help you." He was squeezing my arm. It hurt.

Detective Monroe: And then?

Tiffany Yates: I tried to pull away. I yelled for, I yelled for help.

Detective Carter: Did help come?

Detective Carter: Ms. Yates, we need you to be clear. Was there someone else there?

Detective Monroe: Well? Was someone else there or not?

Tiffany Yates: I didn't see anyone.

Detective Monroe: You didn't see anyone?

Tiffany Yates: I was covering my face. I dropped to the ground and curled up. I was trying not to get hurt. I didn't see anything. Just heard the noises.

Detective Carter: Noises?

Tiffany Yates: Wet sounds. And the rain. Screaming. His screaming.

Detective Monroe: But you didn't look?

Tiffany Yates: No. I was too scared. I thought maybe, I thought maybe it would be worse if I looked.

Ms. Warren: My client is describing a traumatic event. I remind you both she is not obligated to speculate. If she didn't see what happened, she didn't see.

Detective Carter: Tiffany, after the noises stopped, what did you do?

Tiffany Yates: I called my mom. I was scared and I wanted my mom.

Detective Monroe: Did you talk to your mom that night, Tiffany?

Ms. Warren: You don't have to elaborate on that, Tiffany. Your mother already gave her testimony. Ms. Yates, who I will remind you is also my client, clearly stated that she received a twelve-second accidental call from her daughter on the night in question and that during that call there was no intelligible speech.

Detective Monroe: Did you ask your mom to come get you, Tiffany?

Ms. Warren: Detective.

Tiffany Yates: No. I didn't ask her to come.

Detective Carter: What did you do next, after you ended the call to your mom.

Ms. Warren: Objection. We have established it was not a call in the way you are implying.

Detective Carter: Fine. What did you do next, Tiffany?

Tiffany Yates: I wanted to get away.

Detective Carter: Away from what?

Tiffany Yates: From him. From the, from the parts.

Detective Carter: Parts?

Tiffany Yates: I don't want to talk about that.

Ms. Warren: Then she won't.

Detective Carter: Did you see anyone else on the road? Someone running away, maybe?

Tiffany Yates: No.

Detective Monroe: Are you protecting someone?

Ms. Warren: Objection. That's not appropriate. She already stated she saw no one.

Detective Monroe: Look, Tiffany. We're trying to help you. But if something was there, someone, and you're not telling us, that's obstruction. This is your opportunity to be honest.

Tiffany Yates: I told you. I didn't see who hurt him. I only heard noises.

Detective Carter: You're sure?

Tiffany Yates: Yes.

Detective Monroe: Your injuries, your arm. That was from Aaron?

Tiffany Yates: Yes. When he grabbed me. Really hard.

Detective Carter: We're going to request access to your clothing from that night for further analysis. Are there any objections, Ms. Warren?

Ms. Warren: I'll need to review the formal request, but if there's no warrant, we won't be turning anything over today.

Detective Monroe: Understood. Tiffany, if you remember anything else, anything at all, we need you to come forward. We want to help, but we need the truth.

Tiffany Yates: I promise. I didn't see who hurt him.

Detective Monroe: You promise?

Detective Carter: Thank you for your time, Tiffany.

END TRANSCRIPT.

My sister's birthday is in May. So it must have been May when Melissa and I got coffee. Yes, that's right. Because it couldn't have been more than two weeks before I got the call from the principal and had to leave work early to collect Tiffany.

I remember how Melissa looked sitting at the little square table in the middle of the café. There was a mug in front of her, the steam rising from it as she used her fingers to pull a glob of mascara off her lashes. She'd started on a slice of carrot cake, her favorite. There were two forks, and I knew she intended to share it with me. I stood there for a moment, just inside the entrance to the café, my heart full of affection for my older sister. She had been the one who'd hugged me on my wedding day and told me that I didn't have to marry Paul just because our parents had spent all that money. The one who had picked me up and brushed me off every time—from my very first steps until now, as middle-aged women, neck deep in the all-consuming task of raising our kids to be decent humans in a fucking wild world.

I pulled out the seat across from her. She took one look at me and her face fell. "What's happened? What's going on?"

She really does know me better than anyone.

"Is it Tiff? She okay?"

"She's fine," I said. I didn't want her to catastrophize the situation. My anxiety was doing that enough for the both of us. I didn't need her to fuel a fire that was already threatening to burn out of control.

"Fine-ish," I amended.

Her dark eyes searched mine. "Spill it before I lose my shit."

When I'd gotten in the car and driven to the café that morning after dropping Tiffany off with her father, I had resolved that I wasn't going to bring up Emily at lunch. That there was no reason to talk about ghosts. It was enough that she had convinced me to get the house blessed. Who knew what she'd suggest next?

But there was something about that look in her eyes. So eager, so earnest. Before I knew it, my mouth was off and running.

"I think the blessing pissed Emily off."

"Oh God," Melissa said, crossing herself. I snorted. I wouldn't call my sister an atheist to her face, but *heathen* felt pretty accurate.

"The night after the priest came, Tiffany said that Emily thought I wanted her to leave. That she was pissed off that I'd had the priest come."

Melissa leaned forward. Pitching her voice, she said, "Are you serious? Tell me you're joking."

"You didn't tell her about the blessing, right? Did you tell the kids?"

Not that they were really old enough to articulate such a thing to Tiffany. They were only four and two.

"I haven't said *shit*." Melissa crossed herself again.

"Because it all happened when she was at school. She couldn't have known about the blessing unless—"

A café worker appeared at the table in her black apron. She took my drink order and left again. I waited until she was gone before picking up where I left off.

"Unless someone told her about it. And it was only me and the priest in that house."

"Apparently *not*," Melissa hissed, her hands pressed flat to the tabletop. "*Apparently* it was you, the priest, and *Emily*. Emily told her!"

I didn't like the panic in her voice. It was making the hair on the back of my neck rise and my stomach turn.

"What are we thinking?" she whispered, still leaning across the table. "If the blessing didn't work, she can't be a demon. Ghost? Or are there supernatural creatures that attach themselves to little girls? Or maybe Tiffany is a powerful psychic who can—can—"

She snapped her fingers until the word came to her.

"Clairvoyant! She's clairvoyant, and maybe Emily is a guide or a projection to help her understand her gift."

"Why are you whispering?" I asked.

"For all I know, she followed you here!" Missy fisted the paper napkin resting beside the forgotten piece of carrot cake.

"I don't think that's how it works," I said.

"We don't know *how* it works."

She had me there.

"I don't think it's Tiffany," I said.

"Why?" Her eyes were the size of saucers. "What's happened?"

For weeks I'd wondered if the blessing was a mistake. In many ways, the house felt *more* dangerous since the blessing. The energy was different. Believe me, I know how it sounds. I am not the kind of person who believes in energy, chakras, any of that bullshit, but it was hard to deny the fact that when I was alone in the house, there was a feeling in the air. Not only like I was being watched, which was unsettling on its own, but also a hostility. Like the person watching was *glaring* at me.

And that was before the little accidents began.

Before my purse would turn up in weird places with all my shit dumped out on the floor. Before I found holes in my clothes. Strange, bite-sized holes in the fabric as if someone had ripped them with their teeth.

Once I cut my foot open on a nail that was sticking up out of the floorboard. A nail that I *know* had not been sticking out an hour before. The floors had just been redone, and they were smooth and perfect. There was no reason for a raised nail to suddenly jut out of one of the boards.

"It's just a feeling," I said. If I gave her any other details, I knew she'd get scared. There were few ways I could be as useful to my older sister as she was to me. But not scaring her to death was one of them.

She shoved a big bite of cake into her mouth, then lifted a hand. "Wait. Okay. Let's think about this."

"I've done little else for weeks," I said.

"Let's assume that Tiffany is telling us the exact truth. There's a girl named Emily—be her ghost or whatever—and she's Tiffany's best friend. And now her best friend's mom has gone and done something to try and separate them."

I could see how the blessing could be interpreted like that.

"What the hell am I supposed to do?" I asked.

"This psychologist that I like, Dr. Jacqueline French, says that kids grow out of everything. *Everything.* That it's basically what makes kids *kids*, the fact that they change all the time. Maybe Emily—even if she is a ghost—is something

Tiffany will outgrow. You used to see weird shit when you were a kid, and you don't anymore."

"What? What do you mean, weird shit?"

She leaned forward, her fork clattering to her plate. "What? You don't remember Meg?"

The name conjured a vague memory of a lopsided smile, with blood in the corner of her lips.

"Whatever, it doesn't matter. The point is that almost none of us are friends with the kids we knew when we were little—imaginary or not. Maybe we just need to buy time for Tiffany to grow up."

I reached across the table and grabbed the plate, sliding the cake toward me. I shoveled a big bite into my mouth, recoiling inside at the feel of raisins on my tongue. I swallowed. "How the hell do I do that?"

"You need to broker a truce with the little monster living in your house," she said. "I don't know how you do that, but that's the goal. You need to get Emily on your side. The sooner, the better."

I still think about this conversation a lot.

How Melissa had said almost none of us are friends with the kids we knew when we were little.

Almost.

9

Crime Scene Report

Agency: Harbor Bay County Sheriff's Office
Case Number: ME-2006-1110-087
Date of Report: November 8, 2006
Reporting Officer: Officer L. Ramirez, Badge #1427
Time of Arrival: 11:57 PM
Location: State Route 14, approx. 2.6 miles west of M-55 intersection, Harbor Bay, MI
Weather Conditions: Heavy rain, low visibility, 43°F
Type of Scene: Suspicious Death / Possible Homicide

Victim(s):
• **Name:** Aaron Whitaker
• **DOB:** 03/14/1963
• **Status:** Deceased

Initial Observations

Upon arrival, uniformed deputies located a silver 2000 Chevrolet Impala (MI plate #: BYL 4721) pulled partially off the road, front wheels in the ditch. Vehicle was unoccupied. Approximately 25 feet north of the vehicle, a woman (later identified as Tiffany Marie Yates, DOB 07/19/1986) was found kneeling in the middle of the roadway, soaked and unresponsive. She was staring ahead and did not respond to verbal commands. No apparent injuries. EMS called to evaluate.

Note: Yates appeared catatonic and was transported to St. Joseph Mercy Hospital under involuntary psychiatric hold (MCL 330.1401, Person requiring treatment).

Discovery of Body
Trunk of the vehicle was closed but unlatched. Upon opening, officers discovered the body of Aaron Whitaker inside. Subject was severely mutilated. Entire upper torso exhibited extensive tearing and trauma consistent with animal attack, though no known local wildlife could inflict damage of this magnitude.

Notable Observations
• Defensive wounds on forearms and hands.
• Deep, claw-like lacerations across chest and abdomen.
• Face partially obscured by blood and trauma; dental records may be required to confirm ID, pending coroner confirmation.
• Clothing torn, blood-soaked; wallet and ID found in back pocket providing temporary identification
• Car keys missing from person

Scene Processing
Evidence markers placed for:
• Large pool of blood approx. 12 ft from trunk (possibly point of initial attack).
• Drag marks in muddy ground leading to vehicle.

• Unidentified claw marks gouged into rear bumper and trunk lid.

• Fingernail embedded in trunk carpet (possibly human. Sent to lab).

• Partial footprint in blood trail near vehicle.

Vehicle and body transported to lab for further analysis. Wildlife officers and forensic specialists requested to consult on claw/pattern analysis.

Next Steps / Notes

• Interview with Tiffany Yates pending psychiatric clearance.

• Search underway for any local surveillance or witnesses.

• No immediate signs of forced entry or third-party presence, though cause of death appears non-human in nature.

• Possible involvement of unknown animal or person. Further investigation required. Animal control notified.

Filed by:

Officer Ramirez

11/9/2006 08:37 AM

10

It wasn't long after that afternoon in the café with Melissa that I got the phone call from the principal. Of course, they never tell you what's going on over the phone. Just a vague, "There's been an incident. Yes, Tiffany is all right, but we need you to come down to the school immediately."

I explained my situation to my boss, a bitch who acted like me having a child was the biggest inconvenience of her life, and not, say, the fact that Janet was snorting cocaine in the bathroom on her lunch breaks. There were many days back then that I wished they would fire me. I only worked that job as a matter of pride. Paul's alimony and child support were enough to cover all of our bills, and I still had a large nest egg from a business that I built in my twenties then sold when I had Tiffany. I suppose I had a fear that if I didn't do something with my days, I would just sit in that house and rot.

All of this is to say that as I was driving to the school, I was not only worried about Tiffany, but I was also wondering if it wouldn't be better for both of us if I just took her to

Europe for a year or two. I could start an online business while living abroad. Maybe that would fix everything: ghosts, shitty bosses, academic problems, and Paul's lackluster efforts to be a father.

These daydreams ceased the moment I walked into Principal Granger's office, reeling with the realization that Europe may not be far enough, at least not when it came to Emily.

Apparently, Emily had made an appearance at Harbor Bay Elementary that morning, and the school was fourteen miles from our house. If Emily can travel fourteen miles, who's to say she can't travel four thousand?

I also think the principal was pissed that my first order of business was going over to my daughter and confirming she was all right with my own eyes.

It was quite the scene to take in.

Two furious mothers. Two children soaked in what I really hoped was red paint. I knew it couldn't be blood because it was too bright. Real blood, that much of it, at least, dries dark, almost black. This was more like the cartoon red of a clown's nose.

I forgot about the children as soon as I spotted the mark on Tiffany's neck.

"Can someone please tell me who the hell put their hands on my daughter?"

"Ms. Yates—"

"Please answer my questions, Principal Granger. Who made this mark on her neck? And what is this, paint?"

I was referring to the clump of blue matting together a chunk of her chestnut hair.

The mark was too small to be an adult's hand, which was why I still had the will to ask what had happened. If it *had* been an adult, I doubt I would have said anything at all. I would have started making marks of my own.

"I did it," a small voice said.

I turned to see the closest of the red children looking at me. It was a strange sight, seeing a red blob of a child looking back at me, the whites of her eyes bright in contrast against the dark brown pupils set at their center.

"I'm sorry," she added.

The apology took some of the fury out of my sails.

"What happened?" I asked.

The mother burst out with, "I'm sure that it's just—"

"Let her tell me, please," I said. One look from me and the mother closed her mouth. I turned back to the child. "Go on. Tell me what happened."

The mother looked like she was going to object, but I leveled her with what Paul had always called my bitch-from-hell stare, and her mouth shut firmly that time.

"We were playing a prank on Tiffany in the art room. She fell asleep, and so we took her hair and dipped it in the paint."

"Where was the teacher?" I asked.

"The class had ended. No one was in the room but us."

I turned to Principal Granger.

She opened her hands as if anticipating my concern. "Coach Emmett says that he stepped out into the hallway to take a call from his wife between classes and wasn't gone five minutes. He was going to wake Tiffany when he got back. He thought he was doing her a favor by letting her get a few minutes of sleep between classes."

"So you dipped her hair in paint, and what? She threw it on you in retaliation?"

"No! Emily did!" the second girl screamed. "It was—"

"Veronica, hush."

I don't think anyone noticed all the hair rising on my arms or the back of my neck.

It took me a minute to recover my voice. "I-I'm sorry, who?"

Now the mothers looked embarrassed. When I turned to Tiffany, she said nothing. She was doing this thing that she often did when she wanted to see how I was feeling but was struggling to meet my eyes. It was sort of like staring at my nose.

I gave her hand a reassuring squeeze.

"It seems like no one wants to talk about it, but I'm just trying to understand. Tiffany was asleep, you dipped her hair in paint, but that doesn't tell me why you're both drenched or why she has a mark on the back of her neck."

"I was mad about the paint hitting me and I pinched her neck," the little girl admitted.

"And you pulled my hair," Tiffany added.

"I'm really sorry," the girl replied without hesitation. Against my will, I was starting to like this one. I had a weakness for accountability. Though I couldn't tell you what the hell she looked like if she walked up to me on the street.

So where the hell did Emily come in? I wondered.

I had a feeling that no one was going to tell me. Tiffany would, but not until I got her to the car, which I now wanted to do as soon as possible.

"How do we resolve this, Principal Granger?" I asked.

"The girls have apologized to each other, but I think the three of them should stay after school for the rest of the week and clean the art room. It really is a mess now, and it would be unfair to make our janitor, Ms. Cleeves, clean all that up."

"Detention for the remainder of the week. Fine. Are you girls going to get along now?" My question was directed at the two red ones. Call me biased for believing that Tiffany was not the problem here.

"Yes," they intoned.

"Then are we free to go?"

The principal confirmed we were, so I gathered up my

daughter's things and walked out of the office. Halfway down the hallway, one of the girls—the one who'd spoken up—called out.

Imagine my surprise when the little red blob ran to us.

"Tiffany, wait."

Tiffany stopped but wouldn't look up from the floor.

"I *am* really sorry," the girl said, a little breathless. "I promise I won't be mean again. And I won't let anyone else be mean to you either, okay?"

"Okay," Tiffany said, still not looking up from the floor.

"You'll tell Emily, right? That we're friends?"

Tiffany didn't say anything.

And the girl—regardless of whatever else she was hoping to say—was dragged away by her mother.

Once we got to the car, and I turned around in my seat to look at Tiffany sitting there, a pensive look on her face, I'll admit I half expected to find a little ghost girl sitting in the backseat beside her. Fortunately, my daughter was alone.

"What really happened?" I asked.

"What they said."

"*Just* what they said?"

"When Mia grabbed me, Emily didn't like that. She threw the paint on them and pushed them down. They got really scared."

"How the hell did they know her name was Emily?"

"I told them," she said.

Jesus. "What did you say exactly?"

"I said, 'Now you've made Emily mad.'"

"Is this the first time someone has bullied you?"

"No."

"What do you mean no? They were being mean to you before?"

"I told Emily about it, and she said she would take care of it if it happened again."

It was hard for me to hide my anger then. "You should have told *me* about it. *I* would have taken care of it."

"I didn't want you to worry, Mom."

I felt like Emily had stabbed me in the heart.

"It's my job to worry about you. And I love my job. Let me do it."

This earned me a small smile, at least.

"Next thing I know Emily's gonna finish *me* off."

"She would never hurt you, Mom. She promised."

Would you think I'm pathetic if I admitted I was a little relieved to hear her say that? The last thing I wanted was to wake up to a ghost girl standing over me in the dead of night cutting my hair off with scissors or pouring paint down my throat.

"Have you been sleeping in class because you stay up late talking to Emily?" I asked.

Because I couldn't think of any other reason why. I suppose she could have been reading under the covers, but I'd heard the late-night giggling and voices.

"She knows you don't like us being friends, so we can really only talk at night."

Another ice pick to the heart.

"I need to have a talk with Emily."

"No, Mom, please."

"Not a bad talk," I assured her as I put my keys in the ignition. "We just need to agree on what's best for you. Tonight, after dinner, I want you to introduce us, okay?"

She was pulling her hair tie and letting it snap against her inner wrist. Her nervous tell.

"I promise, it's going to be fine. I'll be on my best behavior."

Hopefully Emily will be too.

Believe me when I tell you that I delivered this invitation

with far more bravado than what I was feeling inside. I had no idea what to expect.

She pushed them down. And they got really scared.

Sometimes I still wonder what Aaron Whitaker saw on the side of the road that night, in the pouring rain—assuming, of course, there had been time for him to see anything at all.

11

———

Search Warrant Return & Inventory

Agency: Harbor Bay County Sheriff's Office
Case Number: ME-2006-1110-087
Warrant Number: SW-2006-1116-002
Date Executed: November 16, 2006
Location Searched:
Diane Marie Yates
238 Shoreline Drive
Harbor Bay, MI 49725

Authorized by: Judge Patricia Keegan, 19th Circuit Court
Date Warrant Issued: November 16, 2006
Date of Affidavit: November 16, 2006
Affiant: Officer Ramirez, Badge #1427

Scope of Warrant
Pursuant to the affidavit filed, the following items were
authorized to be seized, if found:

• Any correspondence, documents, or electronic devices belonging to Tiffany Marie Yates or Diane Marie Yates
• Photographs, recordings, or digital files related to Aaron Whitaker
• Any weapons, controlled substances, or biological materials
• Any items containing occult, ritualistic, or supernatural symbology
• Diaries, journals, or printed materials related to anomalous events, animal attacks, or delusions

Summary of Search

Execution Time: 6:32 AM
Entry Type: Knock and announce; door opened provided voluntarily by Diane Yates; keys to shed, garage, and basement provided voluntarily
Present During Search: Diane M. Yates (homeowner), Officer Ramirez, Officer Sharpe, Officer Kowalski, Detective Carter, Detective Monroe, Digital Forensics Unit (DFU) Tech Marla Jensen
Duration: Approx. 2 hrs 15 min

Findings
The residence was thoroughly searched, including:
• Main floor living areas
• Master bedroom
• Secondary bedrooms
• Basement storage
• Garage
• Detached shed
• Attic
• Home office
• Digital devices (2 cell phones, 1 laptop, 1 tablet) scanned on site by DFU

Result:

No items of evidentiary value were recovered.

• No relevant personal belongings of Tiffany Yates found on premises.

• No references to Aaron Whitaker in written, digital, or photographic form.

• No occult or symbolic materials present.

• No weapons, drugs, or biological specimens recovered.

• No evidence of mental illness or delusions.

• No animals found on premises.

• Home appeared clean, organized, and recently dusted

• No signs of hidden compartments or suspicious activity.

Resident was cooperative but declined to answer questions about her daughter without legal representation. No resistance or interference during search.

Notes

• Home security system confirmed, but homeowner claims footage auto-deletes after 24 hours and was unrecoverable.

• Digital devices mirrored but no relevant files found on preliminary sweep.

• Case remains open; Diane Yates may be re-interviewed as investigation continues.

Filed By:
Officer Ramirez
Harbor Bay County Sheriff's Office
November 18, 2006 3:46 PM

12

———

I'm almost embarrassed to tell the next part. Mostly because I will also have to admit how scared I was. There is no way to talk about what happened that night after dinner without also admitting that I nearly shit my pants in terror.

Dinner, homework, and the entirety of that evening had passed without incident. It could have been any spring evening. But once the dishes were done and teeth brushed, I went into Tiffany's room.

"It's time for me to meet Emily," I said.

It was clear that my daughter was worried. She was still indulging in her habit of pulling a hair tie at her wrist only to release it. Pull, release, snap. Pull, release, snap. That and the bounce in her leg were her major tells when it came to her anxiety.

A thin red line formed over her wrist. I placed a hand over it to stop her. "It will be okay. I'm not mad at Emily for what happened. And I don't want to fight. I just want to talk to her."

I looked around the room.

"Is she here now?" I asked. I saw nothing, of course. There was only the large four-poster bed with its thin gossamer curtains. The abundance of stuffed animals because it seemed Paul sent her home with a new one after every visit. The color-coded bookshelves.

"No," Tiffany said. "I don't think she wants to come."

"Why?" When Tiffany didn't answer, I had to push her. "Why won't she come? Because I'm an adult?"

"She doesn't like you," Tiffany said. And she looked truly sorry, as if she'd just insulted me herself.

I had no idea how to explain to my tender-hearted seven-year-old that being disliked wasn't something you worried much about in your forties. That by the time she was my age, she wouldn't have a fuck left to give. True, this would be my first *ghost* hater. I suppose that part was a novelty.

"Why doesn't she like me?" I asked. I tried not to smile or laugh. I had a strong feeling that if Emily was truly that petty, she wouldn't appreciate my sense of humor.

"Because you don't want us to be friends."

"But I'm fine with you being friends. I told you that before."

"You're lying," she said. Her eyes widened. "I-I mean, Emily thinks you're lying."

I wasn't sure if this was any better than being called a liar by my daughter.

I took a slow, deep breath. At least now I was just annoyed and a little amused rather than worried I was about to actually see something.

"Tell Emily I'm sorry about the miscommunication, but no, I don't have a problem with your friendship. But we do need to discuss boundaries and ground rules. That is my right, as the mom. So if she would be so kind, I would appreciate it if she came forward just so we can make sure we're on the same page here. That's how people work it out, you know? They talk to each other."

I wasn't sure if I was trying to sell this to myself, the ghost, or my kid.

After several seconds, in which Tiffany pulled at her hair tie but thankfully didn't strike herself, she finally said, "Emily, my mom wants to talk to you. Can you please let her see you?"

Not how I would have worded it. But it was too late to say that seeing her wasn't a priority. In fact, *not* seeing her was my actual preference. If she really was so scary to look at, I'd be satisfied just knowing that she could hear me.

There was a moment, sitting there on the floor on the pink bean bag, where I did feel something. A barely perceptible shift in the air as if it were suddenly vibrating. But then the heaviness lifted.

Tiffany said, "She doesn't want to come now. She says maybe some other time."

I think any normal parent may have thought their child was lying. That either they were protecting their friend or they were afraid someone was going to get in trouble. But I had felt the strange withdrawal. The way the air had vibrated then settled.

I had also seen the way my daughter's eyes had flicked to the corner of the room and had doubled in size. I'd also seen the slight, almost imperceptible shake of Tiffany's head.

"I understand." I stood and dusted imaginary dust off my knees. "When you see Emily again, please tell her I hope we can talk another time. Whenever she's ready."

And with that, I put Tiffany to bed, completed our bedtime routine, and then went to my room to do my own shower, skincare, and teeth-brushing.

To say I was screaming internally and forcibly trying not

to break into a panicked run would be an understatement. Mostly because *what the hell did Tiffany tell her not to do?*

That question played on a loop in my head, yet somehow, I managed to make it all the way into my bed, the bedside lamp on, filling the room with a comforting glow.

I was reading a book about investing—good, boring stuff to send me off to sleep—when the voices started up.

They were being extra quiet tonight, but I did catch one scrap of dialogue.

"But she actually loves me. Unlike Dad."

My chest compressed suddenly, like a fist closing over my heart.

Goddamn it, Paul. I knew he was a selfish, self-involved prick, but I had hoped he would at least try to hide this from Tiffany better.

I was still fuming about this when the air in my bedroom shifted. It dropped several degrees in temperature. That's when I realized that no sound had come from Tiffany's bedroom in a while. Their discussion had died away while I'd been fuming in my thoughts about Paul and his dickery.

In fact, if I wasn't mistaken, that was Tiffany's soft snoring coming through the walls.

You waited until she was asleep to come to me, I thought. And I wasn't sure if I was happy or terrified about this.

There was a floorboard between the bedroom door and the foot of my bed that if you walked over it, it squeaked.

That night, just after the shift in temperature, it squeaked, and all the hair on my arms and the back of my neck rose.

It wasn't only that it squeaked, it was *how* it squeaked. A slow, drawn-out sound.

Not only was Emily approaching my bed, she was fucking *creeping up on me*.

"Don't do that," I told her before I could stop myself. "I

know you're here and I'm glad you came. But please don't do any spooky shit. Can we just talk?"

I don't know what I expected. A little girl's voice? An apparition? Hell, maybe even a demon no longer pretending to be a little girl since it was just us adults now?

But Emily said nothing.

What she did, however, was sit on the edge of my bed.

The mattress sank under the weight of her. An outline of a girl's legs hanging over the side.

The *will* it took for me to remain perfectly still, calm, as if it were only Tiffany who'd come into the room to talk, was *exponential*. Who knows what my face looked like, but I was sitting in my bed, comforter stretched over me, in the perfect mimicry of a civilized woman in complete possession of herself.

Later I would realize I was gripping the edge of my book so hard I'd actually crumpled it.

"Is there anything you want to say to me?" I asked.

No answer.

"Not the talkative type?"

Still no answer. I waited for a moment to see if Tiffany had woken up to the sound of my voice, but I still heard her snoring.

I had no choice but to go on. I knew she—something—was still here. The air had that weird weight to it, and I could still see her outline on the comforter.

"I wanted to thank you for looking out for Tiffany today. She doesn't have a lot of friends, so it means a lot to me that someone out there is protecting her when I can't."

I didn't say, *I would prefer it if you were alive, but hey, a mom has little say in these things.*

"Now that I know you only have Tiffany's best interests at heart, I'm okay with you two being friends, all right? I'm not trying to separate you guys. I'm sorry if the house blessing upset you. It was something my sister suggested I do. Lots of people do it when they move into a new place. I didn't mean to offend you. From now on, I would like us to be on the same team. For Tiffany's sake."

I had no idea—and still don't—if ghosts know when you lie. But I was honest when I told her I wanted us to form a truce, and hoped that if she *could* really tell what humans thought and felt, she heard the sincerity in my offer.

Still no answer.

The bed shifted and I had a terrible moment of wondering if she was about to pounce on me, but the floor creaked again, and not so slow this time.

She was leaving.

"Before you go," I said, sitting up straight, book forgotten. "There is one thing I need to address as a *mom*."

I had to spit this out before she disappeared again.

"Tiffany is falling asleep in school. That means she's not getting enough sleep. Try not to keep her up late anymore, okay? I don't mind if you guys talk and hang out during the day when you're here and it's just us. You don't have to wait until bedtime to do your chatting."

The cold was dissipating, the static vibrating the air nearly gone.

"You can do that, right? I mean, we both want what's best for Tiffany, don't we?"

My question hung in the air but remained unanswered.

Either Emily couldn't or wouldn't answer me. At least not then.

I don't know how, but I managed to fall asleep—a *miracle* given the adrenaline in my veins.

When I woke the next day, I found that Emily had left me an answer after all.

Above the dresser, a big *Yes* was scrawled across the mirror in my red lipstick. As I stared at the word, I thought for just a moment, I saw a face shift into focus, but it was gone as quickly as it had come.

We both want what's best for Tiffany, don't we? That's what I'd asked.

Yes.

So we had an agreement.

Things did get better after that, but I sometimes still wonder just exactly what I'd agreed to that night. If, unknowingly, I'd signed some sort of permission slip for the dead girl. I'd told Emily to protect my daughter, after all.

And that's exactly what she did.

13

**State of Michigan Office of the Medical Examiner
Forensic Pathology Report**

Case Number: ME-2006-1110-087
Date of Report: November 10, 2006
Name of Deceased: Aaron Michael Whitaker
DOB: 03/14/1963
Age: 43
Sex: Male
Race: White
Date of Death: Estimated between November 9, 2006
11:00 PM and November 10, 2006 2:00 AM
Examiner: Dr. Naomi Trask, M.D., Forensic Pathologist
Autopsy Date: November 10, 2006

I. SUMMARY OF FINDINGS

Cause of Death

Exsanguination and acute trauma due to multiple deep lacerations consistent with a violent animal mauling. Contributing factor: compression-related skeletal trauma.

Manner of Death
Homicide, pending further investigation.

II. EXTERNAL EXAMINATION
• Body recovered from trunk of silver 2000 Chevrolet Impala (MI plate #: BYL 4721).
• Subject nude from the waist up. Denim jeans heavily soiled with blood and plant matter.
• Extensive claw-like lacerations present on anterior torso, neck, and arms. Wounds are jagged, irregular in pattern, with inconsistent spacing and depth.

Notable Details
• Some lacerations appear to overlap in unnatural angles as if inflicted simultaneously from multiple vectors.
• No identifiable animal saliva, hair, or dander detected in or around wounds.
• Claw marks average 2.8 cm apart with talon-like curvature but spacing inconsistent with known predatory mammals in region (e.g., bear, wolf, cougar). Could be consistent with human attack, but humans don't typically possess the strength to deliver such wounds.
• Flesh surrounding wounds exhibits elevated levels of histamine and cortisol, suggesting extreme stress reaction before death. This means subject was alive and aware when attack began.

III. INTERNAL EXAMINATION
• Ribcage crushed inward with force indicative of high-impact blunt trauma, consistent with forced compression or being shoved into a confined space under extreme pressure.

Possibly hit with vehicle at high speed before being shoved into trunk.

• Fractures in clavicle, sternum, and both humeri; spiral breaks suggest forceful rotation or twisting during injury.

• Lungs collapsed. Moderate fluid in airway, subject may have aspirated blood before death.

• Heart intact but adrenal glands highly engorged. Catecholamine surge suggests severe fight-or-flight state prior to death.

Postmortem Notes

• No defensive wounds on hands or knuckles. Subject may have been immobilized or stunned before attack, or it was too quick for subject to react accordingly.

• Liver temperature and rigor suggest time of death approximately 1–2 hours before body discovery.

• Presence of sildenafil detected. No alcohol or other drugs detected in toxicology screening.

IV. ADDITIONAL OBSERVATIONS

• Trace residue under fingernails: black particulate matter, non-biological. Sent to Trace Analysis for identification.

• Wound beds show slight phosphorescence under UV light, currently unexplained. Possible contamination or environmental factor?

• No signs of sexual assault, but there is trauma in the groin area suggesting a violent and likely repeated impact of some kind.

Conclusion

While external trauma is consistent with an animal attack, lack of biological trace evidence and the presence of forceful compression injuries raise the possibility of staged postmortem interference or an unconventional assailant. Findings inconclusive. Investigation is ongoing.

Filed by:
Dr. Naomi Trask, M.D.
Harbor Bay Office of the Medical Examiner
November 10 10:14 AM

From: Dr. Naomi Trask n.trask@washtenawme.gov
To: Det. Lisa Carter l.carter@harborbaypd.gov
Subject: RE: Case ME-2006-1110-087 Aaron Whitaker
Date: November 23, 2006 3:42 PM

Detective Carter,
I know we're trying to wrap this up before Thanksgiving, so I will be brief. Following your request for clarification on the extent and nature of injuries sustained by Mr. Aaron Whitaker, I am formally confirming that the trauma observed during autopsy is *highly atypical* and does not align with wounds inflicted by human means. It is very unlikely that your suspect, Tiffany Yates, or your secondary person of interest, Diane Yates, could be responsible for his death.

This is true even with your proposed theory in which Whitaker was struck with a vehicle and then mauled by an animal, an unlikely scenario.

In particular:
• The depth and shape of the lacerations resemble claw or talon strikes, not knife wounds.
• The spiral fractures in the long bones (especially the humeri

and femurs) suggest torsional force far exceeding normal human strength but not quite so strong as a vehicle strike.
• The compression damage to the ribcage and thoracic cavity indicates blunt-force trauma consistent with being shoved into a small space with *violent force*, but again, this is not consistent with a vehicle strike.

Frankly, there is no physical evidence suggesting that either Tiffany or Diane Yates could have inflicted this level of bodily damage. Neither woman possesses the size, strength, or psychological profile typically associated with such overkill.

Furthermore, your search of the Yates residence yielded no forensic evidence. No blood, no fibers, no weapons, no signs of recent struggle. The black particulate matter found under the victim's fingernails remains unidentified and was not found in any part of the Yates home or on either woman's person.

It is my professional opinion that it was something else entirely.

Respectfully,

Dr. Naomi Trask, M.D.
Forensic Pathologist

14

Fortunately, the police never found the box of bloody children's clothes. I'd had the good sense to throw that shit out years ago. I knew that I was probably making a mistake and throwing out evidence of a crime, but I also knew that the man who owned this house before us was already dead, and likely so were the families who were missing those little girls. The only thing that was going to come of sharing the evidence was turning our home into a murder house on the nightly news. I couldn't have strangers harassing my kid. Not when the chances that Tiffany would admit that *yes*, *actually*, she *did* have a ghost best friend were high.

I felt for the mothers who might be out there, hoping for answers.

But not so sympathetic that I was going to sacrifice my daughter on the slab of sensationalist news to give them peace. And in case you're keeping track, no, I never claimed to be a good person.

I know what you're thinking.

Did I ever try to identify the victims? Or at least Emily?

The answer is yes.

It was after the first time Emily almost killed someone for my daughter.

High schoolers are hard for any mother to handle. That part wasn't Emily's fault. It was just my teenage daughter being a teen girl—which, frankly, was terrifying. The sudden need for makeup, trendy clothes, even the boobs, I could deal with in stride. Not the boys.

Like a lot of moms, I was terrified she was going to get hurt. Physically, sure, but also emotionally. I'd tried to raise her to be strong and independent, but she was still a child in a lot of ways, and it felt like the threats were encroaching on her faster than I could get her ready for the onslaught we call life.

It was tenth grade when I realized my fears weren't unfounded. I remember because she had an art phase that year. Her normally orderly room was becoming overrun with canvasses and dirty glasses of water. She kept getting acrylic paint on the floor, no matter how many times I bitched about it or demanded she use drop cloths.

One afternoon a boy came to the house.

The first question out of my mouth after the front door opened and closed and they entered into the dining room where I'd been sitting at the table double-checking an expense report that a vendor had messed up was a blurted, "How old are you?"

"Seventeen."

"And you'll be eighteen in...?"

"Two months," he said, a grin stretching across his face. I don't know why he thought I would be happy about this.

"I'm Breyden," he said with a little wave. "Nice to meet you, Mrs. Yates."

He was two years older than Tiffany. I was about to ask what the hell an almost grown man was doing here with my kid when Tiffany said, "We have an assignment for physics."

"We're going to build a model with magnets."

I had no idea what that meant, but before I could object, they went up to her room. I screamed up after them, "Keep the door open."

I can't tell you what happened in that room for the next two hours apart from me going to the foot of the stairs every fifteen minutes to look up and make sure the door was still standing open.

It was.

What I *can* tell you was that one minute I was standing in the kitchen, staring into my fridge and thinking I'd rather have a good Indian curry with some warm, buttery naan than make lasagna, when I heard a crash and a scream.

"Emily, no!"

Oh shit.

That was Tiffany's voice.

That meant the overlapping scream must have come from the boy. A heartbeat later, his footsteps thundered down the stairs. I only caught a glimpse of the back of him as he bolted through the front door and out into the twilight.

"Hey—" There was no use in calling after him. He was already throwing himself behind the wheel of a little sedan which I was certain had been borrowed from a parent. His wheels spun gravel for a moment before the car rocked into reverse and shot away.

I went to the front door to close it and saw there was a trail of blood. Not *a lot*. A nosebleed's worth? Or a split lip? It was splashed from the porch across the threshold and into the hallway. I followed it up to Tiffany's room.

She was sitting on the floor surrounded by little gray magnets, a board cracked in half.

There was a larger splash of blood here.

"What happened?" I asked.

"He touched my leg," Tiffany said. She said it as plainly as if she'd asked me for the salt. "Emily didn't like it. I didn't like it."

Like any mother, I seized the opportunity to reinforce the message about consent.

"If a guy touches you and you don't want him to, a bloody nose should be the least of what happens to him."

Static filled the room, and it felt like a cold finger had touched the back of my neck.

I had no idea if that meant Emily agreed with me or if it was some sort of veiled threat.

I bent down in front of my daughter. I took her hand. One of the approved places where she didn't mind being touched.

"Are you okay?"

"How am I going to finish the project? I don't want to get a bad grade. He has a lot of friends. Everyone will say it's my fault."

My heart wilted at that.

"Dickheads usually have lots of friends. But their friends are dicks too." I squeezed her hand. "Why don't you wash up and I'll order takeout. You want chana masala and a samosa?"

She nodded.

"With a side of peas?"

Another nod.

"I'll take care of the guy," I said.

"Emily already said she would."

And she hadn't been wrong about that. When I'd reached out to the teacher the next day on my lunch break to ask about the assignment, the teacher informed me that he already knew about the situation.

I seriously doubted that and asked for clarification.

"I was there this morning," he said. "The school nurse says Breyden will need at least four weeks to recover. He's not going to be able to complete it, given the state he's in. I told

Tiffany to do her best and I'll grade her accordingly. She's had such a terrible day, that poor girl."

The physics teacher went on to explain how the boy had fallen down three flights of stairs in the main atrium of the school. It was between the second and third periods, and most of the students and staff were in the hallway at the time.

His leg broke so badly that it busted through the skin, undoubtedly ending his rising tennis career, or so the physics teacher would have me believe.

Apparently, when he landed at the bottom of the stairs, he started screaming that Tiffany had done this to him.

But several teachers assured me that they knew it wasn't possible. So many people had seen him fall, and Tiffany had been at the bottom of the stairs where he'd landed, not at the top.

"Injured or not, we have a strict no-bullying policy," the principal told me later. "I will get Breyden to write a formal apology for accusing your daughter like that. We were all there. We know what happened. What he said was unkind. How is she doing, by the way?"

When I asked Tiffany what really happened, she replied simply, "He didn't fall. Emily pushed him."

That was when my little hobby launched itself. For months, the hunt was intense. I must have gone to the library a hundred times. But there were no missing children in the Harbor Bay news for decades. No mournful pleas from families to have their kids returned. No one by the name of Emily, with the exception of a sixty-nine-year-old woman who died from a stroke four years ago, after we'd already encountered our Emily.

I found no proof that Emily had ever existed.

At least, not until after Aaron Whitaker was murdered.

15

———

From: Det. Daniel Monroe d.monroe@harborbaypd.gov
To: Det. Lisa Carter l.carter@harborbaypd.gov
Subject: Fwd: Forensics Whitaker case
Date: November 23, 2006 4:15 PM

Hey Carter,

Just got this back from Trask. Read it twice.

Between the search warrant on Diane's place coming up empty and the pathology report confirming what I was already thinking. It's looking less and less like either of the Yates women could've done this. Not physically. Not logistically.

The lacerations look *animal-like*, and yet there's no saliva, no fur, no DNA. Nothing that connects to *any* known predator. And the claw spacing is off. I pressed Trask for details by the water cooler just now, and she says it's like the wounds probably came from something with *asymmetrical limbs*. What the hell does that even mean?

Also, this glowing residue thing under UV? She's sending it out again, but she's already hinting that it's not a known environmental contaminant. We're talking *X-Files* shit.

I stood next to Tiffany that night. Catatonic. Shaking. She couldn't speak, wouldn't move. I've seen shock before. This was different. I still maintain that the mom knows something and isn't sharing, but now I have a gut feeling she might be lying for other reasons.

Maybe she really is just trying to protect her kid from something we don't understand. If this is going the way I think it is, Ms. Yates might just be thinking we won't believe her and so she's keeping her mouth shut.

We need to start considering the possibility that this isn't just a "we don't have the right suspect" situation and that it might be a "we don't know what the hell is going on" situation.

In any case, I have one more idea. It's crazy, but let's talk in person before briefing the captain.

Monroe Out.

16

I hadn't lied about watching a cooking show. The habit of staying up too late after Tiffany moved away for school was a real one. I had talked to my therapist about it—if it was normal to worry so much about your kid after they moved out. She assured me that it was, and that there was no shame in reclaiming that energy for myself now that Tiffany was an adult. And I had certainly tried. I was taking stained-glassmaking classes, like I'd always wanted. I was putting in more time consulting in hopes that I could transition away from the firm and become my own boss again within the next few years. I had even gone on a few dates. There was one guy, Nathanial, who was actually pretty promising in his long-term potential, even if I could never see myself married again.

But there was still a restlessness that lingered when I found myself alone in that house at night.

My routine included opening a bottle of Merlot after dinner and carrying it to the living room with an after-dinner cheese plate, and I would drink my wine and eat my cheese while watching some plump and happy woman show me the best way to dress a duck. I'd get through half the bottle and fall asleep on the couch, the shawl from its back pulled over my shoulders.

This was also what had happened the night Aaron Whitaker had died.

The only difference had been the ringing phone.

There was something in the way it trilled. I know you'll probably think I'm crazy for saying that—assuming you don't already—but it was just a feeling that something was terribly wrong.

Tiffany's name showed on the screen.

"Baby, what's wrong?"

"M-mom." Her voice cracked. "M-m-*mom*."

Her crying made all the hair on my body stand at attention.

"Where are you?" I bolted upright. "What happened?"

"Mom, I—I—Dead. *Dead*."

I threw the shawl to the floor. I found my keys on the hook where they belonged—though later I would replay the memory of leaving them beside the stack of mail I brought in, half convincing myself that I had not been the one to put them by the door—stepped into my slip-ons, and ran out into the rain without a second thought.

By then Tiffany had already hung up.

I opened location services and found Tiffany on the little map. I recognized that stretch of the highway immediately. I almost put the coordinates into my car's navigation system and hesitated.

If the police did get involved, they were going to check my car, perhaps even my phone history if they had a warrant. I didn't know if they had a way to do that, but I also wasn't going to make it easy for them.

I drove from memory to the dot I'd seen, knowing that the tracker could be way off. They weren't as good back then as they are now. She could've been anywhere on that road, but fortunately, she wasn't easy to miss.

I saw the flashers first.

I parked so that my tires were a little in the road. Better they stay on the wet concrete than leave tracks in the muddy shoulders.

Yes, looking back on my actions that night, I can see I was already preparing for the worst.

Especially for the possibility that the *worst* was Emily. There would be no way to convince the police that whatever had happened was done by an angry dead girl. Tiffany would be blamed, and I would rather go to prison for the rest of my life than let that happen to my kid. But I was going to try my damnedest to get both of us out of this unscathed.

At least, that was my plan as I parked the car.

It took me a minute to realize that the huddled form in the middle of the road was Tiffany, crouched down, her hands over her head, gently rocking herself.

"Tiffany! Tiffany!" I screamed as I ran to her.

I grabbed her and pulled her up, trying to get a look at her, but she recoiled.

"Are you hurt? Are you hurt, damn it?"

Yes, I know I'm failing autistic parent 101 here, but I was scared.

Finally, she did wrap her arms around me, and I was able to give her the hard hug that I knew she desperately needed.

Slowly, she relaxed against me.

"What's happened?"

"T-t-t-t—"

Her teeth were chattering in spite of the rain's warmth.

That's when I realized her shirt was ripped.

"Th-the t-trunk."

I wasted no time. Mostly because I didn't think we had any time before someone saw us or the police came.

The trunk wasn't latched, which meant I didn't have to open it with my hand and leave prints. Or maybe the rain would have washed them away. Who knows. But it was partially open, and I saw the blood dripping down over the shiny bumper before hitting the wet pavement. Through the crack I could make out the crumpled form of someone inside.

A dead body. That's a fucking dead body.

Whose, I had no idea.

"Fuck."

Using the tip of my boot, I lifted the lid just enough to get a closer look.

The body was mangled, looking like little more than bloody pulp.

"Em-em—"

"I know," I told her. "I know, and you can tell me about it later. Listen, we don't have any time."

"M-mom."

"Listen!" I grabbed her shoulders again, giving her enough compression to help her focus. "The police are going to come. They're going to ask you questions. Say *nothing*. I don't care if they threaten you or promise you anything. Don't say a single word to them until I get you a lawyer. Even then, don't tell the lawyer about Emily. Don't tell the lawyer much of anything except that you didn't see what happened."

"I d-didn't."

"Even better. Now I have to go home."

"N-no!" She reversed her grip, grabbing on to me now.

"I have to. They're going to come, and if I'm here, I'm going to be a suspect too. It's better if I'm home when they get there, okay? You call the police with your cell phone. Leave it on so they can trace your call. Just wait until they arrive and say *nothing*. They will probably take you with them, and that's okay, but *say nothing*. Do you understand?"

She nodded.

I gave my daughter one more hard hug, kissing her temple, the side of her wet hair sticking to my face as the rain poured down on us. As we stood in the headlights of my car, I said, "It's going to be okay. I promise. We have to be careful, but it's going to be okay. Just don't say a word and we'll get through this."

I released her and ran back to my car. To say I drove home like a demon would be an understatement. I was just grateful that I didn't pass a single car on the way.

I parked my car in the garage and locked it so they couldn't check to see if the engine was warm without a warrant. I stripped as soon as I got inside and put all my clothes—shoes included—in the washer along with a few other items to give the appearance of a full load. I mopped the entryway just enough to remove any tracks but not so much that it couldn't dry in fifteen minutes. I jumped in the shower, scrubbed myself down, put on PJs, and went back to the couch, hair still damp.

I turned on the TV so they would see the light through the front window when they pulled up. I lay down, pulling the shawl over me again. If they came to the window, I wanted them to think I was asleep. I think I was only on the couch five minutes before the lights slid across the living room wall.

I waited until the doorbell rang before getting up. Even then, I was slow, showing the right amount of caution and confusion. No woman living alone would want to open a door at this time of night. Through the closed door, I said, "Who is it?"

"It's Officer Ramirez and Officer Long, ma'am. Are you Ms. Diane Yates?"

"Yes," I said.

"We're very sorry to bother you so late, ma'am, but there's been an accident with your daughter, Tiffany. Can you please let us in?"

"Can you show me your badges?" I called through the door.

"Yes, ma'am, of course."

I took a breath and turned the deadbolt, hoping I had my face in place before the door swung wide.

**Harbor Bay County Sheriff's Office
Vehicle Search Report**

Case #: ME-2006-1110-087
Date of Report: November 14, 2006
Vehicle Search Date: November 13, 2006
Location of Search: Harbor Bay County Sheriff's Office Forensics Garage Bay 3
Reporting Officer: Detective Lisa Carter
Assisting Officer(s): Detective Daniel Monroe, Officer Kelly Stroud (Forensics)
Search Authorized By: Search Warrant HB-21-1109-SW-DY

Subject Vehicle:
- **Registered Owner:** Diane Marie Yates
- **Make/Model:** Lexus RX 330
- **Color:** Black
- **License Plate:** 7RH-88Q
- **VIN:** 4S4BRBCC9D1234567

Reason for Search

In relation to the ongoing investigation into the death of
Aaron Whitaker (ME-2006-1110-087), the subject vehicle was
searched following a signed warrant issued based on prox-
imity and possible connection to witness/suspect Tiffany
Yates. No direct evidence had been recovered from the Yates
residence; the vehicle was processed for potential trace
evidence, weapons, biological fluids, or items of evidentiary
value.

Search Summary

The search began at 11:02 a.m. and concluded at 2:17 p.m. The
vehicle was photographed, logged, and then thoroughly
examined. Components removed for inspection included:

- Floor mats (front and rear)
- Trunk lining
- Front seat cushions (partially lifted)
- Door panels (visual inspection only, no forced removal)
- Air vents swabbed for particulates
- Glove box and center console emptied

Findings

• Biological Evidence

No blood, tissue, or bodily fluids observed or detected via
presumptive testing.

• Fibers/DNA/Trace

Small number of long dark human hairs in passenger footwell
Several dried leaf fragments and pollen spores from local flora

• Weapons or Tools

None found.

• Notable Items Recovered

Two plastic grocery bags
Umbrella
Receipt for gas dated November 9, 2006

Paperback novel in rear seat pocket
Empty Starbucks cup (latte)
Emergency car kit (sealed)

Observations

The vehicle was relatively clean and showed no signs of recent deep cleaning (i.e., no strong chemical smells, residue, or detergent fluorescence under UV inspection). No signs of tampering or modifications. No relevant locations recorded in vehicle's navigation system.

There was no indication that the vehicle had been used to transport a body or any violent activity. No odors consistent with decomposition or bleach were present.

Conclusion

The forensic search of Diane Yates' Lexus RX 330 yielded no evidence linking the vehicle to the crime scene or the body of Aaron Whitaker. Items found were ordinary, expected, and bore no forensic significance to the ongoing investigation.

Report submitted by:
Detective Lisa Carter
Badge #0529
Harbor Bay County Sheriff's Office

18

———

After the third round of interrogations, the search warrants, and the mounting feeling that the damn sharks were just going to keep circling until they scented blood, I had no choice but to finally ask for help.

I waited until after Tiffany was asleep. Yes, she'd moved back in with me after the police released her. She'd tried to spend the first night in her apartment but got so scared that she called me to come and get her at two in the morning.

If we're being honest, I wanted her home too. Whatever had almost happened with Aaron Whitaker was too close a call for me. I felt it acutely in my bones that I'd almost lost my only, beloved child.

And to what fucked-up fantasy, I had no idea.

On the night I asked Emily for help, I almost chickened out. I'd gone through the motions of the evening, spending the hours after dinner on the couch with Tiffany watching a travel show in which they ate food from around the world. This week the host was in Morocco. Tiffany had dozed beside me as I watched spiced dishes of lamb and couscous dance across the screen. Just before midnight, I woke Tiffany and led her up to bed.

Still, I waited until I heard Tiffany's soft snoring through the wall again before finding my voice.

By then I was in my own bed for the night, my comforter pulled up to my chest.

"Emily," I whispered.

Nothing.

"Emily?" I spoke louder this time. "Please. I need to speak to you."

I thought my request for an audience might go unnoticed. I was about to shimmy under the comforter and chase sleep myself when a shadow caught the corner of my eye. I looked up just in time to see the bedroom door shift as if someone slender had slipped through the crack I'd left in case Tiffany needed to sneak into my bed in the middle of the night.

The movement of the door was followed by the slow creak of the floorboard.

She didn't sit on the edge of the bed this time.

Instead, she came closer.

I could feel the cold air of her presence just beside me. I had a terrible feeling that she could reach out and put her hands around my neck if she wanted. She could even do what she did to Aaron Whitaker.

When I tell you that I almost shit myself then and there at the thought, please know I'm downplaying the terror that was racing like frantic white mice beneath my skin.

I took a slow breath.

"Thank you for coming," I said. Can't go wrong with an abundance of politeness. For all I knew, now that Tiffany was grown, Emily could simply kill me and remove the last obstacle between her and her best friend.

Maybe that's what she was contemplating now.

"The police are blaming Tiffany," I said. "Because there

are no witnesses, no one to prove that she didn't hurt him, they are trying to blame her. If they take her to trial or question her too hard, she may end up in a very bad place. You understand that, right?"

No answer.

"Protecting her isn't just about hurting the people who want to hurt her. It's also about protecting her life. Protecting her so she has a chance to live. Surely you know how precious being alive is, Emily."

A cold hand clamped over my thigh.

The pressure was... ambiguous.

I still don't know to this day if she was threatening me—telling me to watch what I said—or if she was assuring me that she did understand.

I rushed on. "You remember that boy you hurt before? You hurt him in front of other people. It looked like an accident, so no one blamed her. Tiffany was safe. I need you to do the same thing, now, Emily. If you don't, then a lot of people are going to try to hurt our girl. Too many for you to protect her from."

The hand tightened.

I bit back a scream. Not because it hurt—it didn't—but my terror was getting the better of me.

"Please, Emily," I rasped, before swallowing hard.

I wasn't above begging. I was a mother. There's nothing I wouldn't do for my kid.

"Please. I don't care what you do, but make sure they know who the bad guy is here. For Tiffany's sake."

A long, dreadful moment dragged on. My breath held, caught in the back of my throat.

Then the hand lifted.

The cold withdrew.

The floorboard creaked slowly once more, signaling Emily's departure.

All at once, the breath I'd been holding left me.

19

────────

From: Capt. Edward Reilly e.reilly@harborbaypd.gov
To: Det. Lisa Carter l.carter@harborbaypd.gov
CC: Det. Daniel Monroe d.monroe@harborbaypd.gov
Subject: Urgent: Meet Me in My Office
Date: November 23, 2006 5:32 PM

Detectives Carter and Monroe,

Why aren't you answering your phones? I need both of you in my office immediately.

New information has come to light regarding Aaron Whitaker, and it's not going to wait for us. I'm warning you both right now, before it hits the press, that Whitaker's background is *far more complex* than we originally believed. You need to be prepared for the fallout.

The story is about to break wide. We need to get ahead of this and get our talking points straight. Come to my office as soon as you read this.

Captain Edward Reilly
Harbor Bay County Sheriff's Office

20

I didn't have to wait long to know if Emily received my message, or if she understood what was on the line for Tiffany. The story broke two days later on the evening news. Tiffany and I had settled down in the living room after dinner with the wine and cheese plate. I'd also brought my sewing kit, hoping to sew a new button on a blouse that had lost one that morning. Tiffany was on the couch beside me, scrolling and absently feeding little cubes of cheese into her mouth every few minutes.

It was his name that made us both look up.

"We have a stunning development tonight in a case that has gripped the Harbor Bay community for weeks. Aaron Whitaker, the man found brutally killed and stuffed into the trunk of his own car earlier this month, may not be a victim after all—but a suspect.

"Authorities confirmed today that Whitaker is now linked to at least three unsolved murder cases, following the discovery of human remains in the woods just outside of town.

"Police say a local dog walker made the grisly find—a

single wrist bone partially buried in the forest floor. Forensic analysis quickly identified the remains as belonging to sixteen-year-old Lily Nash, who disappeared last summer. Whitaker's DNA was recovered from the burial site, linking him to the missing girl.

"The dog walker, Bryan Givens, describes the scene.

"'I take Flapjack out every morning around sunrise, the same trail we always go on. But this time was weird. One minute he was fine, and then he sort of spooked. Ears pinned, hackles up. Then all of a sudden—he just bolts on me. Straight into the trees, like he was following someone. He's *never* done that before. I tried to catch up to him but he's just so fast. That's a Jack Russell for you. By the time I caught up, he was digging like mad. Then he turns around and drops this white thing in my hand. The police told me it was a wrist bone, if you can believe it.'"

The camera returned to the newsroom. The anchor pressed on.

"And that's not all. Investigators have since uncovered at least three more burial sites in the same wooded area. While those remains have yet to be identified, officials say the victims are likely all young women—and all potential victims of Aaron Whitaker.

"Police are calling it a major break in several cold cases and are urging anyone with information about Whitaker's movements to come forward. For now, the Harbor Bay County Sheriff's Office has declined to speculate on a motive —or to comment on how Whitaker met his own violent end. We'll bring you more as this story develops. Back to you, Thomas."

I turned off the television with the remote. Tiffany and I sat in silence for a long time, the shock stretching between us. Then we turned to each other, our eyes locking.

In unison, we said, "Shit."

21

———

From: Chief Raymond D. Talbot rd.talbot@harborbaypd.gov
To: Tiffany Yates starfishcallie@automail.com
CC: Diane Yates diane.yates@automail.com
Subject: Official Clearance from Ongoing Investigation
Date: December 15, 2006
To: Ms. Tiffany Yates and Ms. Diane Yates
Subject: Official Clearance from Ongoing Investigation

Dear Ms. Tiffany Yates and Ms. Diane Yates,

On behalf of the Harbor Bay County Sheriff's Office, including myself, Captain Edward Reilly, and Detective Daniel Monroe and Detective Lisa Carter, I am writing to formally notify you that, following an extensive investigation, and in light of recent developments, you are no longer considered persons of interest in the matter concerning the death of Aaron Whitaker.

The department acknowledges that your cooperation throughout this process has been both forthcoming and valuable. We now understand that Mr. Whitaker was involved in multiple criminal acts, and his death is being reclassified as part of a separate and ongoing investigation into his activities.

We further acknowledge the distress this situation has caused, particularly in light of the public attention and scrutiny. While our initial inquiries were necessary in the pursuit of due diligence, we regret any undue stress or implication this may have caused either of you.

Please be advised that no charges are being filed against you, and your names have been cleared in this matter. A public statement will be issued by our department to reflect this update, and you are entitled to a copy of that release and other relevant documents upon request.

Should you require further documentation for personal, legal, or professional reasons, please do not hesitate to contact our office directly.

Respectfully,

Chief Raymond D. Talbot
Harbor Bay County Sheriff's Office
Office of the Chief of Police
325 North Harbor Drive
Harbor Bay, MI 49701
(231) 555-0198

22

———

In the end they were able to convict Aaron Whitaker, posthumously, of six murders. The rest of girls they dug up from the graves were all co-ed college girls between the ages of eighteen and twenty-three. The first murder took place over fifteen years ago, when Aaron Whitaker would have been twenty-eight. The police didn't seem to know if she was Aaron's first murder or if that was the earliest victim from this area. He went to school out in Arizona and had family there. Last I heard, they are opening a few cold cases there that may belong to Whitaker as well.

What I *am* glad of is that my daughter had not been tortured, raped, and buried out in the woods like the rest of the girls.

I can't say she got away from the experience totally unscathed. She did have PTSD, but after a year off of school and therapy sessions three times a week, she was able to restart classes and finish her degree. Well, she did change her major. From premed to art history, telling me that she never wanted to see the inside of another body for as long as she lived.

Fair enough.

She went to graduate school to get her certificate in museum studies. It didn't surprise me one bit that her new choice of career would allow her to meticulously organize the placement and location of objets d'art in a pleasing atmosphere.

I'm no less proud of my curator than if she had become a doctor, especially after I was invited to the opening of her first collection at the Chicago Museum of Art.

Three years later, after her big debut, she brought home a young man for Thanksgiving, Garrett Pemberly. I liked him very much right away. He was a good egg and nothing like her father. They married two years after that Thanksgiving, and three years after that, my granddaughter Penny was born, just five days before Tiffany's thirty-third birthday.

I went to Chicago to celebrate. I stayed in the spare room of their apartment for a month, helping with the cooking, cleaning, baby care. Just so you know, I was invited and had happily accepted. By then I'd quit my job and was making stained-glass window pieces full time. I asked my boss—me— for a couple months of maternity leave, and she gladly agreed.

I'd never seen Tiffany so happy or exhausted as during those six weeks, and when it was time for me to return to Michigan, she gave me the long, deep, and heartfelt hug that a mother dreams of all her life.

Her desperate *Thank you, Mom* might as well have been the lottery calling to say I won five million bucks. I smiled for the entire five-hour drive back to the house, feeling for the first time in a long time that everything just might be all right after all.

I'VE ONLY FELT EMILY'S PRESENCE ONCE IN THE HOUSE since Tiffany moved to Chicago. It wasn't long after Penny's fifth birthday. They had a big party at some play zone with all their friends and I'd made the drive down for the weekend. When I got home, I was asleep as soon as my head hit the pillow. Chasing ten five-year-olds will do that to an old woman. But I still woke up the instant the floorboard creaked, and that static-y feeling of electricity filled the air.

"Hi, Emily," I said. I bit back, *How have you been?* "Is everything okay?"

The mattress sagged.

Secretly, I was relieved. This was preferred to the menacing hover she'd done the last time she came into my bedroom. Slowly, I recognized a feeling almost like loneliness.

"I miss her too," I said. "But, when everything goes right, kids grow up. We have to be happy for her."

No answer, but she also didn't leave.

"I want to thank you for being such a good friend to my daughter," I told her. "She has built a beautiful life for herself. The kind of life that any mother would be proud of. And it was only possible because of what you did for her. I wish I had a way to repay you for what you've done. To give you some sort of peace. That's my only regret in all of this, actually. I don't suppose you could tell me about yourself, could you?"

I fell asleep long before hearing any sort of answer.

Her reply came a few days later.

I had been cleaning the house when it arrived. Spring was on its way again, and I had that spring-clean fever that I always got when May rolled around and the weather finally started to warm up. The magnolia outside was blooming on schedule, and it was almost time to push out the mower and fill it with fresh gas.

I'd been trying to pull down the living room curtains so I could wash them when the doorbell rang.

From where I stood by the window, I couldn't see anyone

on the porch, but still, I climbed down off my stepladder and went to the door, brushing the dust off my hands by wiping them on my overalls as I went.

When I opened the door, no one was there.

I stepped out onto the porch and looked in all directions but saw not a soul. There was no car in the driveway, and not even any dust from the gravel hanging in the air.

I was about to go back inside when I saw the milk carton.

It was sitting on the first step. I bent down and picked it up.

It was ancient. The red ink was faded and the words rubbed off in places. The expiration date stamped on the side read June 23, 1988.

"What the hell?"

I remembered drinking milk from cartons like this growing up. Mostly the hysteria my mother had over the missing kids printed on the sides and the way she obsessed over our whereabouts because of it.

Missing kids.

I turned the carton in my hand until I saw her face.

Have You Seen Me?
Emily Anne Houte
Last Seen: 10/31/1986
Where: Frankenmuth, Michigan
DOB: 05/06/1978
White Female
Eyes: Brown
Hair: Brown

If you have seen this child, or any other missing child, please report any information you have to (888) 555-1290.

Emily Houte.

She was eight years old when she died. I read the information again, sinking to the steps as I did, one hand over my mouth. I don't know why, but I burst into tears, wondering what I would have done if one Halloween night my daughter simply hadn't come home. How my own baby, Tiffany, had been just three months old, and safe in my arms, whenever Emily took her final breaths.

It wasn't until I'd regained my composure and read the information again that I realized why it had been today.

May sixth.

Today was May sixth.

I wiped my tears with the back of my hand. "Happy birthday, Emily. Happy birthday, baby girl."

I still celebrate it with fresh flowers, every year.

You had better believe I tried to track her family down after that. But as I had suspected, no one was left. Emily's mother had passed away from complications of diabetes in 1992 and her father had died in a car crash later that same year. Emily hadn't had any siblings, and while her mother did have one surviving sister, despite my efforts to reach her, she never returned my calls. The more I thought about it, the more I concluded that Emily had simply been fulfilling my request, not trying to reconcile with her family. I knew she could get around and go wherever she wanted. If she wanted to be with her family—or anyone—that was where she'd be. But since her family was gone, she made a new one. I couldn't decide if that was a happy ending or a terribly sad one.

One Friday morning I was packing for a weekend in Chicago. I'd taken the day off the glass piece I was working on and planned to drive down so that Tiffany and Garrett could celebrate their anniversary without the kiddo in tow. I was trying to decide whether or not I was going to pack a coat when my phone rang.

"Hey there."

"Are you on the road yet?" Tiffany asked, her voice bright with excitement.

"No. But I'll be out the door within the hour, I promise."

"You better. Because the dinner reservation is set and these tickets to *Wicked* are nonrefundable."

"I'll be there before lunch, let alone dinner," I assured her. "I just need to decide on a coat, put on my shoes, and then I'll be out the door."

I didn't add that I would also be stopping at the café for a coffee and a breakfast sandwich. I loved my kid, but she could be a real killjoy when it came to a schedule. Besides, I was right. I'd be there hours and hours before they needed to leave for their tapas reservation.

"Okay, but Mom. Are you—"

"Tiffany. Take a breath. Everything is going to be great. I promise."

She groaned. "I know. You're right. Sorry. I think I'm just worried about Penny."

"Why? Is she sick?"

"No, nothing like that."

Good. Because while I could do it, of course, taking care of a sick kid was not my idea of a good time.

"She just said something weird last night before bed and I can't stop thinking about it."

The little hairs on my arm rose.

"She told me she has a new friend that visits her at night. I know imaginary friends are totally normal, but you'll never guess what she named her."

I knew what she was going to say even before she said it.

"She called her Emily. What a coincidence, right?"

ACKNOWLEDGMENTS

Here we are with *Final Cut: Stories* finished and done.

This is where we drop the curtain and share a round of applause.

First off, endless thanks to my amazing production team. Hats off to The World's Best Editor: Toby Selwyn. And a round of applause for The Most Excellent Cover Designer: Christian Bentulan.

I'm equally grateful for my ever-enthusiastic critique group, *The Four Horsemen of the Bookocalypse*: Katie Pendleton, Angela Roquet, and Monica La Porta.

I can't wrap up these thank-yous without acknowledging my lovely street team. Thank you for reading the books in advance, reporting those lingering typos, and posting honest reviews. Your continued support makes the work worth it.

And last but never least, there's my beautiful wife, Kim, and The Cutest Dog in the World, Maximus Courage—without whose company I'd be too sad to write stories like these.

Everyone listed above is perfect and can do no wrong. Therefore, any remaining errors in the book are entirely my own.

ABOUT THE AUTHOR

USA TODAY bestselling author Kory M. Shrum has published more than thirty books including the bestselling *Shadows in the Water* and *Dying for a Living* series.

She is the host of two podcasts: *Who Killed My Mother?* a true crime podcast about her mother's tragic death, and a second show, *A Well Cared For Human*, which focuses on debunking self-care myths, while offering concrete strategies for improving one's mental health and personal power.

She also publishes poetry under the name K.B. Marie.

When not writing, podcasting, or planning her next adventure, she can usually be found under thick blankets with snacks.

She lives in Michigan with her equally bookish wife, Kim, and their very spoiled rescue dog, Max. Learn more about Kory and all the mischief she gets up to at www.korymshrum.com

ALSO BY KORY M. SHRUM

Dying for a Living series

Dying for a Living

Dying by the Hour

Dying for Her: A Companion Novel

Dying Light

Worth Dying For

Dying Breath

Dying Day

Shadows in the Water series

Shadows in the Water

Under the Bones

Danse Macabre

Carnival

Devil's Luck

What Comes Around

Overkill

Silver Bullet

Hell House

One Foot in the Grave

Blood Rain

First Light

Castle Cove series

Welcome to Castle Cove

Night Tide

The City 2603 series

The City Below

The City Within

The City Outside

The Borderland series

Blade Born: A Borderlands Novel

Standalone Novels

Jack and the Fire Eater

Short Fiction

Thirst: new and collected stories

Final Cut: stories

Nonfiction

Who Killed My Mother? a memoir

A Well Cared for Human: self-love strategies for transforming pain into power

Poetry (as K.B. Marie)

Birds & Other Dreamers

Questions for the Dead

You Can't Keep It

Learn more about Kory's work at www.korymshrum.com